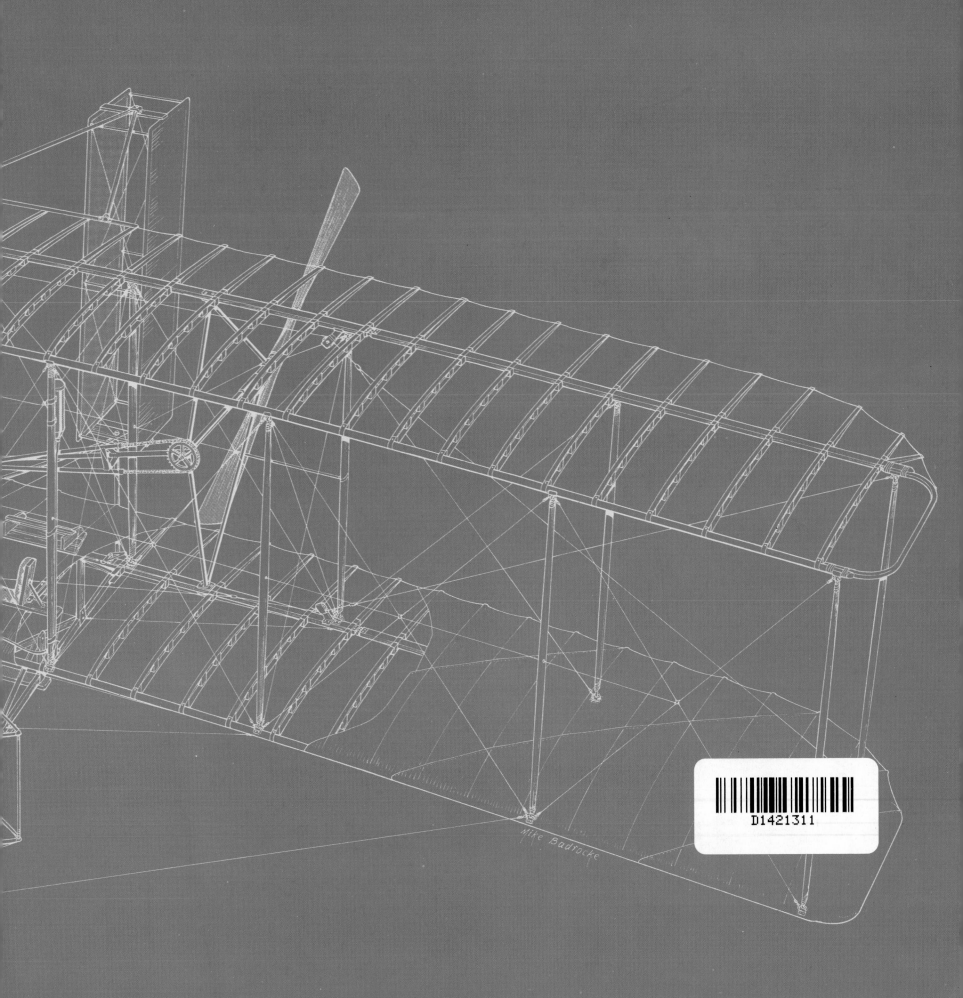

Mike Badrocke

D1421311

A CENTURY OF
MANNED
FLIGHT

15. 10. 98

A CENTURY OF
MANNED
FLIGHT

RICHARD TOWNSHEND BICKERS

This book belongs to

Dale Martin

32, Mount S.T.

Dromore,

Co. Down.

N. Ireland

(01846) 699091

BT25 1AT

Bramley Books

5056 A Century of Manned Flight

Produced by PW Publishing Limited, Broadstone, Dorset, UK
for Quadrillion Publishing Limited

This edition published in 1998 by Bramley Books,
an imprint of Quadrillion Publishing Limited,
Woolsack Way, Godalming, Surrey, UK

Project co-ordinator / Geraldine Christy
Design / GoodallJames, Bournemouth, Dorset, UK

Conceived and commissioned by Jasper Spencer-Smith
Editorial and picture consultant / Philip Jarrett
Proofreader / Martyn Bramwell
Indexer / Michael Forder
Production / Neil Randles, Karen Staff, Ruth Arthur

Reprographics by The Faculty Ltd, Broadstone, Dorset, UK

Printed in Spain.

ISBN 1-85833-851-4

Foreword

To research a book on aviation that spans nearly a hundred years of manned, controlled flight is a supremely enjoyable, but weighty, undertaking. Diligently delving in numerous sources for information, I found myself frequently distracted from the pursuit of facts by the romantic and adventurous allure of the story. It is a narrative of immense human endeavour encompassing high intelligence, bravery, persistence and total belief in what is achievable however impossible it may seem. The saga of heavier-than-air flying machines encompasses superb feats of skill and courage in the service of mankind and in the terrible annals of warfare. Both are equally enthralling and revealing of man's ingenuity.

From a flimsy aircraft that barely rose off the ground, briefly staggered through the air and covered only a few yards before landing, mankind has achieved the nonchalant frequency of space flights.

In the second century AD, the Roman Emperor Hadrian posed a pertinent question:

> *Friend and associate of this clay*
> *To what unknown regions borne*
> *Wilt thou now wing thy distant flight?*

The answer was provided first by the Wright brothers and amplified by the astronauts of the 20th century.

The information necessary for this account of the first century of the aeroplane and of long-distance flight could not have been completed without the encouragement of Jasper Spencer-Smith, the help of Philip Jarrett, and their encyclopaedic knowledge of the subject; the information provided by the Royal Aeronautical Society, the Royal Air Force and the Public Record Office; and those whose abundant photographs grace this volume. Jean Webber tirelessly carried out the typing of corrections to the copy. All of these have my thanks.

Richard Townshend Bickers
Shoscombe, Somerset
May 1998

9

Contents

Introduction

On 17 December 1903 the Wright Brothers flew the first manned, powered, heavier-than-air flying machine.

Throughout recorded time mankind has envied birds their gift of flight. As an ability it has been held in awe. The biblical prophet Jeremiah, describing his vision of the Seraphim, wrote, "Each one had six wings ... with twain he did fly".

Fascination with free flight bred legends about self-propelled aerial exploits centuries before man conquered the air. In Greek mythology, Daedalus was an Athenian craftsman of superhuman genius, who, for treachery to King Minos, was imprisoned with his son Icarus in a labyrinth from which no one had ever escaped. Daedalus made wings of wax and feathers for them both and away they flew: Daedalus landed safely on the island now called Icaria; Icarus, forgetting the warning not to fly too near the sun, lost his wings as the wax melted and plunged to his death in the sea.

Persian legends tell of King Kai Kawus harnessing eagles to his throne in the hope that they would raise him aloft. In literature, even space flight was invoked in 1638 by the English Bishop of Llandaff, Francis Godwin, an imaginative writer, one of whose characters was the first man on the moon, towed there by a gaggle of geese.

The evolution of flight has followed a logical sequence. In France, in 1763, Madame du Deffand, in a letter to the eminent philosopher d'Alembert, stated, in another context, the basic fact

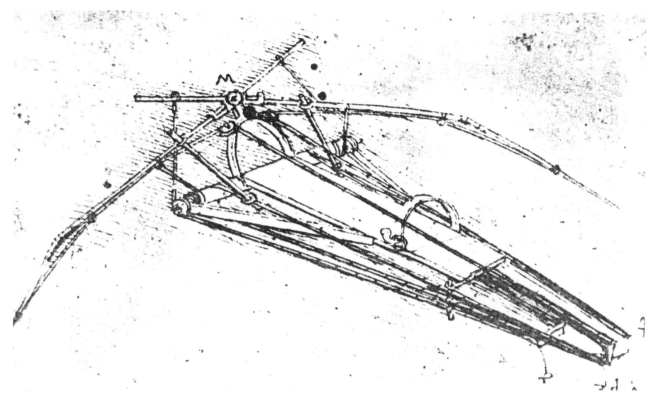

about aeronautical history: "The distance is nothing; it is only the first step that counts." It began with kites, which had been flown in China since about 200 BC and were the earliest aerial transporters. The first European to see one was Marco Polo in the 1290s on his travels there. It was huge and made of woven reeds. Sailors used kites as a prognostic by sending a man aloft borne by one. If it rose straight, the omen for putting to sea that day was good; if it tilted (often fatally), it was not – emphatically for the unfortunate whose turn it was to make the test. In the Middle Ages, kites were already familiar in many regions of the Orient, notably Japan, and used for landing soldiers on enemy terrain or spying. It was not until 1326 that seamen who had travelled to the Far East introduced them to Europe as playthings, with no aspiration to take a human being aloft.

In the Western world, the earliest practical approach to some means of aerial conveyance appeared in designs drawn by the polymath genius Leonardo da Vinci (1452–1519). The thoroughness with which he undertook all tasks led him to study air currents and pressures, the relevance of which had not occurred to any other hopeful designer of the world's first manned flying machine. Like most who aspired to conquer the air, Leonardo focused on bird flight and its emulation in the form of ornithopters. The basic impediment, however, power to weight ratio, did not occur to him or anyone else. No such machine driven by human arms and legs could become airborne: the muscles that enable birds to flap their wings constitute about 50 per cent of their bodyweight, whereas those of a man burdened with the same task amount to only some 22 per cent.

A misadventure befell the Frenchman Abbé Desforges in 1792. He was presumably confident of divine protection, but it is a cautionary tale. He had a wicker-

ABOVE: **This prone-piloted ornithopter was just one of many proposals by Leonardo da Vinci (1452–1519) for man-carrying flying machines, all of which were to be powered by human muscle power.**

BELOW: **Daedalus watches helplessly as his son, Icarus, plunges to his death after flying too close to the Sun, which melted the wax securing his feathers.**

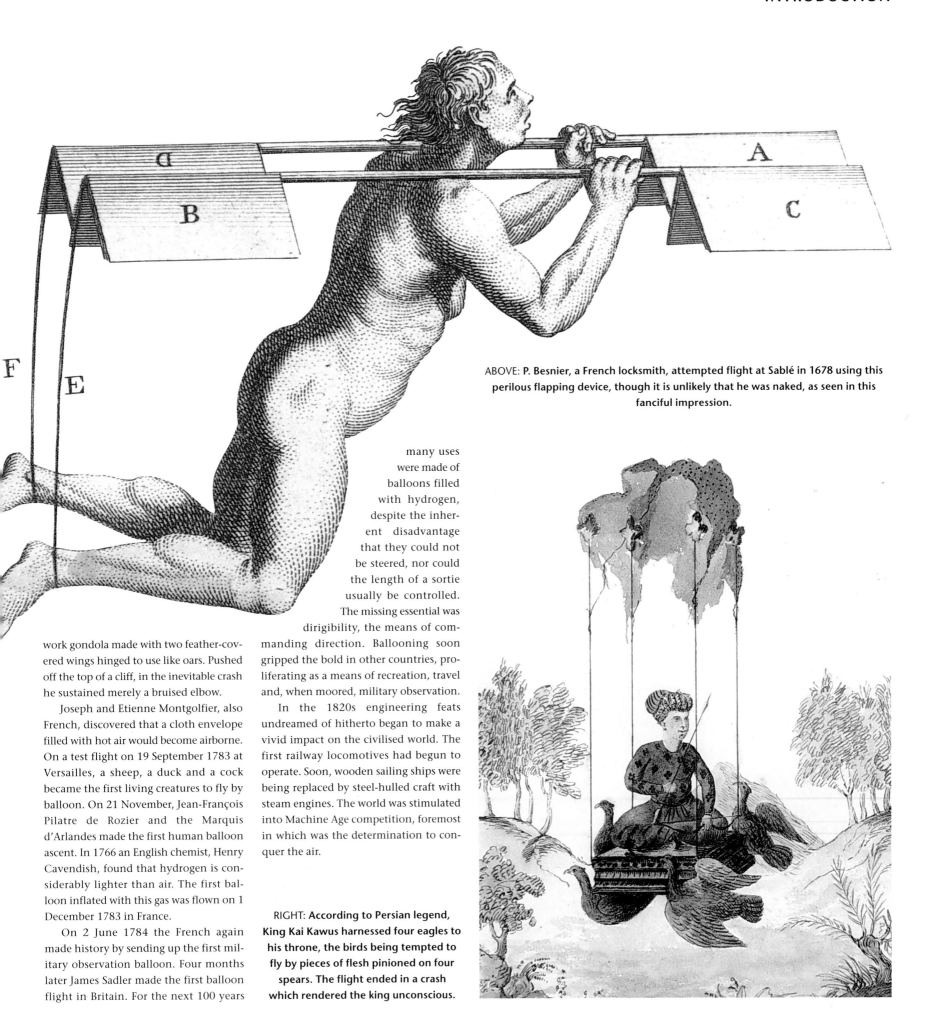

ABOVE: **P. Besnier, a French locksmith, attempted flight at Sablé in 1678 using this perilous flapping device, though it is unlikely that he was naked, as seen in this fanciful impression.**

work gondola made with two feather-covered wings hinged to use like oars. Pushed off the top of a cliff, in the inevitable crash he sustained merely a bruised elbow.

Joseph and Etienne Montgolfier, also French, discovered that a cloth envelope filled with hot air would become airborne. On a test flight on 19 September 1783 at Versailles, a sheep, a duck and a cock became the first living creatures to fly by balloon. On 21 November, Jean-François Pilatre de Rozier and the Marquis d'Arlandes made the first human balloon ascent. In 1766 an English chemist, Henry Cavendish, found that hydrogen is considerably lighter than air. The first balloon inflated with this gas was flown on 1 December 1783 in France.

On 2 June 1784 the French again made history by sending up the first military observation balloon. Four months later James Sadler made the first balloon flight in Britain. For the next 100 years many uses were made of balloons filled with hydrogen, despite the inherent disadvantage that they could not be steered, nor could the length of a sortie usually be controlled. The missing essential was dirigibility, the means of commanding direction. Ballooning soon gripped the bold in other countries, proliferating as a means of recreation, travel and, when moored, military observation.

In the 1820s engineering feats undreamed of hitherto began to make a vivid impact on the civilised world. The first railway locomotives had begun to operate. Soon, wooden sailing ships were being replaced by steel-hulled craft with steam engines. The world was stimulated into Machine Age competition, foremost in which was the determination to conquer the air.

RIGHT: **According to Persian legend, King Kai Kawus harnessed four eagles to his throne, the birds being tempted to fly by pieces of flesh pinioned on four spears. The flight ended in a crash which rendered the king unconscious.**

13

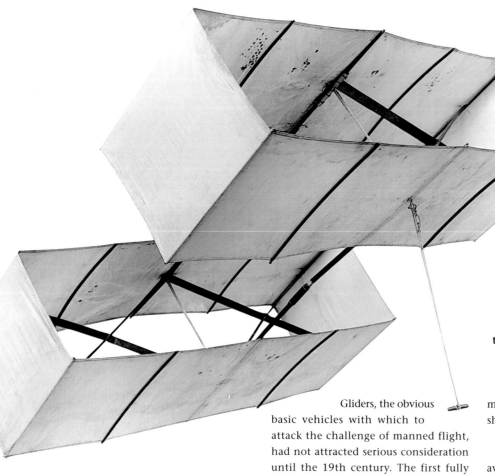

ABOVE: **The boxkite invented by Australian Lawrence Hargrave in 1893 was influential in establishing the biplane layout, but Hargrave's own experiments with numerous powered model flying machines brought no real success.**

RIGHT: **Sir George Cayley described his "governable parachute" in 1852, and this faithful reproduction was flown (under tow) in 1973. The sole means of control was the tiller-operated "influencer" projecting behind the nacelle.**

Gliders, the obvious basic vehicles with which to attack the challenge of manned flight, had not attracted serious consideration until the 19th century. The first fully thought-out aerodynamic experiments were made by Sir George Cayley, who built his best-known glider in 1853. He forced his reluctant coachman to make the maiden flight in it, across a shallow valley. Cayley's grand-daughter, who was present, recorded a tactful understatement: "I think it came down in rather a shorter distance than expected."

The coachman gave notice.

France was still leading the world in aviation research. On 9 August 1884 the airship *La France* made the first flight by a manned, powered and controlled craft. It was 170ft (51.8m) long, completely manoeuvrable, powered by a 9hp electric motor and flew at 12mph (19kph).

Germany was destined to surpass France. The name that became, and remains, synonymous with airships is Zeppelin. On 2 July 1900, Count Ferdinand von Zeppelin, who adhered to the belief that "biggest is best", took LZ.1, the first airship he built, on its maiden flight. It was 420ft (128m) long, 38ft 6in (11.7m) in diameter, had a gas capacity of 400,000cu ft (11,320 cu m) and two 16hp Daimler engines. Adequate control was still lacking; the rudders were too small for efficient steering and, to climb or dive, weight had to be shifted forward or aft. After many vicissitudes, including a disintegrating accident with LZ.2, on 9 October 1906 LZ.3 flew at 33mph (53 kph) propelled by two 85hp engines.

A compatriot, Otto Lilienthal, who started as usual by seeking to emulate birds, was the first to perceive that success lay in a thorough study of control systems before applying power to a flying machine: putting the horse before the cart instead of vice versa as others had persistently done. Getting airborne was futile unless one knew how to steer and to gain and lose height. Between 1891 and 1896 he built five monoplane and two biplane gliders. He steered by shifting his body-weight and, launching himself from hills or a man-made mound, made flights of distances up to 750ft (230m).

At the turn of the century the richly textured story of man's conquest of the air began to accelerate towards its climax. The internal combustion petrol engine, which had been invented in 1884, was by now small and light enough to install in an airframe. There were many ingenious rivals in competition to be the first to pilot the controlled flight of a heavier than air flying machine. In the USA the Wright Brothers, Wilbur and Orville, built their first glider in 1899. In France, Louis Blériot, the brothers Charles and Gabriel Voisin, and an expatriate Brazilian,

LEFT: **In Germany, Otto Lilienthal made countless flights in his monoplane and biplane hang gliders during the 1890s, but finally lost his life in August 1896 when one of his monoplanes stalled and crashed.**

ABOVE RIGHT: E. P. Frost of Cambridge, England, was convinced that the birds had the answer, and spent a great deal of time and money on elaborate experimental ornithopters. This example was tested in 1906–7.

RIGHT: Lilienthal's greatest disciple was Englishman Percy Pilcher, seen here in the Hawk glider with which he made his most successful flights. He sustained fatal injuries following an in-flight structural failure of this machine on 30 September 1899.

Alberto Santos-Dumont, and others, were striving towards the same distinction. A sense of compulsion held them and others in thrall.

The ebb and flow of setbacks and progress met triumph at last on 17 December 1903, when Wilbur and Orville Wright achieved their goal. They had each in turn taken off twice from level ground aboard the aeroplane they had built, under its own power, and flown it over increasing distances up to 120ft (35m). In one day, the Air Age had dawned.

In 1909 Louis Blériot crossed the English Channel in a monoplane, and the first aviation meeting took place.

Chapter One
First Flights

England, France, Russia and later the United States of America were the countries in which the greatest efforts were made to achieve manned, powered flight during the 19th century. Early experiments with scale models led only to full-scale approximation of what was intended. In France, Félix du Temple de la Croix built a model monoplane that made short hops in 1857, first driven by clockwork and later by steam. In 1874 a full-size aeroplane of similar design but with a hot air engine, took off downhill and flew a short, unrecorded distance; but this did not count, as it could not become airborne from a run along level ground. In Russia 12 years later, an aeroplane designed by Alexander Feodorovich Mozhaiski and fitted with two English steam engines made a hop of 65–100ft (20–30m) from a ramp. It had made the same kind of assisted take-off, so also failed to comply with the parameters.

Clément Ader, a French electrical engineer, claimed that he had made a hop on 9 October 1890 after taking off from a level surface in a machine powered by steam, with a tractor airscrew (propeller). Although there was no eyewitness confirmation of this, and Ader could not say how long the flight had been, the French Army gave him financial help for further development of the aircraft. This was the first instance of practical military interest in aero-

planes: a logical progression from the various armies' use of balloons, with an interim attraction to airships. Eventually the subsidy ceased, Ader exhausted his own funds and that was the end of another false start – even, perhaps, a myth.

In 1894 an American electrical engineer who lived in England, Hiram Maxim, inventor of the eponymous machine gun, came close to being the first man to fly a powered aeroplane. His creation was an enormous biplane with two 180 hp lightweight steam engines, two propellers 17ft 10in (5.44m) in diameter and an all-up weight of 3.5 tons (3,556kg). To ensure that it could not make a free flight, it was run along rails with guard rails to restrain it. It did lift, but an axle failed and fouled the rails; Maxim's trials with it ceased.

The man who made the greatest progress towards the feat that everyone knows was at last accomplished by Orville and Wilbur Wright, was a German engineer named Otto Lilienthal.

Reasoning with what appeared to be indisputable logic that birds should be taken as the perfect model for the technique of flight, Lilienthal had a fascination with ornithopters – wing-flapping aircraft. In 1889 he published a book, *Bird Flight As The Basis Of Aviation*, which is a classic of aeronautical literature and provided the Wright brothers with inspiration. Intending always to return to ornithopters, in the interim Lilienthal built a fixed-wing hang glider in 1891 and, in the next five years, five more vari-

ants of monoplane gliders and two biplanes were built.

He first launched himself aloft from a springboard, but soon gave this up in favour of running downhill. He was supported by his arms, his legs dangling so that he could swing his torso in order to balance and control the craft. Next, he fitted a means of working a rear elevator by body movement; altering the centre of gravity in this way, he was able to rise and descend. He was fatally injured when he crashed in August 1896, but remains admired as the leading contributor to the science of aeroplane design in the pre-Wright era.

ABOVE: **In the USA, Professor Samuel Langley launched his man-carrying "Aerodrome" from a catapult atop a houseboat on the Potomac River in December 1903, but it was underpowered and suffered a structural failure, plunging into the water on both launch attempts.**

ABOVE: **Hiram Maxim's massive steam-powered test rig suffered severe damage when it broke free of its restraining rails during a trial in July 1894, and was thereafter relegated to giving strictly earthbound joyrides.**

MILESTONES

1903

First powered flight by the Wright Brothers at Kitty Hawk, North Carolina, USA.

1906

First powered flight in Europe by Alberto Santos-Dumont at Bagatelle, Paris, France.

1909

Louis Blériot crosses the English Channel, a flight lasting 47 minutes, from Calais to Dover.

AMERICAN PIONEERS

Versatility was a gift given to many of those who designed aircraft of all types: kites, balloons, gliders, aeroplanes and helicopters. Professor Samuel Langley, an American, clearly had the gift. A railway surveyor, engineer and distinguished astronomer, he was employed on aeronautical experiments at the Smithsonian Institution in Washington. In 1891 he began concentrating on steam-driven model aeroplanes. After four failures, his fifth and sixth constructions, launched by catapult from a barge on the Potomac River, made many flights, of which the longest was 4200ft (1,280m). The models were metal, with two sets of dihedral wings in tandem. A steam engine drove two propellers.

He had intended to abandon experimenting with flight, but, as could be expected, his country's President offered him a government subsidy to build a full-size aeroplane that could be developed for military use. His opening move, in 1901, was to make a quarter-scale model with a petrol engine: the first aircraft of any type or size to have one. Two years later Langley and his assistant, C. M. Manly, presented a full-size aeroplane. It had a petrol engine designed by Manly that was extraordinarily efficient and light – from which radial engines were developed.

Manly was the pilot when the aircraft, in which so much hope and so many dollars were invested, was tried out. Two trials were attempted and both were failures. This contraption suffered a structural failure and flopped into the river, but Manly suffered no injury. Not only did Langley's experiments end there, but so also did the government subsidy.

Ocatave Chanute, an American of French extraction, was another railway engineer and builder of successful gliders. In 1894 several articles he had written were published as a volume titled *Progress In Flying Machines*. It was largely the influence of Chanute, and of course the work of the aviation experimenters, notably including Lilienthal, which encouraged the two bicycle makers, Wilbur and Orville Wright, in their own many experiments that led to these brothers achieving the historic feat of building a powered machine capable of sustaining flight.

Alberto Santos-Dumont was Brazilian and a flamboyant extrovert: he sometimes moored his airship outside his club in Paris and, once, at his house on the Champs Elysées. He was a sprightly little man not short of courage, determination and intelligence: essential qualities in all pioneers of flight.

On 13 September 1906 he made the first successful aeroplane flight in Europe. He called his machine the 14bis (14 modified) because he had first tested it by carrying it slung beneath his No14 airship. It was an unattractive contraption, a boxkite of the type usually called tail-first or canard. The aircraft flew only 23ft (7m) before returning to earth with a crunch. He then fitted an octagonal aileron to each

17

first decade of the 20th century there was a plethora of other daring men in their flying machines deserving of mention. A prize for the weirdest-looking aircraft would perhaps go to Horatio Phillips. His research into aerofoils (wing sections) was fundamental to the theory of flight. His experiments with aerofoils that differed greatly in shape brought him to the correct deduction that the low pressure on top of a wing contributes more to lifting it than the high pressure below. In 1907 he constructed a multiplane aircraft that had four banks of wings, arranged in tandem, which were dubbed "Venetian blinds". It made a flight of 500ft (152m), but was too cumbersome to be a practical proposition. Such trials showed that one long, narrow wing would give as much lift as multiplane wings of similar ratio.

In 1906 a national British newspaper, the *Daily Mail*, encouraged aircraft

outboard wing box. These were connected to a harness he wore, so that he could control them by leaning left or right.

Hitherto the early aeroplanes, with few exceptions, had been biplanes. Trajan Vuia, a Romanian who lived in Paris, designed and built two monoplanes that had a great influence on the development of this type. Both were bat-like in shape and had tractor propellers. The first was controlled by wing warping, with a forward fin and rear rudder. A heavy landing in it persuaded Vuia to add a rear elevator and a framework under the wing, with a

four-wheel undercarriage, from which he operated the controls. In 1906 and 1907 he made several short hops after taking off from level ground.

Trajan Vuia's second machine, flown in 1907 with a 24hp Antoinette engine, achieved only two short hops.

The next year Santos-Dumont made another biplane, but it did not fly; so in November he started testing a monoplane that did, the No 19. In 1909 he made an improved version, the Demoiselle (Dragonfly), with a 20hp two-cylinder engine and 18ft (5.5m) wingspan. Three

bamboo poles formed the framework and the pilot sat on a canvas sheet stretched between two of these, under the wing on which the engine was mounted. The moveable tail was on a ball-and-socket joint. It was difficult to fly but has an exalted place in aeroplane history. It was the first design that was in the public domain, free for anyone to copy and build: deliberately, its inventor did not patent it.

As well as the famous names of the Wright brothers, Santos-Dumont and Louis Blériot (of whom more later), in the

LEFT: The "Venetian blind" multiplanes built by Horatio Phillips in the late 1890s to early 1900s were distinctive but unsuccessful. This is his 1904 model.

BELOW: Alliott Verdon Roe's first full-size aeroplane was this tail-first biplane, which eventually achieved limited hop-flights at Brooklands, Surrey, England, in June 1908.

constructors and pilots by offering money prizes for the best model aircraft. A. V. Roe, who became famous as Sir Alliott Verdon Roe, founder of Avro, one of the earliest aeroplane manufacturers, won £75.

In the USA, Glenn Curtiss designed and flew the "June Bug". On 4 July 1908 he won a magazine prize for the first officially recorded flight of 1km to be made in that country.

The first aeroplane flight in Britain was made at Farnborough on 16 October 1908, over a distance of 1390ft (424m), and ended in a crash landing. The pilot was a colourful, extrovert American ex-patriate, Samuel Franklin Cody, who later became a British citizen, but not for long: he was killed in a flying accident in 1913, aged 52. He designed and built the aircraft, which was named British Army Aeroplane No 1.

It was a Frenchman, Louis Blériot, who was the most influential designer of monoplanes. His No VII, built in 1907, had a 50hp Antoinette engine, a tractor airscrew and an enclosed fuselage. His concentration on monoplanes won him a place in aviation history that is second only to that of the Wright brothers in the annals of the early days.

Italy lagged behind the other European nations in developing an aircraft industry, but Gianni Caproni was emerging as their best designer. His first powered machine was the Ca 1, which appeared in 1910.

TECHNOLOGY FORGES AHEAD

On 26 January 1910 Glenn Curtiss made the first three seaplane take-offs, from California's San Diego Bay in a machine of his own design. The eight-cylinder engine drove a pusher propeller and the aircraft had a broad main float for hydroplaning. A later product was a flying boat whose wooden hull replaced the seaplane's floats and outriggers. On 28 March 1910 Henri Fabre made the first take-off from water in his float plane (hydravion) and was credited with a hop of 1640ft (500m) at

about 37mph (60kph). The first seaplane to take off and land safely was the Lakes Flying Co.'s Waterbird biplane, on Lake Windermere in the northwest of England. The first amphibian was the Sopwith Bat Boat, which won the £500 Mortimer Singer Prize for being the first all-British aircraft to make 12 landings alternately on land and water, within five hours.

The first flight over the Alps was accomplished on 23 September 1910 by the Portuguese, George Chavez, in a Blériot monoplane, though he crashed to his death at the end of the flight. Year by year astonishing feats were being performed by pilots whose small number of flying hours made their accomplishments all the more remarkable. In 1913 Roland Garros made the first crossing of the Mediterranean. On 1 January 1914, the world's first scheduled passenger-carrying service by aeroplane was inaugurated. A Benoist flying boat, carrying one passenger, now plied between two Florida towns, Tampa and St Petersburg.

On 30 July 1914 a Norwegian, Tryggve Gran, in a Blériot monoplane, became the first to cross the North Sea.

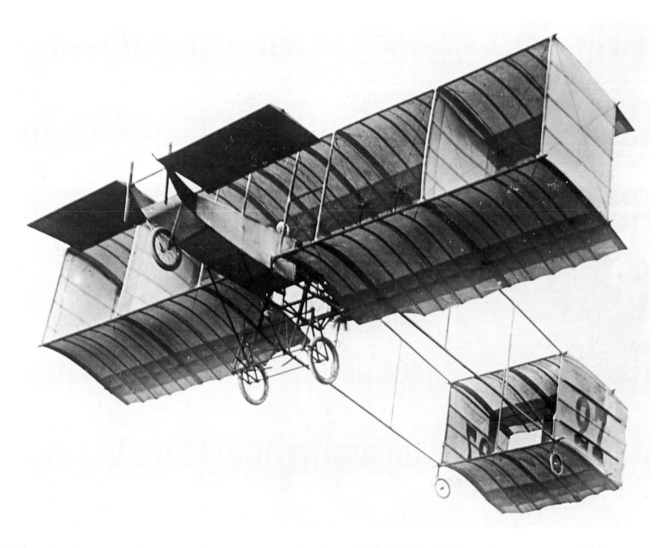

LEFT: The primitive Voisin boxkites of 1909–10 had no lateral control, and could only be turned in flat, wide, skidding curves if the pilot was to avoid sideslipping into the ground.

BELOW: French-domiciled Englishman Henry Farman bought an early Voisin, removed the "side-curtains" between the wings and later added ailerons to produce a controllable aeroplane in which he made the first official kilometre circular flight in Europe, on 13 January 1908.

ABOVE: **An evocative study of a Paumier biplane making a sunset flight at France's celebrated flying ground at Issy-le-Moulineaux.**

L'AÉROPLANE "LATHAM" AU DÉPART

RIGHT: **The celebrated pilot Hubert Latham taxies out in his Antoinette IV monoplane, 1908. This aileron-equipped machine spanned 12.80m (42ft), weighed 460kg (1,014lb) and was powered by a 50hp Antoinette engine driving a two-bladed metal propeller.**

ABOVE: British designer J. W. Dunne produced a succession of inherently stable, tailless swept-wing aircraft. This D.8 flown by the French military in 1913–14 was powered by an 80hp Gnome rotary engine, had a span of 46ft (14m), weighed 1,900lb (862kg) loaded and could attain 56mph (90kph).

ABOVE RIGHT: The Antoinette VII of 1909 had wing warping instead of ailerons, but lateral control was still exercised by means of handwheels on either side of the pilot. Its improved 60hp Antoinette engine gave it a speed of 52mph (84kph).

ABOVE: "Colonel" S. F. Cody made the first officially recognised powered flight in Great Britain on 16 October 1908 in his British Army Aeroplane No 1. This is one of his later products, the biplane on which he won the Michelin Cup on 31 December 1910 for a 4hr 47min flight that covered just over185 miles (296km) and established new British records for duration and distance over a closed circuit. It had a 60hp ENV "F" engine, spanned 46ft (14m) and weighed 2,950lb (1,338kg) loaded.

LEFT: By 1910 A. V. Roe was making successful flights in the latest of a series of triplanes. Here, he takes a passenger (back to the radiator) for a flight in the Roe III. This machine had a 35hp Green engine, spanned 31ft (9.45m) and had an all-up weight of only 750lb (340kg).

RIGHT: Based on the Farman design, the Bristol Boxkite of 1910 was used by both civilian and military operators. Powered by a 50hp Gnome engine, it spanned 34ft 6in (10.5m), had an all-up weight of 1,050lb (476kg) and flew at 40mph (64kph).

The Wright Brothers

On 17 December 1903 a flight of 12 seconds covering a distance of 120 ft (37m) changed history. The Wright Brothers had flown the first manned, powered heavier-than-air flying machine. The location was Kitty Hawk, North Carolina, USA.

Not only were the Wright brothers intuitive engineers; they were also scientists, test pilots and mathematicians. In addition to their unprecedented glider trials, they carried out meticulous windtunnel tests, and designed their own propellers, which were more efficient than any yet produced.

Like others, they studied bird flight; but it was soaring, not wing flapping, that held their attention. In 1899 they made a biplane kite with a 5ft (1.5m) wingspan and a new feature – wing warping – which enabled it to maintain lateral stability. This was a consequence of noticing that buzzards, when soaring, maintained equilibrium by a torsion of the tips of their wings: so they made a kite's wingtips twistable. A fixed foreplane gave fore and aft stability.

The following year they built a 17ft (5m) wingspan glider and took it from Dayton, Ohio, their home, to the sand dunes at Kill Devil Hills on the North Carolina coast, some 500 miles (800km) away, a site carefully chosen for its sandy surface and steady winds. In 1901 they advanced to a bigger one, which had a 22ft (6.7m) wingspan and anhedral wings and whose longest flights were over 100 yards (90m). The wingspan of the glider that they flew a year later was 33ft (10m). It had two pivoted rudders astern of the wings, which prevented yaw and enabled it to make balanced turns.

In 1903 they at last built the aircraft towards which all their efforts had been directed: a 40ft 4in (12.3m) wingspan biplane with skids, not wheels, which they named "Flyer". They also made the 12hp petrol engine that drove two pusher propellers. On 17 December they tossed a coin for first go and 36-year-old Wilbur won: but as it was launched he pulled the nose up too steeply and stalled. It was now the turn of Orville, four years his junior. This time the take-off was successful and the aeroplane flew for 12 seconds, during which he covered 120ft (37m): the first successful powered, controlled flight in history. Wilbur made the second on the same day. Each made another flight that day before a gust of wind wrecked the "Flyer 1".

They returned to Dayton and, using a more powerful engine, built Flyers 2 and 3,

> **"it was soaring, not wing flapping, that held their attention"**

which they flew from a nearby field at speeds up to 35mph (55kph). By now the aircraft could be banked and turned, so they were able to fly figures of eight. The secrecy with which they had conducted their experiments proved detrimental to their prospects of profiting immediately from their historic accomplishments. Not even their compatriots, let alone the world, were aware of their achievement, although details of their earlier work with gliders had been communicated to European pioneers by Octave Chanute. From 1905, trying to sell their aeroplane,

> **"the Flyer was far superior to any European aeroplane"**

LEFT: A series of glider trials to perfect the control system and piloting techniques had preceded the first powered flight. This is the No 3 glider in modified form being launched with Orville aboard in 1902.

MAIN PICTURE: **Orville Wright circling the parade ground at Fort Myer on 9 September 1908 during demonstrations for the US army.**

BELOW: **The Wright Model R or "Baby Wright" of 1910–11 was a smaller, racing version of the Wright biplane format. This is the one flown by Alec Ogilvie in the 1911 Gordon-Bennett Race at Eastchurch, powered by a 50hp NEC engine.**

which was turned down by their own military authorities and the British War Office, they did no flying. By 1908 they had built a two-seater flyer, which was crated and taken to Europe by Wilbur. He made no sales, so returned home after a few months, leaving the crated aircraft at Le Havre.

In 1908 the US War Department invited them to demonstrate their machine and, a month later, the Wrights arranged to manufacture Flyers in France. Wilbur returned there to give demonstration flights. These astonished the French aircraft industry and pilots: the best that had been achieved in Europe were flights of no more than 90 seconds made only a few feet off the ground. The Flyer was far superior to any European aeroplane, let alone French ones, in all respects. One basic difference between the Wrights' and the Europeans' was that the former did not have inherent stability. Presently Wilbur and Orville further improved their aeroplane by fitting a fixed tailplane behind the double rudder at the rear. Their final type was the Model L of 1915. ●

WRIGHT F

Wright Flyer

The first manned, power-driven, heavier-than-air flying machine.

SPECIFICATION
Wingspan
40ft 4in (12.29m)

Length
21ft 1in (6.43m)

Height
8ft 0in (2.44m)

Weight
750lb (340kg)

Engine
Four-cylinder 12hp Wright water-cooled petrol engine

Simple wooden propellers, mounted behind the wings, were driven by sprocket wheels and chains from the engine.

As a result of no suitable engine being available to power their aircraft, the Wright brothers designed and built their own. The result was a lightweight four-cylinder 12hp water-cooled petrol engine with magneto ignition.

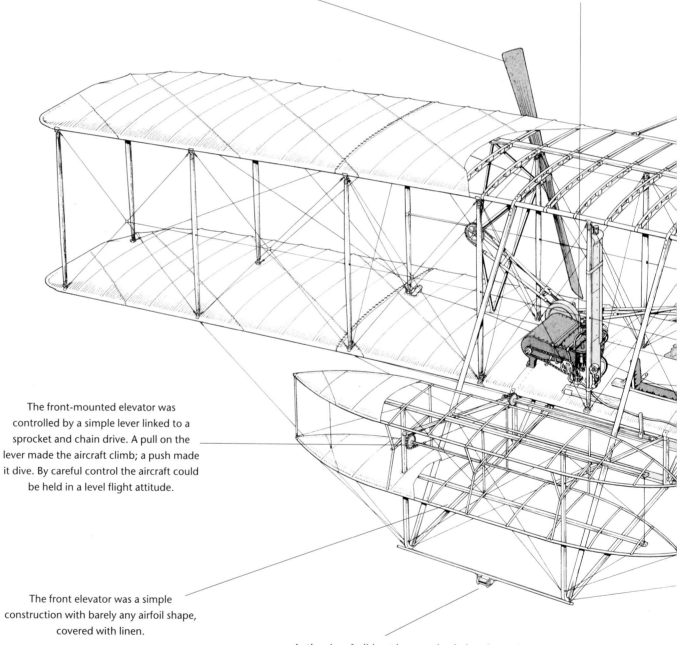

The front-mounted elevator was controlled by a simple lever linked to a sprocket and chain drive. A pull on the lever made the aircraft climb; a push made it dive. By careful control the aircraft could be held in a level flight attitude.

The front elevator was a simple construction with barely any airfoil shape, covered with linen.

As the aircraft did not have a wheeled undercarriage, it was launched from a ground-mounted rail. Rollers were fitted to the front and rear of the airframe to guide the aircraft along the launching rail.

illustration © Mike Badrocke

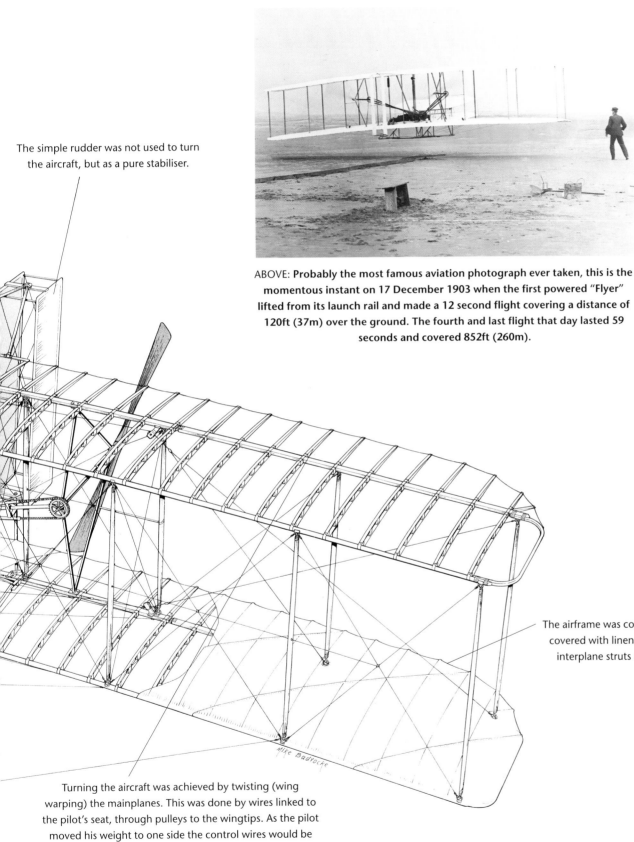

The simple rudder was not used to turn the aircraft, but as a pure stabiliser.

ABOVE: **Probably the most famous aviation photograph ever taken, this is the momentous instant on 17 December 1903 when the first powered "Flyer" lifted from its launch rail and made a 12 second flight covering a distance of 120ft (37m) over the ground. The fourth and last flight that day lasted 59 seconds and covered 852ft (260m).**

KEY FACTS

1900–01
The Wright brothers build their first two gliders, No 1 and No 2.

1902
Glider No 3 is successfully flown at Kitty Hawk.

17 December 1903
The first manned, powered flight in history is made by Orville Wright in a Flyer at Kill Devil Hills, Kitty Hawk, North Carolina, USA.

1905
Flyer No 3 is built and successfully flown.

1908
Wright Model A is flown and later tested by the US Army at Fort Meyer in July 1909.

1910
Wright Model B is built and for the first time a Wright aircraft has a conventional tailplane and rudder assembly. The model R (Baby Wright) is flown for the first time in this year.

The airframe was constructed from ash and spruce wood, then covered with linen. The two mainplanes were connected by interplane struts and the complete assembly stiffened by bracing wires.

Mike Badrocke

Turning the aircraft was achieved by twisting (wing warping) the mainplanes. This was done by wires linked to the pilot's seat, through pulleys to the wingtips. As the pilot moved his weight to one side the control wires would be tensioned, thus twisting the wings, which resulted in a gentle banking turn.

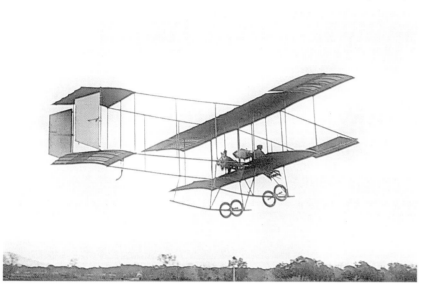

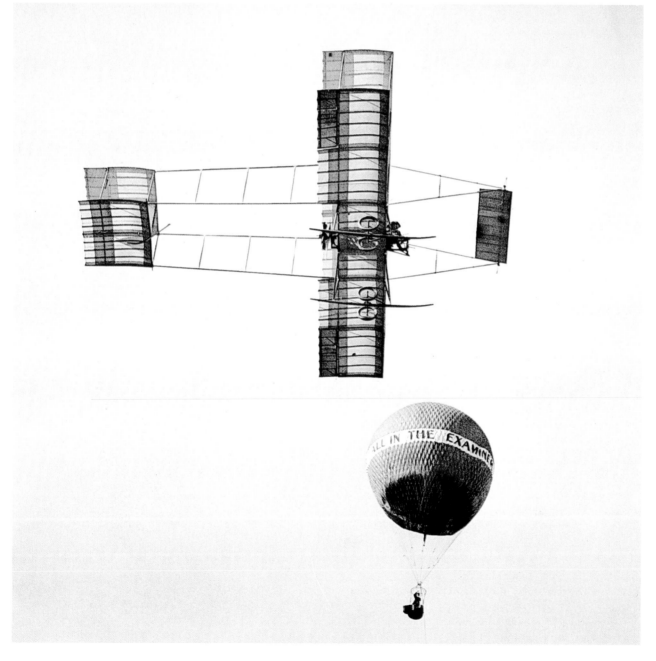

ABOVE: Aviation fever was widespread, and often provided inspiration for carnival floats. This "exact model of M Henri Farmen's [sic] Aeroplane", based on an adult tricycle, won third prize in the 1909 carnival at Taunton, Somerset, in England.

ABOVE LEFT: It was on this Farman biplane in April 1910 that the French airman Louis Paulhan won the *Daily Mail* newspaper's £10,000 prize for the first flight from London to Manchester, in a hard-fought race with Britain's Claude Grahame-White.

LEFT: The USA's first international aviation meeting was held at Dominguez Field, Los Angeles, in January 1910. One of its star attractions was Louis Paulhan, seen here on the way to attaining a record-breaking altitude of 4,146ft (1,264m) in his Farman biplane on 12 January. The balloon in the background is tethered.

ABOVE: Among the fastest aeroplanes of 1912–13 were the Deperdussin monoplanes designed by Louis Béchereau, with their sleek, streamlined monocoque fuselages. This one is being flown by the celebrated French pilot Maurice Prévost.

ABOVE RIGHT: A moody sunset study of an Antoinette VII of 1909 captures the aeroplane's delicate lines and the romantic appeal of aviation in the pioneer years. Antoinettes were among the prizewinners at the Reims meeting in France that year.

RIGHT: The sound of an aeroplane was sufficient to stop people in their tracks and draw all eyes skyward, as in the case of these holidaymakers at Weymouth, Dorset, England, as Grahame-White's bright blue Henry Farman seaplane, emblazoned with the slogan "Wake up, England" passes overhead in 1912.

LEFT: Despite its ungainly appearance, the Voisin canard, or tail-first, biplane of 1911 was flown in both landplane and seaplane forms, but the aeroplane failed to find favour.

RIGHT: At Eastchurch, England, in 1911 the Short brothers produced the Triple Twin, with a pair of 50hp Gnome engines (one at the front end and one at the rear of the nacelle), driving one pusher and two tractor propellers. It flew successfully.

BELOW: In 1910, when it appeared at Dunstall Park racecourse, Wolverhampton, in England, the aptly named Seddon Mayfly tandem biplane was one of the largest aeroplanes in the world, with a wing area of about 1,000sq ft (92.9sq m) and 2,000ft (610m) of steel tubing in its structure. Persistent trouble with the two 65hp NEC engines prevented its creator from attempting flight.

ABOVE: **Seen at the 1912 Cicero International Air Meet in Illinois, USA, the circular McCormick-Romme "Umbrellaplane" initially had no ailerons and could not turn in the air; but it did fly.**

ABOVE: **"Colonel" S. F. Cody (real name Cowdery), an expatriate American, is credited with making the first powered, sustained and controlled flight in an aeroplane in Britain, at Farnborough on 16 October 1908.**

RIGHT: **It seems unlikely that the pilot of the optimistically named Kauffmann No 1 monoplane of 1910 attained any greater altitude than seen here.**

ABOVE: By 1911 the latest Farman "Circuit" biplane had lost the type's prominent forward elevator, and its pilot and passenger were carried on a rather precarious framework extending from the lower wing.

LEFT: On the Blériot stand at the 1914 Olympia Aero Show in London the company's new Parasol monoplane, so called because of its high wing, was displayed alongside two No XI-type monoplanes not far removed from the machine in which Blériot had crossed the English Channel in 1909.

RIGHT: Sightseers on the beach at Filey, Yorkshire, in 1911 admire the Blackburn Flying School's Mercury II two-seater monoplane, powered by a 50hp Gnome rotary engine.

ABOVE: The aeroplanes built by "Colonel" Samuel Cody in Great Britain were noted for their sturdy construction and the use of seats normally associated with agricultural machinery. Here Cody shows off his 1911 Circuit of Britain biplane for the benefit of spectators at Hendon Aerodrome, near London.

RIGHT: While this means of testing the strength of the wings of a Bristol Coanda monoplane in 1912 with a sandbag load might seem primitive, similar techniques were still common practice many years later.

ABOVE: The first really successful aeroplane built by Frederick Handley Page was the crescent-winged Type E of 1912, nicknamed "Yellow Peril" owing to its yellow-varnished wings and tail. Its fuselage was blue.

LEFT: American Glenn Curtiss produced some of the first successful seaplanes. The example seen here is the Paulhan-Curtiss Triad, competing in the Monaco Hydro-Aeroplane meeting of March 1912.

ABOVE: Night flying was a new adventure, and special events were put on at Hendon Aerodrome, when the aircraft were flown with arrays of light bulbs along their wing leading edges. This illuminated Farman biplane was photographed in 1912.

RIGHT: Another participant in the 1912 Hydro-Aeroplane meeting at Monaco was this Maurice Farman biplane flown by Renaux, with its extremely staggered wings.

Louis Blériot

Louis Blériot, who contributed greatly to the development of aviation, is best remembered for making the first heavier-than-air flight across the English Channel, in response to the *Daily Mail*'s offer of a £1000 prize. His age at the time was 37. Taking off at 4.35am on 25 July 1909 in a monoplane of his own design, the Blériot No XI, with a 22/25 hp Anzani engine, he entered cloud 10 minutes later and flew blind for another ten miles before the Dover cliffs came in sight. The wind had blown him off course and his intended landing place was far to the west. He turned towards it but lost speed in the headwind, so entered an opening in the cliffs. Here the wind caught him and, he wrote, "I stop my motor and the machine falls". It was 5.12am. Within two days Blériot had received orders for over one hundred XIs. Some of these were for the British War Office.

This great feat had been preceded by much endeavour. In 1905 Blériot had collaborated with Gabriel Voisin in designing a glider. In 1907 he built his first powered monoplane, progenitor of the many that would make him world famous. In 1908 he made his No VIIIbis, which he flew for 8 minutes 24 seconds, followed by VIIIter, which he flew for 28km (17 miles) in 22 minutes, with two landings.

In May 1909 Blériot produced his first passenger machine, the No XII, powered by a 60hp ENV engine, in which he took two passengers up at the Reims Meeting of 22–29 August that year and was awarded a special prize.

The No XIII, with a 40hp Anzani engine, was built in 1910. Henceforth, Blériot concentrated on development and sales, while leaving the flying to Adolphe Pégoud, a great aerobatic pilot and the first man to perform a loop.

BELOW: **The cross-Channel machine on display after its epoch-making flight. Its Chauvière propeller was one of the most advanced designs for its time.**

LEFT: **Louis Blériot poses in the No XI monoplane in which he made his celebrated cross-Channel flight in 1909, under the power of a small 25hp three-cylinder Anzani engine.**

ABOVE RIGHT: **Blériot prepares to depart from Les Baraques on 25 July 1909. He was walking on crutches at the time, owing to a mishap at a flying meeting shortly before.**

RIGHT: **The widespread adoption of the Blériot No XI following the Channel crossing is typified by this study of one such aircraft in use in Russia.**

Альб. Гюйо. на моноплане „Блеріо"

Булла СПБ

FAR LEFT: Bathers wave to M. Salmet as he flies his Gnome-engined Blériot XI monoplane, named "Entente Cordiale" along the beach at Scarborough, Yorkshire, England.

LEFT: On 10 January 1912 Lt Charles Samson took off from HMS *Africa* in the Short S38, using a wooden runway mounted over the vessel's forward gun turret. The flotation bags proved unnecessary: Samson made a safe landing at Eastchurch, England.

RIGHT: Dutchman Anthony Fokker's first machines were a series of monoplanes with marked dihedral to their wings and named Spin (Spider). This is the M1 of 1912, with an enclosed fuselage and a 100hp Argus engine.

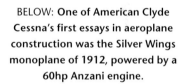

LEFT: The most successful prewar product of the Royal Aircraft Factory at Farnborough was the BE2 designed by Geoffrey de Havilland, which proved stable and reliable. It is seen here during tests of "fin struts" and an early oleo undercarriage.

LEFT: The Avro Type D of 1911 was a breakthrough for the company, and led ultimately to the famous Type 504. This Type D, seen at Brooklands, Surrey, England had a 35hp Green engine, which gave it a speed of 45–50mph (72–80kph).

BELOW: One of American Clyde Cessna's first essays in aeroplane construction was the Silver Wings monoplane of 1912, powered by a 60hp Anzani engine.

The progressive understanding of aerodynamics and structures allowed the aeroplane to be developed into a formidable fighting machine.

Chapter Two

The Pace Quickens

The Air Battalion of Britain's Royal Engineers had been created on 1 April 1911 to equip with both airships and aeroplanes. The following year, the Royal Flying Corps (RFC) came into being. France and Germany also formed air forces and aeroplanes figured in war for the first time. The Italian Army had acquired its first aeroplanes in 1910; in 1911, when the Italo-Turkish War erupted in Libya, Italy sent seven aeroplanes by sea to Tripoli: two Blériots, two Etrichs and three Nieuports. She also possessed a few Farmans. Belligerence and colonial ambition had been quick to put the most advanced method of locomotion to destructive use.

In 1912, Bulgaria, Serbia, Greece and Montenegro had formed an alliance to free Macedonia from Turkish rule. The Bulgars, having few aeroplanes or pilots, hired mercenaries who brought their own aircraft. An American pilot, Riley Scott, had already invented a bomb sight and bomb rack, a great convenience: hitherto, the pro-Bulgaria pilots had tied a bomb loosely to one foot and simply kicked it off over the target.

When the First World War began, the RFC's only airship squadron, No 1, was in the process of re-equipping entirely with aeroplanes. Henceforth there would be no more airships on the Battle Order. Four aeroplane squadrons already existed, numbered from 2 to 5, and there were 110 aeroplanes on the strength. Nos 6 and 7 Squadrons were being formed. The squadron establishment was 12 aircraft and 12 pilots. They flew a variety of types with maximum speeds of 65 to 75mph (120kph). There were Blériot No XIs like the one that first flew the Channel, and four makes of biplane: the Farman Shorthorn, which had a 75hp Renault engine and a speed of 66mph (106 kph); the Martinsyde, with an 80hp Gnome or a Le Rhône engine; the Bristol Scout, with a Le Rhône; and the BE2c, most favoured because its 90hp engine was made, like the airframe, in the Royal Aircraft factory at Farnborough, Hampshire, in southern England.

The RFC's greatest handicap was that the other British engine manufacturers, of whom the leaders were Wolseley, Beardmore and Rolls-Royce, were producing very small quantities. All aircraft constructors had to depend mostly on small rotary air-cooled French engines, Le Rhône, Clerget and Renault. Later that year the Avro 504, a biplane that was the first modern-looking military type, with an enclosed fuselage and clean lines, came into service. With a 110hp Le Rhône nine-cylinder engine that gave it a speed of 95mph (153kph), it could climb to 18,000ft (5,486m). Improvements were made over the next four years, including the addition of a Lewis gun mounted on the upper mainplane.

The Royal Naval Air Service (RNAS) faced the same equipment problems.

France entered the war with a total of 160 aeroplanes in 25 Escadrilles, each established for six aeroplanes. Some were flying Farman Longhorns. Other types were: Farman F20 with a Gnome or Le Rhône 80hp engine that gave a maximum speed of 65mph (105kph); Voisin LA with a 130hp Salmson engine and speeds up to 65mph; Caudron G III with a Gnome engine and 65mph speed; Morane-Saulnier L, Le Rhône-engined, capable of 72mph (116kph). Only the Voisin was armed with a machine gun.

Germany had 246 aeroplanes, of which 198 were sent to the Front in 33

ABOVE: **An early attempt to fire through the propeller arc. This French Morane Type N monoplane, flown by pre-war pilot Jules Vedrines, has an unsynchronised Hotchkiss machine gun with 25-cartridge strip feed. Steel deflector wedges have been attached to the wooden propeller blades to deflect mistimed bullets.**

ABOVE: The Sopwith Camel entered service with the Royal Flying Corps in 1916, and was armed with two synchronised 0.303in Vickers machine guns. It was powered by a 130hp Clerget 9B, 150hp Bentley or 110hp Le Rhône; all were nine-cylinder rotary engines.

MILESTONES

1915

The Morane-Saulnier Type N and the Fokker E-I, effectively the first single-seater fighters, enter service.

1917

The formidable Albatros DIII enters service with the Imperial German Air Force.

1918

Handley Page O/400 night bombers attack German targets

Field Service Units, each with six aeroplanes. Ten Home Defence Units of four aeroplanes each remained in the Fatherland. The Germans enjoyed high-volume production of two excellent makes of engine, Mercedes and Benz, both of which were heavy, in-line and water-cooled. The German Military Aviation Service was flying two-seater biplanes capable of 65 to 76mph (105 to 122kph), the Albatros and AEG; and two single-seater monoplanes: the Taube, which was made by the Albatros works, and Fokker.

Russia had 300 aeroplanes in her air force, Belgium 25 and Austro-Hungary 35.

DEADLY RACE

The function of aeroplanes was at first limited to reconnaissance and artillery spotting – reporting to the gunners the fall of shells in relation to the target. Air fighting had not been seriously contemplated by any of the air forces. The first type that could defend itself and attack enemy aircraft was the Voisin: a machine gun was mounted in its cockpit. Because the pilot and observer sat side-by-side instead of in the usual tandem seating and the propeller was a pusher type, there was no obstruction to the field of fire. The British, French and Germans often carried bombs of roughly 20lb (9kg), which they dropped by hand.

The deadly race to dominate the world in air power began in Europe at a rate and on a scale of progress that demanded total application to military aviation requirements. Only in the USA could development in the civil – essentially commercial – sector be pursued.

The Italian Military Air Service had been formed on 7 January 1915 and Italy declared war on Austro-Hungary on 24 May that year. Turkey had by now declared itself on the German side, so Britain's RFC was in action over Mesopotamia (now Iraq). The Austro-Hungarians, allied to Germany, equipped themselves with German aircraft. In the words of Generale Felice Porro, the Italian air arm was "in an embryonic state": it had only 58 aeroplanes. By 1915 Britain had 161, France 1,150 and Germany 764.

The Italian Macchi factory was manufacturing the French Nieuport under licence, but the Italians designed and built their own bomber, the Caproni, with three 190hp Isotta-Fraschini engines, giving it a maximum speed of 85mph (137kph). By early 1918 the Caproni C4 triplane, which had three 270hp water-cooled V-type Isotta-Fraschini engines, was operational. Its wingspan was 98ft 1in (29.9m), length 49ft 6in (15m); it had a maximum speed of 87mph (140kph) and seven hours' endurance. By the summer, a development from it, the Ca5, had entered the air battles. This had three 30hp Fiat A-12bis water-cooled engines, its wingspan was 76ft 9in (23.4m), length 41ft 5in (12.65m) and its maximum speed was 94.4mph (152kph). The endurance was four hours.

In the same year a fighter of Italian design and build, the Ansaldo SVA5, joined the Battle Order. With a water-

ABOVE: **Another way to avoid propeller damage was to mount the gun to fire clear of it. This Nieuport 27 of 1 Sqn, RFC, in France in the winter of 1917, has a Lewis gun on a Foster mount, aimed through an Aldis sight.**

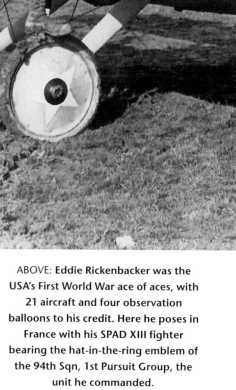

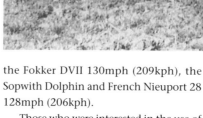

ABOVE: **Eddie Rickenbacker was the USA's First World War ace of aces, with 21 aircraft and four observation balloons to his credit. Here he poses in France with his SPAD XIII fighter bearing the hat-in-the-ring emblem of the 94th Sqn, 1st Pursuit Group, the unit he commanded.**

cooled engine, it attained 136.7mph (220kph).

Not all designs incorporated the latest improvements. The ultimate purpose of a warplane designer is to achieve maximum lethality: armament and bomb load, high speed and ceiling are the priorities, coupled with the shortest possible production time. Aesthetically pleasing form is secondary. The French Morane-Saulnier Type L parasol monoplane, the British BE2 and Avro 504, and German Fokker E III of 1914–16 had enclosed fuselages and tractor propellers, but the British Vickers FB5 Gunbus, the Royal Aircraft Factory FE8 and de Havilland DH2 all had booms between the nacelle and tail unit, and a pusher propeller.

A young Dutchman, Anthony Fokker, was establishing himself as a brilliant aviation engineer. He was also an aircraft designer, but above all, he was an outstanding businessman. Although he was educated in Holland, he studied aeronautics in Germany and in 1912, when aged 22, set up a company there. His first aeroplane (though there is an unresolved argument that attributes the design to another Dutchman, Jacob Goedekker) was the Spin – which means spider in Dutch (in German it is Spinne). This monoplane had first flown in 1911. Its wingspan was

36ft 1in (11m), and length 25ft 2in (7.70m). Powered by a 25hp Argus engine, it reached a maximum speed of 56mph (90kph). A German named Rheinhold Platz was Fokker's chief designer; he was responsible in 1917 for the Fokker Triplane, based on the British Sopwith Triplane.

The latter, which first flew in 1916, was the most interesting and innovative aeroplane of the mid-war period. Its three wings imparted superb manoeuvrability and a ceiling of 20,000ft (6,096m), with a top speed of 120mph (192kph). Unfortunately for many German fighter pilots, the Fokker imitation initially had a fatal defect: structural weakness caused a number of in-flight failures of the top wing.

DIVERSITY IN DESIGN

The most handsome and streamlined aeroplanes that began to appear in 1916 were the Morane-Saulnier Type N and, even more pleasing to the eye, Germany's Albatros DV with its sleek torpedo shape. The Albatros DIII was powered by a Mercedes 160hp engine and had a top speed of 110mph (177kph). By the end of the war the French SPAD XIII (acronym for La Société pour l'Aviation et ses Derives) had attained 133mph (214kph),

the Fokker DVII 130mph (209kph), the Sopwith Dolphin and French Nieuport 28 128mph (206kph).

Those who were interested in the use of aeroplanes for commercial purposes looked to the biggest. Multi-engine bombers had attained formidable dimensions and good speeds. By 1918 there was a rich diversity of makes. In Russia, Igor Sikorsky's Ilya Mouromets variant, IM-G3, was powered by two 220hp Renault inner engines and two 150hp RBZ-6 outers. It carried a bombload of 2,000lb (907kg) and there were three machine gun positions. In Italy, when the Caproni Ca42 entered service in 1918, its bombload was 3,000lb (1,360kg).

Germany operated two behemoths. The Friedrichshafen G.III had 260hp Mercedes engines, pusher propellers, a maximum speed of 87mph (140kph) and five hours' endurance. Its bombload was 2,200lb (998kg). The twin-engine Gotha G.V. had the same power units, bombload and pusher airscrews, a top speed of

87mph (140kph) and six hours' endurance.

In 1917 the massive bulk of the Handley Page O/100 heaved itself into the air and set about pulverising the enemy with the 2,000lb (907kg) bombload it carried. With twin Rolls-Royce Eagle engines, it could make 95mph (153kph) and had six hours' endurance. The following year the O/400 entered squadron service with the same engines and bombload, of the same dimensions, but was credited with 2mph (3kph) greater speed, 22lb (10kg) greater gross weight and four hours' endurance.

Seaplanes and the design of flying boats also benefited from the hothouse

ABOVE: A German pilot poses with his Fokker D VII, armed with a pair of synchronised Spandau machine guns. The controlability and responsiveness of the D VII, which entered service in the spring of 1918, made it an excellent fighter.

17, whose top speed was 103mph (166kph), Spad VII with 120mph (193kph) and the Spad XIII with a speed of 133mph (214kph). Italy was engaged mostly on bombing, but manufactured French fighters under licence: Nieuport in 1915, Caudron in 1916, Spad in 1917–18. By the time the armistice was declared, every aspect of aeronautics had made unprecedented progress.

of war. The Felixstowe F.2A flying boat of 1917, a much refined development of the Curtiss America series and powered by Rolls-Royce Eagle 375hp motors, carried a crew of four to six, according to its armament. It had a Lewis gun in the nose and on either side at the waist, plus either a 13in (33cm) torpedo or two 230lb (104kg) flat-nosed anti-submarine bombs.

The type still most ahead of its time was the Junkers J1, which not only had a metal airframe covered with thin sheet iron, but also, being a cantilever monoplane, was much stronger than biplanes with wooden airframes and fabric-covered wooden wings. It was not until the mid 1920s, however, that other manufacturers began to design for all-metal construction.

The aeroplanes that attracted the greatest interest were the Fokker E I– E III Eindeckers, which cost the RFC and French Air Force heavy losses in 1916, and the de Havilland DH2, which was the first to turn the tables. The Albatros DI, which appeared in late 1915, was steadily improved and the Fokker D VII was capable of 130mph (209kph) by the end of the following year. The Bristol Fighter had a maximum speed of 120mph (193kph). The Sopwith Camel could attain 115mph (185kph) and had the most remarkable agility. The SE5 was another great fighter and was 5mph (8kph) faster than its contemporaries. The DH4 and DH9 were two-seater light bombers. Rolls-Royce engines were the best in the world, closely followed by the Mercedes; Wolseley and Armstrong Siddeley engines were also giving good service. However, the British still relied mostly on French engines. France's outstanding aeroplanes were the Nieuport

RIGHT: A German DFW C.V two-seat reconnaissance aircraft goes about its business over the Western Front. Powered by a 200hp Benz Bz VI water-cooled engine, the C.V served in large numbers from the end of 1916.

LEFT: **A fine take-off study of a Royal Aircraft Factory BE2e two-seat reconnaissance aircraft of 1916. Wingspan** 40ft 9in (12.4m), **length** 27ft 3in (8.3m), **height** 12ft (3.6m), **weight** 1,430lb (650kg), **engine** RAF 1a, 90hp 8-cylinder vee air-cooled, **maximum speed** 90 mph (145 kph), **endurance** 4 hr, **crew** 2.

BELOW: **Seaplane carrier HMS** *Ark Royal* **in 1914–15, with a Sopwith Type 807 seaplane on deck.**

LEFT: **The Farman F40 entered service with the French in 1915 as an army and artillery co-operation aircraft. Wingspan** 58ft (17.69m), **length** 30ft (9.1m), **height** 13ft (3.96m), **weight** 1,650lb (748kg), **engine** Renault 8C, 130hp 8-cylinder vee air-cooled, **maximum speed** 84mph (135 kph), **range** 263 miles (423km), **crew** 2.

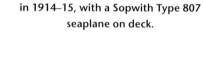

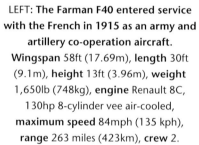

RIGHT: Initially used as a reconnaissance and bomber aircraft, the Avro 504 became one of the greatest trainers of all time. This is a 504K. **Wingspan** 36ft (11m), **length** 29ft 5in (9m), **height** 10ft 5in (3.2m), **weight** 1,100lb (500kg), **engine** Gnome Monosoupape 100hp or Le Rhône 110hp 9-cylinder rotary air-cooled, **maximum speed** 80–90mph (130–145kph), **range** 250 miles (400km), **crew** 2.

BELOW RIGHT: A Henry Farman F27 used by 30 Sqn RFC in Mesopotamia for supply dropping and reconnaissance. **Wingspan** 53ft (16.15m), **length** 30ft (9.1m), **height** 12ft (3.65m), **engine** Salmson 140hp or 160hp 9-cylinder radial water-cooled, **maximum speed** 92mph (148kph), **endurance** 2hr 40min, **crew** 2.

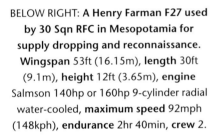

RIGHT: **The Airco DH2 scout, produced to counter Fokker's Eindecker, entered service on the Western Front early in 1916.**
Wingspan 28ft 3in (8.6m), **length** 25ft 3in (7.7m), **height** 9ft 6in (2.9m), **weight** 943lb (428kg), **engine** Gnome Monosoupape 100hp or Le Rhône 110hp 9-cylinder rotary air-cooled, **maximum speed** 90mph (145kph), **endurance** 3hr, **crew** 1.

ABOVE: **This Nieuport XI fighter of 1916 is fitted with launching tubes for eight Le Prieur rockets for use against enemy observation balloons.**
Wingspan 25ft (7.6m), **length** 18ft (5.5m), **height** 8ft (2.4m), **weight** 705lb (320kg), **engine** Le Rhône 9C 80hp 9-cylinder rotary air-cooled, **maximum speed** 100mph (161kph), **range** 156 miles (250km), **crew** 1.

BELOW RIGHT: **The Fairey Campania of 1917 was a carrier-borne patrol seaplane for the RNAS.**
Wingspan 61ft 7in (18.77m), **length** 43ft 4in (13.21m), **height** 15ft 1in (4.59m), **weight** 3,725lb (1,690kg), **engine** Rolls-Royce Mk IV 250hp 12-cylinder vee water-cooled, **maximum speed** 80mph (129kph), **endurance** 6hr 30min, **crew** 2.

BELOW: **Leutnant Walter von Bülow with his Fokker E III Eindecker escort fighting scout in 1916.**
Wingspan 31ft 3in (9.52m), **length** 23ft 8in (7.2m), **height** 7ft 11in (2.4m), **weight** 1,342lb (610kg), **engine** Oberursel UI9 100hp 9-cylinder rotary air-cooled, **maximum speed** 81mph (130kph), **endurance** 1hr 30min, **crew** 1.

Fighter versus Fighter

Aeroplanes were at first limited to reconnaissance and artillery spotting. Later the battle for air supremacy began, with pilots trained for combat and more sophisticated aircraft.

On 5 October 1914 history's first air-to-air victory was recorded. A mechanic, Louis Quenault, as air gunner, with Sergeant Joseph Frantz as pilot, shot down a German Aviatik.

Two-seater British aircraft were ill equipped for air fighting. The observer, at the machine gun, sat in front, with only 180 degrees field of fire: a pusher's tail was unprotected and a tractor's foward arc of fire was restricted by the propeller.

On 1 April 1915 air gunnery made a prodigious advance: Lieutenant Roland Garros, flying a Morane-Saulnier H with a fixed forward-firing Maxim machine gun, introduced a feature which revolutionised air fighting. He perfected a device

invented by Raymond Saulnier: the fitting of steel wedges to the wooden propeller blades so that bullets that did not pass between them were deflected. Garros scored three victories in 18 days before being shot down.

Anthony Fokker and his team devised a mechanism that dispensed with the deflectors by synchronising the firing of the gun with the revolutions of the propeller. The Fokker E I, the E signifying Eindecker (monoplane), thus equipped was the first real fighter and became the scourge of the Allies despite its low maximum speed of 81 mph (130 kph). The success prompted the design of the Fokker E II only a month after the E I had entered

BELOW: Despite its size, the doughty Bristol F2B Fighter, which entered service with the RFC in 1917, was fast and agile. A single, fixed synchronised 0.303in Vickers machine gun fired forwards, while the observer/gunner in the rear cockpit had one or two 0.303in movable Lewis guns on a Scarff ring mounting (inset). Up to twelve 25lb (11kg) bombs could also be carried.

ABOVE: Typical of late-war German two-seater reconnaissance aircraft, the LVG C.VI was powered by a 200hp Benz Bz IV six-cylinder water-cooled engine, and its armament comprised a single fixed forward-firing Spandau machine gun and a movable Parabellum machine gun in the rear cockpit. Compared with the Bristol Fighter it was slow and sluggish in the air.

ABOVE LEFT: Captain Albert Ball, VC, RFC, was Britain's first widely recognised heroic figure in air warfare. A master of air combat, he amassed a tally of at least 44 combat victories in a mere 14 months, flying Nieuport and SE5 scouts, before his death on 7 May 1917 in mysterious circumstances.

" Be above your opponent with the sun behind you and shoot from as close as possible"

service. The definitive E III became a most feared fighter in the hands of German pilots, such as Boelcke and Immelmann. By the end of 1916 the Albatros D III entered service, and although an improvement on the earlier D I and D II it was prone to structural failure. Later in early 1918 the Albatros D V, a rakish torpedo-shaped aeroplane with twin machine guns firing through the propeller, appeared in action.

The RFC's first single-seater squadron, flying the 93mph (149kph) Airco DH2, a pusher with a Lewis gun, had arrived in France in January 1916. The pilot was kept busy, having to change the ammunition drum after every 47 rounds, aim and pull the trigger while working the joystick and throttle. Several months later the gun was mounted rigidly in front. This aeroplane and the 97mph (156 kph) Nieuport II Bébé, with its machine gun on the upper wing and firing over the propeller, did well against the Fokker.

The most successful pilots then were German; Boelcke, the first great fighter leader, and Immelmann. Boelcke's rules for success were, "Be above your opponent with the sun behind you and shoot from as close as possible". In January 1916 each shot down his eighth victim. On 18 June Immelmann died attacking a Bristol FE2b, whose gunner shot his aircraft in half. On 28 October, Boelcke, leading his Jasta (squadron) of Albatros DVs against two DH2s, collided with one of his own pilots and was killed, after 40 victories.

The most successful French pilots to date were Jean Navarre, who used to stand up in his Nieuport to fire its Lewis gun and shot down 12 enemy machines before being wounded and grounded in late 1916; Charles Nungesser, wounded or injured in crashes 17 times in the course of destroying 45 opponents, survived the war; Georges Guynemer, killed in 1917 with a score of 53; René Fonck, France's top scorer with 75, six of them in one day.

The first RFC pilot to receive vivid publicity was Albert Ball, who went into battle in 1916 aged 19 and was killed, flying a SE5a, 16 months later with a score of 44.

A Canadian, Major William Barker, shot down one hostile as an air gunner and, as a pilot, 25 in France and 27 in Italy. The 1917 Sopwith Camel he flew was worthy of the man. It had two Vickers machine guns. Its rotary engine made it difficult to master but enabled it to turn with lightning speed. The Sopwith Triplane was a nimble, formidable fighter. Fokker successfully copied the formula in his Dr. I, which proved a formidable opponent in fighter combats.

At the war's end, Manfred von Richthofen, with 80 victories, was the top-scoring pilot. The RFC/RAF's best were Mannock with 73, and two Canadians, William Bishop 72 and Raymond Collishaw 68.

Vickers FB5

The "Gunbus" was one of the first combat aircraft to enter military service in the First World War.

SPECIFICATION
Wingspan
36ft 6in (11.13m)

Length overall
27ft 2in (8.28m)

Height
11ft 6in (3.51m)

Weight
1,129lb (512kg) empty
2,050lb (930kg) loaded

Engine
One nine-cylinder 100hp Gnome Monosoupape rotary

The aircraft's flying surfaces were constructed of wood and covered with a fine-cotton fabric. This was then finished, to weatherproof and camouflage it, with a lightweight paint known as dope.

The complete airframe is braced with tensioned wires to provide rigidity and strength. The structure was strong enough to carry a light bomb load under the wings.

The pilot sat in a separate cockpit, behind the observer. The aircraft was controlled by a conventional "joystick" column and rudder bar, and the engine was operated by a simple 'on-off' electrical ignition switch.

Armament was a single .303in Vickers or Maxim belt-fed machine gun mounted in the observer's front cockpit. Later models were fitted with a single drum-fed Lewis gun.

Long skids were fitted to the undercarriage to prevent the aircraft from tipping nose-over when landing on rough grass airfields.

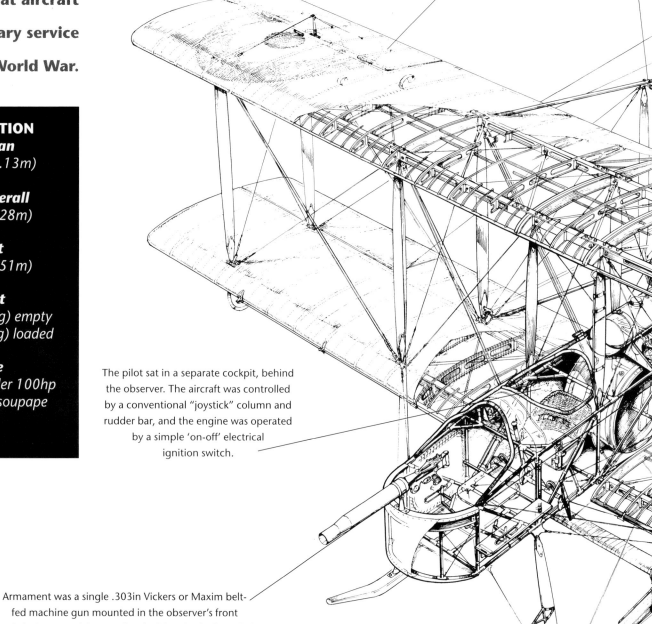

Illustration © Frank Munger

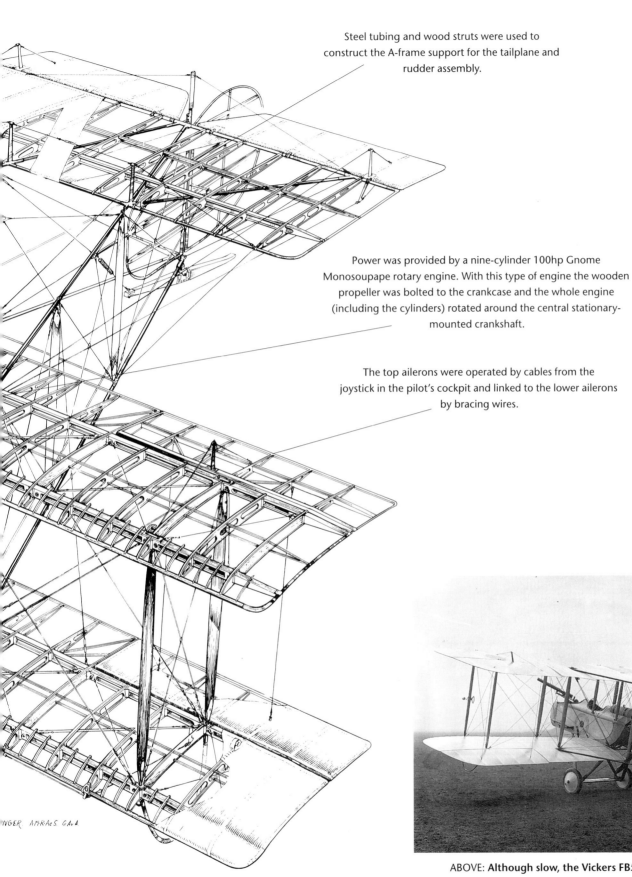

Steel tubing and wood struts were used to construct the A-frame support for the tailplane and rudder assembly.

Power was provided by a nine-cylinder 100hp Gnome Monosoupape rotary engine. With this type of engine the wooden propeller was bolted to the crankcase and the whole engine (including the cylinders) rotated around the central stationary-mounted crankshaft.

The top ailerons were operated by cables from the joystick in the pilot's cockpit and linked to the lower ailerons by bracing wires.

KEY FACTS

1913
Originally designed as the Vickers Type 18 Destroyer in 1912, it is first flown as the EFB1 (Experimental Fighting Biplane).

October 1914
First flight of the production FB5.

25 July 1915
Entry into service with No 11 Squadron Royal Flying Corps on active service in France.

December 1915
First flight of the FB9, an improved version of the FB5.

1916
Last FB9 delivered after a total of 300, of both types, has been built by Vickers and Darracq.

ABOVE: Although slow, the Vickers FB5 was an extremely sturdy machine. Nicknamed "Gunbus" by its crew, it served well until the Germans introduced proper Fokker scouts armed with forward-firing synchronised machine guns.

LEFT: **Sopwith 1¹/₂-Strutter bombing, fighting and reconnaissance aircraft of No 3 Wing, RNAS, at Luxeuil, France in November/December 1916.** Wingspan 33ft 6in (10.2m), **length** 25ft 3in (7.62m), **height** 10ft 3in (3.12m), **weight** 1,259lb (570kg), **engine** Clerget 110hp 9-cylinder rotary air-cooled, **maximum speed** 106mph (170kph), **endurance** 4hr 30min, **crew** 2.

BELOW: **The Airco DH4 day bomber and fighter-reconnaissance aircraft entered service with the RFC in 1917.** Wingspan 42ft 5in (13m), **length** 30ft 2in (9.2m), **height** 10ft 2in (3.1m), **weight** 2,300lb (1,043kg), **engine** BHP 200hp six-cylinder inline, Siddeley Puma 230hp six-cylinder inline or Rolls-Royce 250hp 12-cylinder vee water-cooled, **maximum speed** (Rolls-Royce) 113mph (180kph), **endurance** 3hr 30min, **crew** 2.

RIGHT: Loved by all who flew it for its delightful handling qualities, the Sopwith Pup scout of 1916 served with both the RFC and RNAS, on land and at sea.
Wingspan 26ft 6in (8m), length 19ft 4in (5.9m), height 9ft 5in (2.9m), weight 787lb (357kg), engine Le Rhône 80hp 9-cylinder rotary air-cooled, maximum speed 105mph (169kph), endurance 3hr, crew 1.

BELOW RIGHT: Making its appearance in the summer of 1917, the Albatros DV fighter proved a formidable opponent and saw wide usage.
Wingspan 29ft 8in (9.04m), length 24ft (7.32m), height 8ft 10in (2.7m), weight 1,511lb (685kg), engine Mercedes D IIIa 180/200hp 6-cylinder inline water-cooled, maximum speed 116mph (187kph), endurance 2hr, crew 1.

ABOVE: Once the reconnaissance crews had photographed the enemy positions, prints of their pictures were assembled into a mosaic to provide overall coverage of the required battlefield area. Here, an interpreter positions individual photos over a map to the same scale. A completed mosaic is visible on the left.

LEFT: Albatros DI fighters of Jasta 2 lined up ready for operations. Introduced in the winter of 1916–17, the DI and DII accounted for many allied reconnaissance aircraft.
Wingspan 27ft 11in (8.5m), length 24ft 3in (7.4m), height 9ft 6in (2.9m), weight 1,423lb (645kg), engine Benz Bz III 150hp or Mercedes D III 160hp six-cylinder inline water-cooled, maximum speed 109mph (175kph), endurance 1hr 30min, crew 1.

RIGHT: **A Sopwith F1 Camel of A Flight, No 9 Naval Squadron, with a portrait of music-hall comedian George Robey. Wingspan** 28ft (8.5m), **length** 18ft 9in (5.7m), **height** 8ft 6in (2.6m), **weight** 962lb (436kg), **engine** Clerget 9B 130hp or Le Rhône 9J 110hp 9-cylinder rotary air-cooled, **maximum speed** 108mph (174kph), **endurance** 2hr 30min, **crew** 1.

CENTRE RIGHT: **Albatros DIIs of Jasta 14 lined up outside their tent hangars. The DII had its upper wing mounted closer to the fuselage than the DI to minimise obstruction of the pilot's view.**

BOTTOM RIGHT: **Swinging the propeller of a Fokker Dr.I triplane of Jasta 11. Wingspan** 23ft 8in (7.19m), **length** 18ft 11in (5.77m), **height** 9ft 8in (2.95m), **weight** 893lb (405kg), **engine** Oberursel UR II 9-cylinder rotary air-cooled, **maximum speed** 103mph (166kph), **endurance** 1hr 30min, **crew** 1.

BELOW: **During the interwar years the Bristol F2B Fighter was used principally in the army co-operation role. Wingspan** 39ft 3in (12m), **length** 25ft 10in (7.8m), **height** 9ft 9in (3m), **weight** 1,934lb (877kg), **engine** Rolls-Royce Falcon III 275hp 12-cylinder vee water-cooled, **maximum speed** 113mph (182kph), **endurance** 3hr, **crew** 2.

LEFT: The Breguet 14 was the principal French bomber/reconnaissance aircraft of the later war years, and subsequently served with many other nations' air arms. **Wingspan** 49ft (14.94m), **length** 29ft (8.84m), **height** 11ft (3.4m); **weight** 2,242lb (1,017kg), **engine** Renault 12Fcx 300hp 12-cylinder vee water-cooled, **maximum speed** 120mph (193kph), **endurance** 2 hr 45min, **crew** 2.

BELOW: Soldiers examine an Albatros DV that has made a forced landing in the British lines. This aircraft was subsequently test flown in Britain to enable its performance and handling to be assessed and compared with its Allied counterparts.

RIGHT: **This captured Hansa-Brandenburg W29 monoplane sea fighter of 1918 displays a curious mixture of German and British markings.**
Wingspan 44ft 3in (13.5m), **length** 30ft 8in (9.36m), **height** 9ft 10in (3m), **weight** 2,200lb (1,000kg), **engine** Benz Bz III 150hp 6-cylinder inline watercooled, **maximum speed** 109mph (175kph), **endurance** 4hr, **crew** 2.

BELOW: **One of the great fighters of the First World War, the Royal Aircraft Factory's SE5a was the mount of several leading 'aces' including Ball, Mannock and McCudden.**
Wingspan 26ft 7in (8m), **length** 20ft 11in (6.4m), **height** 9ft 6in (2.9m), **weight** 1,399lb (635kg), **engine** Hispano-Suiza 150hp or Wolseley W.4A Viper 200hp 8-cylinder vee watercooled, **maximum speed** 114mph (183kph), **endurance** 2hr 20min, **crew** 1.

The Giant Bombers

The first heavy bomber in history was the Ilya Murometz Type V, built in 1914, a variant of Igor Sikorsky's design for the first four-engine passenger aircraft, which had made its entrance in 1913: Le Grand (it was fashionable in Russia to speak French), was much the biggest aeroplane then in existence. The Type Vs, of which between 70 and 80 were built, equipped the world's first heavy bomber unit, the EVK Squadron. Ultimately there were seven versions, all with ski or multiple-wheel landing gear. They operated by night and day, making sorties of up to six hours. The later ones had the first self-sealing fuel tanks. Only one was shot down, after having downed three fighters.

Germany's Gotha G IV and V, which began bombing London in June 1917 by day and night, had the advantages of speed and height. The RFC and RNAS had no fighters with a fast enough rate of climb or maximum speed to intercept them, until SE5a squadrons entered the scene. The biggest was the Staaken R VI, which appeared in June 1917. Each of four 260hp Mercedes D IVa engines in tandem pairs drove one tractor propeller and one pusher propeller.

Italy, which entered the war on the Allies' side in May 1915, manufactured two types of heavy bomber for its Military Air Corps, the Caproni Ca5 biplane and Ca42 triplane. The latter was delivered in 1918 and sold also to Britain's Royal Naval Air Service in the same year.

In April 1918 the RAF formed the Independent Force, a bomber unit based in Northern France and devoted to the destruction of targets in Germany, France and Belgium. The unit comprised five night squadrons and four day squadrons. Operating the Handley Page O/100 and O/400, as well as the de Havilland DH4, it flew a total of 650 raids.

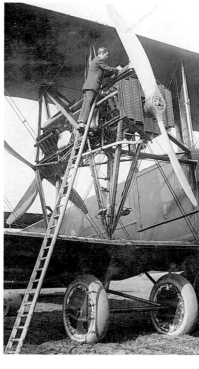

BELOW: **Ministering to one of the four 375hp Rolls-Royce Eagle VIII engines of a Handley Page V/1500, intended to bomb Berlin but rendered unnecessary by the Armistice.**

BELOW: **The DFW RI, one of a number of extraordinary Riesenflugzeug (giant aircraft, or R-planes) built and flown in Germany, had four 220hp Mercedes D IV engines and spanned 97ft (29m).**

ABOVE: **The Handley Page O/400 night bomber, which entered service with the RAF Independent Force in 1918, was used to deliver the 1,650lb (748kg) bombs which were the "blockbusters" of their day.**

RIGHT: **No fewer than six 160hp Mercedes D IIIs powered the Staaken VGO III, which spanned 138ft 5in (42m) and had a duration of 6hr. It carried its seven-man crew on some seven bombing missions against railway installations, troop encampments and depots in the vicinity of Riga, Latvia.**

BELOW: The RNAS pioneered operations from aircraft carriers. Here, a Sopwith 2F.1 Camel makes a smart take-off from HMS *Pegasus* in the Firth of Forth. The steam issuing from the vessel's bows was provided to give the aircraft's pilot and handlers an indication of wind direction.

RIGHT: Captain Reid Chambers of the US Air Service's 94th Aero Sqn poses with his candy-striped SPAD XIII fighter in 1918.

BELOW:The Sopwith Triplane of 1917, with its Clerget rotary engine of 110hp or 130hp, provided the inspiration for the Fokker Dr.1 of similar configuration.

BOTTOM: A captured Fokker D VII, one of the great fighters of the late war period, on display at the Hotel des Invalides, Paris, in 1918.

LEFT: Open cockpits offered scant protection from the elements, and pilots needed to be well wrapped for long missions over the lines at night, especially in winter. Here, the pilot of a Royal Aircraft Factory FE2d fighter-reconnaissance aircraft is donning a Sidcot suit, while his observer wears fleece-lined "fug boots" and long leather coat.

RIGHT: Felixstowe F3 flying boats of the RNAS patrolled the North Sea on the watch for enemy submarines and aircraft, and despite their size could engage the latter in combat. This F3, based at Catfirth, is seen at Lerwick Harbour in the Shetlands in 1918, minus its starboard propeller.

LEFT: The Royal Navy's cruisers had take-off platforms mounted on gun turrets, enabling the aircraft to be pointed into the wind for launch. This Sopwith 1½-Strutter is just departing HMS *Malaya*.

RIGHT: Like the unit seen here, most Jagdstaffeln (fighter squadrons) on the Western Front were re-equipped with the formidable Fokker D VII during the summer and autumn of 1918.

With the signing of the Armistice, commercial aviation services began to be established, using converted military aircraft.

Chapter Three
Peace Returns

The ceasefire on 11 November 1918 did not mean a total cessation of activity by Britain's Royal Air Force (formed by the amalgamation of the RFC and RNAS on 1 April 1918). Even before the war had ended, the RFC started long-distance flights for the ultimate benefit of civilians. The first was made by a Handley Page O/400, which took off from England on 28 July 1918 and landed in Egypt on 7 August. On 29 November 1918 an O/400 left from Cairo for Baghdad, with a night stop at Damascus. On 13 January 1919 an HP V/1500, Britain's biggest bomber, which was about to enter squadron service when peace was declared, set off from Britain for India. It arrived 32 days later after frequent engine trouble.

On 14 December 1918 the RAF, at the request of the Foreign Office, began two daily courier flights by DH9s (two-seater bombers) between London and Paris. Up to seven passengers were also carried in an HP O/400.

On 27 July 1919 No 1 (Communications) Squadron was formed for long-distance trips – A Flight was equipped with DH4s, two-seater bombers, while B Flight flew two Avro 504s and two BE2es. On 13 December that year an entire Communications wing came into being with two squadrons, each operating one HP O/400 carrying eight passengers, and four DH4s that carried two.

Britain, France, Italy and, to a lesser extent, the USA had been distracted from applying progress to commercial aviation. Now they could resume. Instead of merely taking people up for short pleasure flips, companies were acquiring bombers converted to carry passengers and baggage, or purpose-built passenger aircraft. In the immediate aftermath of war, however, RAF types were much used. One of the passenger carriers, Aircraft Transport and Travel, used DH9Bs in 1919 and 1920. It equipped its passengers with thick coats, helmets, goggles and gloves, and, in the autumn and winter, hot-water bottles.

In Germany all military flying came to a dead stop: the peace treaty compelled her to disband her air force.

In the USA the design and production of military aircraft languished during the war years. When the USA entered the war on the Allies' side in April 1917, her air force had to be equipped with the Spad XIII and DH4. Civil flying had been able to advance without interruption and on 15 May 1918 the first regular airmail service was introduced. Curtiss JN4s flown by Army pilots plied between Washington, Philadelphia and New York until the Post Office took over on 12 August 1918 with purpose-built Standard JR1B mailplanes. By 31 December the US Aerial Mail Service was operating with 91 per cent regularity.

Immediately after the armistice the US Post Office bought war-surplus aeroplanes that included 100 US-built DH4Bs with 400hp Liberty engines, which made it possible to begin a coast-to-coast service on 15 May 1919. The first experiment with flying part of the cross-continental route from San Francisco to New York by night was made when two aeroplanes took off from each terminal city on 22 February 1921. One of the eastbound pilots crashed fatally in Nevada and bad weather forced one westbound pilot to abandon his flight at Chicago. The flight to New York was ultimately completed in 33 hr 20 min.

PASSENGER FLIGHTS

Civil flying was permitted to resume in Britain on 1 May 1919. However, it had already resumed in Germany. In February 1919 Deutsche Luft-Reederei (German Air-

ABOVE: **An array of civil aircraft on display at the Olympia Aero Show in London in 1920. Most new designs failed to gain a foothold in the market, owing to the ready availability of huge numbers of cheap war-surplus aircraft.**

ABOVE: **This Fairey IIIC seaplane, carried by HMS *Nairana*, served with the expeditionary Syren Force sent by the British to North Russia in 1919 to support the Imperial Powers in their unsuccessful struggle against the Bolsheviks.**

MILESTONES

1918

The first regular international airmail services, between Vienna and Kiev, begin.

1919

Aircraft Transport and Travel inaugurates the first London–Paris service.

1919

Alcock and Brown make the first nonstop transatlantic flight by a heavier-than-air aircraft.

line) instituted a daily service between Berlin and Weimar. In March, the manufacturers of Junkers aircraft began a service between Dessau and Weimar with J10 all-metal monoplanes. The same month, scheduled Berlin–Hamburg flights were started, and soon after, Nuremberg –Leipzig–Berlin and Augsburg–Munich. In 1926 the companies still in business joined to form Deutsche Luft Hansa.

In Britain, the first flights to take advantage of this commercial opportunity were not between the capital and major provincial cities. On 24 May, Avro Civil Aviation Service started daily flights between Manchester, Southport and Blackpool. Again, the Avro 504 was the chosen aircraft. This service, which had received no subsidy, ended 18 weeks later.

On 25 August 1919 Aircraft Transport and Travel began a daily service between London and Paris. At 12.30pm a DH16 left the airfield at Hounslow and arrived at 2.50pm at Le Bourget. A DH4A bound for London also took off at 12.30pm – from the airfield at Le Bourget and bound for London. It landed at 2.40pm. Both pilots were RAF officers.

On the same day, an HPO/7 of Handley Page Transport made the same flight between London and Paris. On 2 September it began its scheduled service between the two capitals.

In March 1919 the Farman Line began a weekly passenger flight between Paris and Brussels. In the following month, Cie des Messageries Aeriennes (CMA) launched a Paris–Lille cargo operation. A daily Paris– London service opened in co-

operation with Handley Page Transport in September.

Such cautious beginnings were not the style of another French company set up in the same year and based at Montaudran, near Toulouse: Lignes Aerienne Latécoère (soon known simply as La Ligne). It was the creation of Pierre Latécoère, an armament manufacturer who had ventured into the field of aircraft construction. By July he was running an experimental mail service between Toulouse and Rabat, in Morocco. A year later, with Gallic dash, he had stretched the operation to Casablanca. He recruited wartime aircrew, as did all the growing airlines in the former Allied countries. By 1925 La Ligne was running a scheduled operation between Toulouse and Dakar, in French West Africa.

While the war had dominated the attention of Britain and her allies, two important innovations unconnected with the conflict were introduced. On 11 March 1918 the first regular international airmail service began: between Vienna and Kiev. On 24 June 1918 the first domestic airmail was started; this time, between Mon-

ABOVE: **Spectators watch as a Vickers Virginia bomber taxies past during the RAF Display at Hendon, the annual highlight of interwar aviation in Britain. As well as seeing the industry's latest products, they were treated to exhibitions of aerobatics, parachute jumping, crazy flying and mock combat "set pieces".**

treal and Toronto in Canada. It is indicative of the dearth of civilian pilots that the aircraft was flown by an RAF officer. On 12 August that year, the USA's first airmail route opened, between New York and Washington. The first USA–Canada air mail was established on 3 March 1919, between Seattle and Victoria.

PRIZE FLIGHTS

The ending of the war incited an abundance of ambitious ventures. In 1913 the *Daily Mail* had offered a £10,000 prize for the first crossing of the North Atlantic by air. Contestants would be displaying a confidence that, only three or four years previously, would have seemed absurd. Even the two first flights to India, only a few months earlier, had not covered such a distance on any of the refuelling stages – and they were across land, with only a comparatively short crossing of the Mediterranean. Those in search of fortune and fame needed to be the greatest of optimists. In the spring of 1919 12 crews were preparing in Newfoundland to make the attempt.

The first Atlantic crossing was made by a US Navy crew in a Curtiss NC4 flying boat. Three boats (the usual way of referring to this type of aircraft), each with a crew of six, left Trepassey Bay, Newfoundland, on 8 May. US Navy destroyers stationed every 50 miles (80km) marked their route. Two of the NC4s were wrecked. The route took the surviving aircraft via the Azores, where it refuelled, and Lisbon, where it fuelled again. On 31 May it arrived in England, having covered 3,925 miles (6,317km) in 57hr 16min, at an average speed of 78mph (126kph). This was a fine achievement, although it was neither nonstop nor across the North Atlantic.

The weather delayed the competitors for the *Daily Mail* prize until 18 May, when Harry Hawker and Mackenzie Grieve set out in the Sopwith Atlantic. They had to make a forced landing on the sea, about halfway across, near a Danish steamer, which rescued them. An hour after the first departure, Frederick Raynham and William Morgan, in a Martinsyde, crashed on take-off.

On 14 June two ex-RAF officers, John Alcock as pilot and Arthur Whitten Brown as navigator, made their start in a Vickers Vimy bomber with extra fuel tanks. With a great quantity of petrol aboard, the aircraft was barely able to leave the ground, but became airborne at 4.28pm. Electricity for the radio was provided by a wind-driven propeller, which soon fell off.

Until shortly after midnight, Alcock and Brown were either climbing through cloud in search of clear sky, or flying between cloud layers, which made it impossible to fix their position accurately. Some 11 hours into the journey, they found themselves in a thick cloud bank. This disoriented the pilot so much that the aircraft began to spin. The rudimentary instruments did not enable him to regain control until, when they were down to 500ft (152m), they broke through cloud base and regained level flight. Another hour passed in clear air, then they were assailed by hail, sleet and snow. Brown had to climb onto the fuselage and wipe off ice that was masking the fuel gauge.

Breakfasting on sandwiches at 8.15am, while they were at only 250ft (76m), they had their first glimpse of land, ten minutes before crossing the west coast of Ireland. The clouds were low and the terrain ahead was hilly. It would be folly to fly on, so Alcock set the Vimy down – on what looked like dry ground but was a bog, which tipped the aeroplane on to its nose

but did not do much damage. The time was 8.40am: they had been airborne for 16hr 27min, their average speed had been 121mph (195kph) and the distance covered was 1,890 miles (3,034km). They were both rewarded with a knighthood. Alcock was killed in an accident when flying over France on 19 December.

The next to share a £10,000 prize were the Australians Ross and Keith Smith. It was their government that offered it, for a flight from England to Australia, a distance of 11,290 miles (18,170km), to be completed within 30 days.

They took off from Hounslow, near London, in a Vickers Vimy on 12 November 1919 and landed at Fanny Bay, Darwin, on 10 December with 52 hours to spare. Only one other crew completed the trip.

In the same month as the maiden England to Australia flight, Britain's Air Ministry announced the RAF's completion of its survey of a route to South Africa. On 4 February 1920 yet another Vickers Vimy, this time in the hands of Lieutenant Colonel Pierre van Ryneveld and Squadron Leader Christopher Quintin Brand, was airborne from Brooklands in southern England on its way to the Cape of Good Hope, South Africa. Both men were South Africans and the venture was

BELOW: **A display parachutist shows the position he will adopt on the trailing edge of the biplane's lower wing when he jumps off to make his descent.**

ABOVE: **One way to attract customers was to put on a display of wing walking. Here, a bold stuntman clutches an outer interplane strut of an ancient Airco DH6 belonging to Maylands Flying School of Romford, Essex, England in 1928. This ex-First World War trainer was ideal for such stunts, being sedate and slow.**

financed by their government. Their aircraft, named *Silver Queen*, did not behave as regally as hoped: she crashed at Wadi Haifa when making an emergency landing in the dark, and was written off. The government replaced her with another of the same type, which was optimistically christened *Silver Queen II*. This one crashed at Bulawayo, in Southern Rhodesia (Zimbabwe), and was succeeded by a war surplus DH9 bearing the name *Voortrekker* (Pioneer), with which they resumed their flight on 17 March. They landed at Cape Town three days later.

LIGHT AIRCRAFT

The category of aircraft that has introduced a wide variety of men and women to the pleasure that can be obtained by

the acquisition of a pilot's licence is the light aeroplane. One of the earliest was the Sopwith Dove, evolved from the famous Pup fighter. In 1923 the English Electric Wren made a great impression by flying 85 miles (137km) on one gallon (4.5 litres) of petrol with a 3.5hp engine that also powered motorcycles and managed 50mph (80.5kph). The Cygnet, first flown in 1924, was the first aircraft that Sidney Camm, designer of the Hurricane, designed for Hawker.

The definitive light aircraft that set the standard for this genre was the DH60 Moth, powered by a 60hp ADC Cirrus engine, which first flew on 22 February 1925. With a replacement Gipsy engine it became known as the Gipsy Moth. On 26 October 1931 the Tiger Moth made its first flight. It differed from its predeces-

sor in three ways: it had staggered and sweptback wings, to aid egress from the front cockpit when wearing a parachute; and an inverted engine to improve the forward view. Its 120hp Gipsy III engine was replaced by a 130hp Gipsy Major in the second production batch. Britain's Air Ministry ordered it after its first flight, to be the RAF's *ab initio* trainer.

MILITARY AIRCRAFT

While civil aviation was thrusting ahead all over the globe, military aircraft were developing more slowly. In 1924 the Vickers Virginia bomber entered squadron service with the RAF. The US Army Air Corps flew the Martin MB-2 bomber. It had two 420hp Liberty engines and carried 2,000 lb (907kg) of bombs. Light day bombers still

had their uses. The first new type built for the RAF was the two-seater Fairey Fawn, which had a top speed of 114mph (183kph) and a 460lb (209kg) bombload.

Japan's first indigenously built light bomber, a Mitsubishi, appeared in 1927. Concurrently, the Italian Air Force received the Fiat BR1 two-seater, whose top speed was 153mph (246kph) and bombload 1,000 (454kg).

The RAF's last biplane heavy night bomber, the Handley Page HP 38 Heyford, first flew in June 1930.

The first post-war fighter ordered in quantity for the RAF was the Gloster Grebe, which entered service in October 1925. It had two Vickers machine guns and a maximum speed of 152mph (245kph). The Armstrong-Whitworth Siskin had also been ordered, and joined its first squadron in May 1924; its maximum speed was 134mph (215.6kph), and it had two Vickers guns. It was flown by Bomber Command until mid 1939, when it was withdrawn from frontline service.

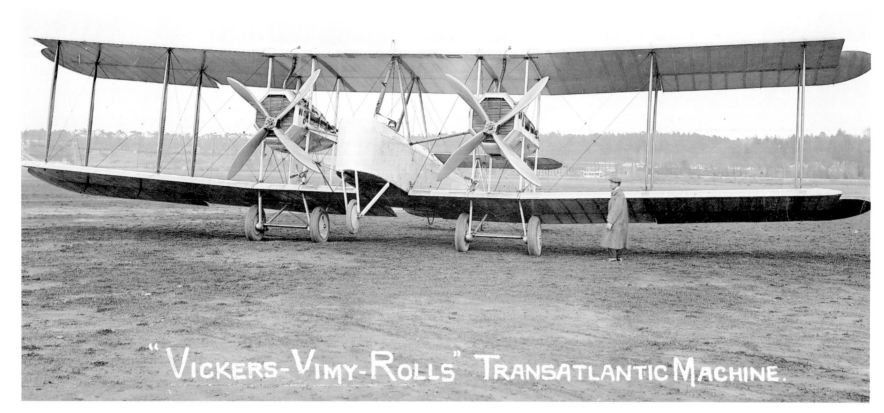

"Vickers-Vimy-Rolls" Transatlantic Machine.

LEFT: Designed as a bomber, the Vickers Vimy became famous for record-breaking flights: this is the one in which Alcock and Brown made the first nonstop transatlantic flight, in June 1919.

RIGHT: An Airco DH4A of Aircraft Transport and Travel is made ready to depart Heathrow on an early postwar cross-Channel flight. Like many early commercial aircraft, it was a converted bomber.

BELOW LEFT: The first transatlantic flight by a heavier-than-air aircraft was made by the Curtiss NC-4 flying boat, which completed the flight in stages.

BELOW: Passengers queue to board a Handley Page O/10 at Croydon in 1920, for a flight to the Continent. The inset picture shows the spartan interior of an earlier passenger conversion of the O/400 bomber.

ABOVE: **France's first real passenger carrier was the Farman Goliath, which began life as a bomber design but was quickly given a passenger cabin. Wingspan** 86ft 10in (26.45m), **length** 47ft (14.33m), **height** 16ft 4¾in (5m), **weight** 10,515lb (4,769kg), **engines** two 260hp Salmson 9-cylinder radial liquid-cooled, **cruising speed** 75mph (120kph), **range** 250 miles (402km), **crew** 2, **passengers** 12.

LEFT: Another French product of the 1920s was the Nieuport Ni.D 29 fighter, powered by a 300hp Hispano-Suiza 8-cylinder water-cooled engine and armed with a brace of 7.7mm Vickers guns. Built in large numbers, it was also successfully converted for racing.

ABOVE: The Zeppelin-Staaken E.4/20 of 1919 was an amazingly advanced all-metal commercial transport weighing 18,740lb (8,500kg) and powered by four 245hp Maybach engines, which gave it a cruising speed of 125mph (200kph). Intended for Friedrichshafen–Berlin services, it was broken up in late 1922 after the Control Commission ordered suspension of test flying.

LEFT: The prototype Vickers Vimy Commercial arrives at Amsterdam for the First International Air Transport Exhibition, held in July and August 1919. A mating of the Vimy's engines, wings and tail unit with a new monocoque fuselage to accommodate passengers, the Commercial was not an oustanding success, but a military version, the Vernon, became the RAF's first troop carrier.

Ross and Keith Smith

Every aspect of aviation had made a great advance during the First World War, which enabled pilots to embark with confidence on long-distance flights that would have been impossible four years earlier. The *Daily Mail*'s offer of a £10,000 prize in 1913 for the first crossing of the North Atlantic by air was won on 14/15 June. This prompted the Australian Government to offer the same amount for a flight from England to Australia, to be completed in 30 days.

Six crews entered. The winners – the only ones to meet the time limit – were two ex-officers, Ross Smith, aircraft captain, who had been in the Royal Australian Air Force during the war, and his elder brother Keith, navigator and second pilot, who had served in the wartime RFC/RAF. Their mechanics, still serving in the RAF, were Sergeant J. M. Bennett

and Sergeant W. H. Shiers. Their aircraft was a Vickers Vimy bomber, a type that had first flown on 30 November 1917; it had two 360hp Rolls-Royce Eagle VIII engines driving four-bladed propellers. Its maximum speed was 103mph (166kph) at sea level – hardly a relevant altitude for any major journey.

They took off from Hounslow, on the western outskirts of London, for their 11,290 mile (18,170km) venture on 12 November 1919. Their route took them via Taranto, Cairo, Ramadie, Bandar Abbas, Karachi, Delhi, Muttra, Allahabad, Calcutta, Akyab, Moulmien, Bangkok, Singora, Singapore, Soerabaya, Bima and Atamboes to Darwin. They had expected to cover 600 miles (966km) a day, but storms over the Mediterranean, in the Middle East and in south-east Asia reduced their average to a daily 400 miles

(644km). They landed at Fanny Bay, Darwin, Australia, on 10 December 1919, two days and four hours within the time limit. They flew on to Adelaide, their home town, via Melbourne and Sydney, among other places. Both were knighted.

Only one other crew completed the journey, well outside the time limit.

Ross Smith was killed in 1922 when flying a Vickers amphibian with which he planned to make a flight round the world.

BELOW RIGHT: **Ross and Keith Smith pose in the snow at Hounslow Aerodrome with their Vimy, G-EAOU, on 12 November 1919, shortly before embarking on their epic adventure. They jokingly said that the aeroplane's registration letters stood for "God 'elp all of us".**

BELOW: **The refuelling of big aircraft was not a simple process under the best of circumstances, but in primitive conditions the fuel for the Smiths' Vimy had to be poured into the aircraft's tanks can-by-can through a large funnel with a chamois leather filter.**

RIGHT: Approaching the end of their 27-day flight, members of the Vimy's crew enjoy a cup of tea near a small Australian town. Owing to the dearth of prepared landing grounds en route, the aircraft often had to be put down in rough fields.

LEFT: A classic small airliner of the 1920s, the Junkers F13 employed the all-metal structure developed by the German manufacturer in the First World War, with characteristic corrugated aluminium skinning. This one was operated by Swedish Airlines.

RIGHT: Dutch manufacturer Anthony Fokker produced the aerodynamically clean FIII, which first flew in the early months of 1921. This is one of 12 of the type to serve with KLM. Wingspan 57ft 9½in (17.62m), length 36ft 3¾in (11.07m), height 12ft (3.65m), weight 4,188lb (1,900kg), engine one 240hp Armstrong Siddeley Puma 6-cylinder inline water-cooled, cruising speed 84mph (135kph), range 420 miles (676km), crew 1, passengers 5.

BELOW: Handley Page W8b G-EBBH of Imperial Airways runs up its two uncowled 360hp Rolls-Royce Eagle VIII engines. Carrying 12 passengers, the W8b first flew in August 1921.

INTERIOR OF A HANDLEY PAGE
TWIN ENGINE AEROPLANE.

ABOVE: The "passenger saloon" of the
W8b, showing the lightweight wicker
seats in common use at the time.

RIGHT: The first Handley Page W8, with
neatly cowled 450hp Napier Lion
engines, on display at the Paris Aero
Show in late 1919/early 1920.

ABOVE LEFT: As with many of its kind in the 1920s, the de Havilland DH34 had an enclosed cabin for its nine passengers, but the two pilots had open cockpits in the forward fuselage. The engine was a 450hp Napier Lion 8-cylinder vee water-cooled.

LEFT: Passengers in a Handley Page W8b enjoy the view. Note the refinements: a water dispenser and glasses, instruments to provide flight information, a fire extinguisher, overhead baggage racks and a box of publicity pamphlets above the window.

ABOVE: **A relic of the war years, the Sopwith Snipe served in RAF fighter squadrons until 1926.**
Wingspan 31ft 1in (9.49m), **length** 19ft 10in (6.09m), **height** 8ft 3in (2.51m), **weight** 2,020lb (916kg), **engine** one 234hp Bentley BR2 9-cylinder rotary air-cooled, **maximum speed** 121mph (195kph), **range** 310 miles (499km), **crew** 1.

RIGHT: **This four-passenger Blériot Spad 33, with a 230hp Salmson radial engine, was operated by Cie des Messageries Aériennes on its London-to-Paris service in the early 1920s.**

Vickers Virginia Mk X

This aircraft was the standard heavy bomber of the Royal Air Force from 1924 until 1937.

SPECIFICATION
Wingspan
87.8in (26.72m)

Length overall
62ft 3in (18.97m)

Height
18ft 2in (5.54m)

Weight
9,650lb (4,377kg) empty
17,600lb (7,983kg) loaded

Engines
Two W-12 cylinder 570hp
Napier Lion V

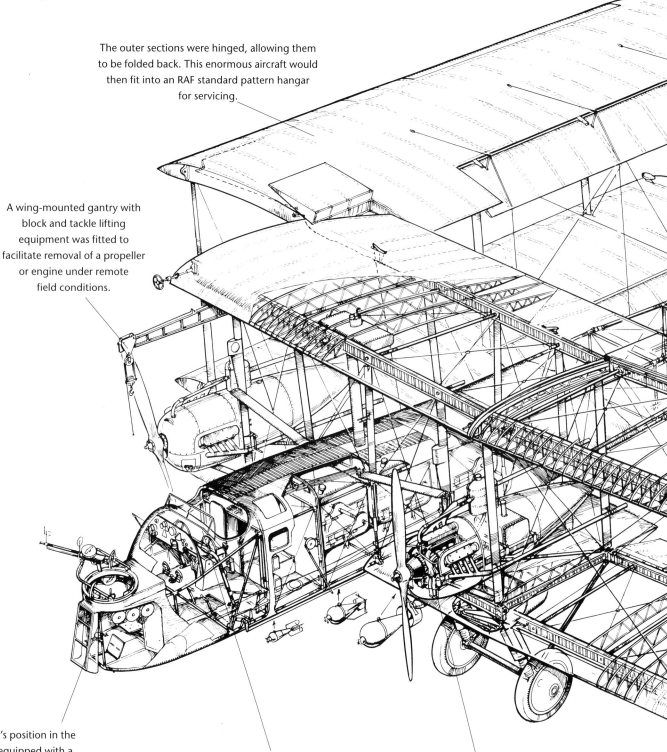

The outer sections were hinged, allowing them to be folded back. This enormous aircraft would then fit into an RAF standard pattern hangar for servicing.

A wing-mounted gantry with block and tackle lifting equipment was fitted to facilitate removal of a propeller or engine under remote field conditions.

The gunner/bomb aimer's position in the nose of the aircraft was equipped with a rudimentary bombsight and a single drum-fed .303in Lewis machine gun mounted on a fully traversing and elevating Scarff-type ring mounting.

A captain and co-pilot occupied the open cockpit, which was equipped with conventional flying and engine controls. The Virginia Mk X was also equipped with an autopilot system.

Power was supplied by two W-12 (W-broad arrow configuration) 570hp Napier Lion water-cooled engines. The two-bladed wooden propellers were attached, without reduction gearboxes, to the engine's crankshaft.

Illustration © Frank Munger

Situated in the extreme tail of the aircraft the tail gunner's position was equipped with a single (occasionally two) drum-fed .303in Lewis machine gun.

Early marks of Virginias were constructed of wood and metal tubing. Later, the completely redesigned Mk X was built of metal, but as in earlier marks was covered in fabric material.

A "jump-off" platform was fitted to each lower wing for the training of parachutists. The person carried aloft standing on the platform would, at a suitable altitude, stream their parachute and be pulled off by the developed canopy and descend to the landing zone.

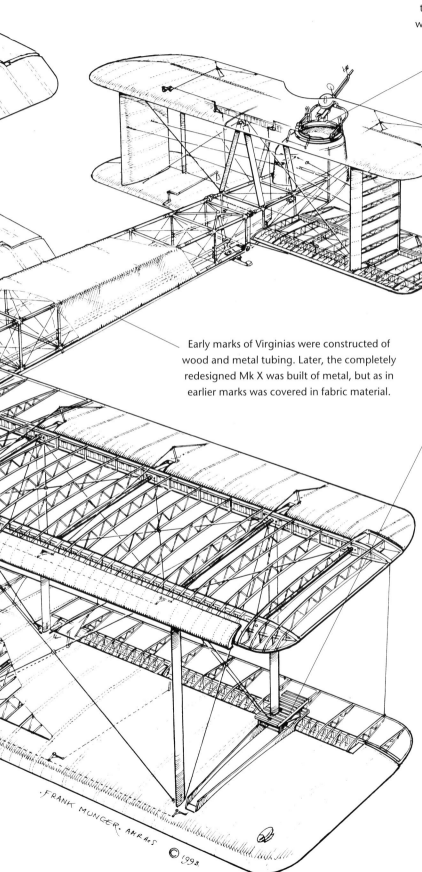

ABOVE: **An unusual view of a Vickers Virginia Mk X of No 500 "County of Kent" Squadron, Royal Air Force, in the 1930s.**

ABOVE: **Trainee RAF parachutists demonstrate the "pull-off" technique, whereby they were taken aloft standing on a small platform at the Virginia's outer rear struts, and at a given signal deployed their parachutes and let them pull them off the wing.**

LEFT: **This Swallow biplane with a 200hp Wright Whirlwind radial engine, operated by Varney Airlines on its Pasco–Boise–Elko route during 1926–34, is typical of the aircraft adopted for the privately operated US airmail services.**

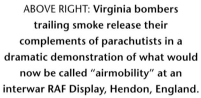

ABOVE RIGHT: **Virginia bombers trailing smoke release their complements of parachutists in a dramatic demonstration of what would now be called "airmobility" at an interwar RAF Display, Hendon, England.**

RIGHT: **A Dornier Wal flying boat of Deutsche Luft Hansa awaits launch from the catapult of the depot ship** *Westfalen* **during trials for the airline's South Atlantic mail service in May 1933. Wingspan** 73ft 10in (22.49m), **length** 56ft 7¼in (17.25m), **height** 17ft (5.18m), **weight** 12,556lb (5,559kg), **engines** two 350hp Rolls-Royce Eagle IX 12-cylinder vee liquid-cooled, **cruising speed** 87 mph (140kph), **range** 1,350 miles (2,172km), **crew** 2, **passengers** 10.

The Barnstormers

Flying daredevils first appeared in the early 1900s, but the real heyday of the aerial stuntmen came in the 1920s, when all manner of tricks were performed at airshows and for the movies.

The word "barnstormer" evokes high jinks and daring. It was coined for the touring theatrical companies in the late 19th-century USA, who had to make do with barns in which to set up stage. The aerial barnstormers were also entertainers, but their calling involved an element that did not threaten actors – the risk of injury and death.

Today's aerobatic displays by fighters emitting coloured smoke evolved from the early-day daring men, mostly British and American, in their primitive flying machines. Effectively, they were also the first test pilots, and provided aircraft designers with valuable information. Moreover, from the First World War onward fighter pilots have benefited from the antics they initiated, which are the basis of all the manoeuvres for attack and defence used in air fighting.

Lincoln Beachey is considered the best of the first generation. Flying a Curtiss biplane, his repertoire included vertical power dives and scooping up a scarf or handkerchief with a wingtip. When he flew low over the Niagara Falls and under the suspension bridge below them, he provided valuable evidence of how to contend with severe air turbulence. He gave up his death-defying avocation in 1913, but was lured to resume when he heard that the outstanding French pilot, Adolphe Pégoud, on 2 September 1913, had demonstrated a loop. As communications between Russia and the Western world were slow, the USA and Europe were unaware that the first loop had already been performed on 20 August 1913 by Lieutenant Peter Nikolaevich Nestarov of the Russian Air Service, flying a Nieuport IV. Beachey was killed in 1915 when, at 2,000ft (610m), his machine's wings folded.

An article in *Flight* magazine in 1913 spoke warily of the barnstormers. "Several accidents have resulted from the deliberate performance of tricks in the air, such as were at one time notorious in America,

> ## "these men would display the most amazing nerve"

where several pilots have been killed in front of spectators. Catering to the sensations of the crowd, these men would display the most amazing nerve in making steep dives followed by banked turns in which the wings would approach to a vertical position. On one occasion the machine actually turned turtle through over-banking and the pilot was killed."

Pégoud, an employee of the Blériot company, had also demonstrated a parachute jump. One of his aerobatics began with a bunt (outside loop), out of which he half-rolled upright at the bottom, then half-looped up, thus performing an 'S'. Another stunt was to stall at the top of a 45-degree climb and let the aeroplane slide back in a parabola. He had trained for inverted flight by having his aeroplane hung upside down with him in it. An ingenious innovation of his that enabled take-offs and landings on confined and bumpy areas failed to arouse interest. It entailed flying under a cable stretched between two posts and climbing to engage a quick-release gear with a longitudinal cable, which brought him to a stop. In the First World War he was the first pilot to be dubbed an Ace (a term invented by the French press), for having

LEFT: **Curtiss test pilot Roland Rholfs poses with the company's Model 18T Wasp triplane, in which he gained the world climb and altitude records on 18 September 1919, attaining 34,910ft (10,640m).**

ABOVE: **Aircraft of Alan Cobham's National Aviation Day Display encouraging airmindedness at Dagenham, Essex, England, in 1934. Many people had their first flights in the Airspeed Ferry seen on the ground, or the Handley Page Clive overhead.**

scored five victories. He was shot down in 1915 while reloading his Lewis gun.

After the war, great numbers of young men who learned to fly in the air forces could not settle to humdrum civilian jobs, so they turned to barnstorming. There was also an abundance of surplus aircraft to be bought cheaply, of which the most popular were the Curtiss Jenny and Avro 504. They did valuable public relations work by taking people up for short, cheap flights as well as thrilling spectators with wing-walking, riding astride the tail, dangling from the undercarriage and mock combat. The first instance of flight re-fuelling was a stunt; a pilot with a can of petrol strapped to his back moved from one aircraft to another. Many graduated from barnstorming to air racing and long-distance pioneering flights.

ACROBATIES AÉRIENNES VUES D'UN AUTRE AVION

INSETS, ABOVE: **The slow and stable Curtiss Jenny and Standard biplane trainers made ideal mounts for US stunt pilots. The man on the left hangs by his teeth from a trapeze attached to the undercarriage, while the one on the right changes from aeroplane to automobile on a mercifully clear road.**

LEFT: **The choice of aeroplane for Roland Toutain, a French daredevil of the 1920s, is a Caudron C60 biplane trainer, powered by a 130hp Clerget rotary engine.**

Chapter Four

Spanning the World

Britain, France, Italy, Germany and the USA, war-weary but commercially and technically ambitious, were competing to design and produce the world's most advanced aeroplanes. These were to be bigger, faster, safer, with a greater capacity for both passengers and freight than their competitors, and capable of flying ever-increasing distances without refuelling.

The US aircraft industry was slow to develop in these postwar years. Commercial airliners were either purchased or licence-built from European manufacturers. In the 1920s the famous companies such as Boeing and Curtiss began manufacturing aircraft to their own design.

The routes on which the British company Air Transport and Travel was so solicitous about its passengers' protection from the cold had multiplied rapidly. The London–Paris route was soon also being flown by Handley Page Transport and in 1922 Daimler Airway began competing with the others. In May the next year, in collaboration with the Dutch airline KLM, it began a London–Amsterdam service.

By 1924 the various British airlines were working between London and Amsterdam, Basle, Berlin, Brussels, Cologne, Paris and Zurich. Several small companies were formed to carry passengers between Britain and continental Europe, and one, British Marine Air Navigation, operated a flying boat

between Southampton and Jersey. There was not enough custom to make them all financially viable: in consequence, only four were still in business by 1924, so were amalgamated as Imperial Airways on 31 March that year.

A clever and forceful man of authority, Sir Sefton Brancker had figured prominently in all aspects of aviation since 1911. At that time a Captain in a cavalry regiment in India, with characteristic originality Brancker flew in a Bristol Boxkite during cavalry manoeuvres. In 1913, Brancker, having returned to England, learned to fly (officers had to do so at their own expense before joining the RFC), followed a course at the RFC's Central Flying School and was put on the RFC Reserve. He was soon appointed Deputy Director of Military Aeronautics at the Military Aeronautics Directorate. In 1915 he was given command of a wing on the Western Front and rose to the rank of Major General before leaving the RAF to become Director of Civil Aviation. Priority then was given to establishing air routes for Imperial Airways between Britain and her far-flung empire.

AROUND THE WORLD

In 1921, Alan Cobham, a wartime RFC pilot, took his first big step up the ladder of fame when he made a 5,000-mile (8,047km) flight around Europe.

On 6 April 1924 two US Army Air Service crews, flying two-seater Douglas

World Cruisers with interchangeable wheel and float landing gear, took off from Seattle to make the first flight round the world. They landed on 28 September, having flown via the Aleutians, Japan, India, Europe, Iceland and Greenland. Their flying time was 15 days, 11 hours and 7 minutes.

On 20 November 1924 Alan Cobham, with Sefton Brancker aboard, took off from Croydon, south of London, in a DH50 with a 230hp Siddeley Puma engine, on a return journey to Rangoon. They landed back at home on 18 March 1925 after flying a total of 17,000 miles (27,360km). In 1926 Cobham flew to

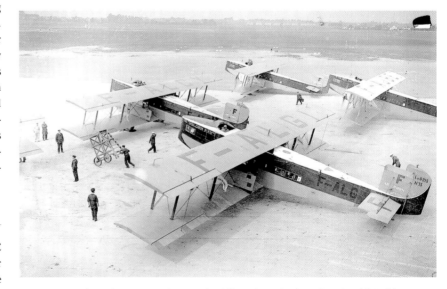

ABOVE: **Lioré et Olivier 213s, in French airline Air Union's red and gold Golden Ray livery, prepare to leave Croydon Airport in June 1932 with celebrities bound for Reims to celebrate the 250th anniversary of the discovery of champagne.**

MILESTONES

1921

Alan Cobham makes a 5,000-mile (8,047 km) tour of Europe.

1923

A US Army Fokker T-2 makes the first nonstop flight across the USA.

1924

Two Douglas World Cruisers complete the first round-the-world flight.

ABOVE: The all-metal Ford 5-AT Trimotor saw widespread use in the USA from the early 1930s. Here, an aircraft of National Air Transport, powered by Pratt & Whitney Wasp radials, takes aboard its cargo of mailbags.

Cape Town and back, followed by a flight of 23,000 miles (37,015km) around Africa. His next trail-blazing venture was a round trip to Australia. His experience exemplified the ardours and perils suffered by flyers in the 1920s, when navigational aids were few and primitive, there was no long-range radio communication between ground and air, and searing heat in the tropics and sub-tropics caused fatigue and illness at the altitudes at which most long flights were made.

An early innovation was flight refuelling, but it did not become general practice until the 1940s. It was first used by the United States Army Air Corps when a pair of DH-4Bs set a new world endurance record of 37hr 15min 43.8sec on 27/28 August 1923. None of the airlines took advantage of the facility because the methods employed were still very primitive.

Britain gave priority to establishing a regular passenger and mail air service between London and India. The route was being put together in stages. In June 1921 the RAF had begun a mail run between Baghdad and Cairo. The entire route was surveyed between December 1926 and January 1927 by Imperial Airways with a DH66 Hercules. On 7 January 1927 the company took over the first link in the chain of communication from the RAF and added Basra and Gaza to the sector. In 1920 the Compagnie Franco-Roumaine de Navigation Aérienne began running a Paris–Prague service; the following year Paris–Budapest and Paris– Stamboul were added. In 1922 another new service was flown by the USSR–German Deruluft, between Königsburg, Kowno, Smolensk and Moscow. By 1923 some airlines were even making night flights. Flying boats were being used by the Belgian line SNETA – later taken over by Sabena – on routes in the Congo.

Australia, with its 2,974,000 square miles (7,702,660sq km), was an obvious candidate for coverage by air routes. December 1921 marked the first flights of the mail service between Geraldton and Derby, both in Western Australia but over 1,000 miles (1,600km) apart. Two years later Qantas started a passenger service between two Queensland towns, Charleville and Cloncurry.

Passenger and mail services, flown by night as well as day, proliferated all over the United States of America during the 1920s. As early as 1921 it was possible to fly from coast to coast between New York and San Francisco in 33hr 20min. Ernest Gann, a giant figure in the pantheon of air pilotage and navigation, described a typical winter's night flight carrying mail when this was a government monopoly. Flying the US Mail in an open cockpit, he said, was a job for young men already matured beyond their numbered years.

Most of the aircraft were war-surplus De Havilland DH-4s built in America under licence, with a 12-cylinder Liberty engine replacing the Rolls-Royce Eagle. On a winter night the cold was intense. The exhaust pipe had not been extended

ABOVE: **This British-registered Sikorsky S-38B amphibian, powered by a pair of 420hp Pratt & Whitney Wasp radials, was the private transport of millionaire Francis Francis, who bought it in 1932.**

beyond the cockpit, but ended 12 inches (30.5cm) or so astern of the engine block. This, Gann said ironically, gave the pilot the dubious advantage of judging his engine-fuel mixture by the colour of the exhaust flame without getting a stiff neck from constantly turning to look behind him. The carbon monoxide exuded was, fortunately, swept away by the slipstream. In 1926 in the course of flying two million miles (3,218,600km), two pilots were killed, 59 had minor injuries and nine aeroplanes were lost. By 1927 flying the mails had been completely contracted to private companies.

The HP O/100 and O/400, converted from bombers to passenger carriers, had been a boon to the nascent airlines; but, like all makeshifts, they had to be succeeded as soon as possible by aeroplanes specifically designed for their function.

The first of these was the twin-engine Handley Page W8, which appeared in 1921. It was quickly followed by the W8E and W8F Hamilton and W9a Hampstead, each of which had a third engine in its nose. On 10 February 1926 the HP W10, ordered by Imperial Airways, made its first flight. The reversion to twin motors proved short sighted: two out of the four that were built crashed.

SPIRIT OF ADVENTURE

Countries with smaller populations were also contributing to the conquest of the air. Portugal, with only some six million inhabitants, showed the spirit of adventure that had lured Vasco da Gama to make his great sea voyages in the late 15th and early 16th centuries. Two Portuguese naval officers took off from Lisbon on 30 March

1922 in a Fairey IIID floatplane to cross the South Atlantic against the prevailing wind. They staged through Las Palmas, the Cape Verde Islands and Porto Praia, delayed at each by adverse weather. At last, on 18 April, they were able to depart for Fernando Po, 200 miles (320km) east of Brazil, but had to force-land at St Paul's rock, which badly damaged the aeroplane. An escorting Portuguese cruiser took them aboard until a replacement Fairey IIID was delivered. This one also came to grief, at Fernando de Noronha. Yet another seaplane was provided and they reached their destination on 16 June.

On 14–15 October 1927 the South Atlantic was crossed non-stop by two French Air Force officers. Their aircraft was a Breguet XIX and in 19hr 50min they covered the 2,125 miles (3,420km) between St Louis, in Senegal, and Natal, in Brazil.

Two resounding triumphs in the second decade of the 20th century caught the world's attention probably more than any other feat of aviation during those ten years. Twenty-five-year-old Charles A. Lindbergh, a native of Detroit, won the $25,000 prize offered for the first non-stop flight between New York and Paris. He made the take-off run in his purpose-built Ryan NYP (Ryan New York–Paris), named *Spirit of St Louis*, from Long Island on 20 May 1927, not sure that the 237hp Wright Whirlwind engine would lift it into the air with the weight of 450 US gallons (1,705 litres) of petrol in the fuselage and wings. However he landed safely at Le Bourget, the Paris airfield, on 21 May after a flight of 33hr 39min that had covered 3,590 miles (5,776km).

The other of the two greatest triumphs in aviation during the 1920s was Charles

Kingsford Smith's flight with his co-pilot, C. T. P. Ulm, from San Francisco to Brisbane, Australia, between 31 May and 9 June 1928 – the first full crossing of the Pacific Ocean. Both men were Australians, and their aircraft was a Fokker F VIIB/3M, named *Southern Cross*. The flight began at Oakland, California, on 31 May 1928 and ended at Brisbane on 9 June, having covered 7,389 miles (11,890km) in 83hr 38min flying time, via Honolulu and Fiji.

The *Daily Mail* newspaper, which had been so generous in awarding prizes for feats that advanced man's mastery of the air, introduced a remarkable innovation in August 1928. This not only exploited the rapid advances that aircraft design and performance had made, but was also a masterstroke of journalistic genius. In August 1928 the newspaper bought a DH61 Giant Moth, a cabin biplane that was an airborne extension of its London Fleet Street headquarters. A darkroom was fitted out, an office desk installed and, most ingenious of all its features, a motorcycle was carried. Photographs of events in the news could now be developed and printed, and the stories typed, in flight. On landing, the motorcyclist aboard would then make a speedy delivery of the whole package to head office.

Two years earlier, this newspaper had also, in unforeseen circumstances, initiated the delivery of bulk air freight. In 1926

BELOW: **Passengers disembark from a Blériot 165 of Air Union at Croydon about 1928. Only two of these biplanes, powered by 420hp Gnome-Rhône Jupiter 9Ab 9-cylinder air-cooled radial engines, were built. This one was named after aviation pioneer Octave Chanute.**

RIGHT: **This Vought O2U-1 floatplane of the US Navy was attached to the cruiser USS *Raleigh* during 1928. An observation biplane, it was powered by a 450hp Pratt & Whitney air-cooled radial.**

there was a general strike in Britain during which coal miners, printers and many others ceased work and neither trains nor buses ran. The *Daily Mail* was the only British paper that had an office in Paris. The British editions were therefore printed there, flown to the airfields near London and taken thence by car to newsagents. No such quantity of cargo had previously been carried by aircraft, and this initiative introduced a type of service that spread quickly for all manner of goods.

POLAR FLIGHTS

Such was the grip that flying had on men and women of adventurous spirit, not least on those for whom exploration was an irresistible lure, that it seemed inevitable that someone would want to fly over the North and South Poles. In 1897 three Swedes had made a foolhardy attempt to fly over the North Pole in a balloon, which vanished without trace until its wreckage was found in 1930. By then both poles had been reached on foot. Veteran Norwegian explorer Roald Amundsen, who had been the first to trudge to the South Pole, tried to make it to the North Pole three times in an aeroplane during 1925. His companions were an American, who financed him, and two Norwegian pilots.

The first flight over the North Pole was eventually made by Amundsen (and an Italian crew) in the airship *Norge* on 11–14 May 1926. US Commander Richard Byrd made the first crossing of the South Pole in a Ford 4-AT Trimotor on 28 November 1929.

One typical instance will convey the ingenuity and toughness demanded of bush pilots who flew over "The Frozen North". One of the best known was

RIGHT: **The Boeing Model 40A of 1927 was designed expressly to fly with the new Boeing Air Transport Corporation on the San Francisco–Chicago portion of the transcontinental airmail route, recently awarded to the carrier.**

"Punch" Dickins, who set off from Edmonton, Alberta, one morning in 1929 to deliver mail on a 1,500 miles (2,414km) trip following the Mackenzie River to Aklavik. En route, landing on frozen snow, an undercarriage strut broke and the tips of the propeller were bent. Dickins and the mechanic who accompanied him repaired them. A wrecked boat yielded piping to replace the strut and they sawed 6in (152mm) off the propeller blades.

The aircraft that were flown over the huge, uncharted wilderness of northern Canada were fitted with wheels that could be interchanged with skis or floats, and had to be high-winged for stability and for convenience when loading and unloading. A typical one was the Fairchild 71, which made its maiden flight in 1929. Wingspan was 50ft (15.24m), length 32ft 10in (10m), and its 430hp Pratt & Whitney engine gave a top speed of 129mph (208kmh). The pilot flew solo and the cabin had capacity for six passengers or the same weight in mail or freight.

On 6 November 1929, the Junkers G-38 took to the air for the first time. It was a typical Dr Hugo Junkers design: he believed fervently in a "flying wing" shape, which enabled most of the fuel and payload to be carried within the wing structure. In this instance, six passengers were seated in the wing centre-section, which had windows forward, and 28 passengers in the fuselage. Only two of this type were built; they operated with Deutsche Luft Hansa until one crashed in 1936 and RAF bombs destroyed the other in 1940.

ABOVE: When it first appeared in 1925, the de Havilland DH60 Moth heralded a revolution in privately owned light aeroplanes. Here the prototype, G-EBKT, displays its folding wings at the company's Stag Lane Aerodrome in Middlesex, England. The engine was the specially created 60hp ADC Cirrus I 4-cylinder air-cooled inline.

BELOW: The French Breguet 19 general-purpose biplane was one of the most prolific and successful military aircraft of the interwar years, being used by many national air arms and for many record-breaking long-distance flights.

ABOVE: Junkers' first trimotor transport, the G23, was followed in 1925 by the G24, powered by three 280/310hp Junkers-L5 inline engines. This Deutsche Luft Hansa G24 at Tempelhof, Berlin, shows the now-familiar corrugated skinning.

LEFT: Probably the most inelegant transport aircraft of the interwar years were the Farman Jabirus. This is the first production F-3X, built in 1924, which had four 180hp Hispano-Suiza 8Ac engines.

ABOVE: The Fokker line continued with the F VII. This one, powered by a water-cooled 450hp Napier Lion, was used by Fokker for demonstrations in England.

LEFT: Although it originated in the First World War, the doughty DH9A served with the RAF into the early 1930s. These aircraft, built from reconditioned stored fuselages, belong to 39 Squadron, based at Spittlegate, Yorkshire, England, in the mid-1920s.

BELOW: Despite their unconventional float-incorporating fuselages, the interwar line of Loening amphibians were successful. This OL-5 was the first aeroplane delivered to the newly established US Coast Guard Air Service in 1926.

ABOVE: **The Armstrong Whitworth Argosy airliner entered service with Imperial Airways in 1926, carrying 20 passengers on the airline's Silver Wing service to Paris.**
Wingspan 90ft 8in (27.64m), **length** 65ft 10in (20.07m), **height** 19ft 10in (6.05m), **weight** 18,000lb (8,165kg), **engines** three 386hp Armstrong Siddeley Jaguar III 14-cylinder radial air-cooled, **cruising speed** 90mph (145kph), **range** 330 miles (531km), **crew** 2, **passengers** 20.

RIGHT: **The Boeing FB-1 shore-based fighter equipped US Marine squadrons from the mid-1920s. A 435hp Curtiss D-12 12-cylinder water-cooled inline engine gave it very clean lines and a top speed of 159mph (256kph).**

ABOVE: **From April 1926 three 420hp Bristol Jupiter 9-cylinder air-cooled radial engines formed the powerplant of the Handley Page W9 Hampstead, which carried 14 passengers in a heated cabin. Only one was built, but the Jupiter was used to power the next generation of Imperial Airways airliners.**

RIGHT: **Four Focke-Wulf A38 Möwe (Seagull) ten-passenger aircraft were built for Luft Hansa in 1931. Wingspan** 65ft 7¼in (20m), **length** 48ft 0in (14.63m), **height** 13ft 1in (3.99m), **weight** 8,818lb (4,000kg), **engine** one 480hp Siemens Jupiter VI 9-cylinder radial air-cooled, **range** 500 miles (805km), **crew** 2, **passengers** 8.

LEFT: The Armstrong Whitworth Siskin single-seat fighter served with the RAF in various marks from 1924 to 1932. Here, mechanics and riggers tend to Siskin III J7758 and its 325hp Armstrong Siddeley Jaguar III 9-cylinder air-cooled radial engine.

BELOW: The ubiquitous Avro 504 was given a new lease of life when it was modified and re-engined with an Armstrong Siddeley Lynx radial to become the 504N trainer, which remained in production until 1933. This one belonged to the Cambridge University Air Squadron.

Douglas World Cruisers

In 1924 eight US Army airmen, crewing four aircraft based on a US Navy torpedo bomber design, set off to attempt the first round-the-world flight, and two crews were successful.

Arthur Hugh Clough, the 19th-century poet and moraliser, if alive today would have given hearty support to the rivalries that have always infused the aviation world with such vigour; and, on the whole, the same kind of friendliness that is traditional in clubs devoted to a sport or game. His lines:

Thou shalt not covet; but tradition
Approves all forms of competition

suggest that he would have been rooting for British supremacy in every facet of aeronautics; such as the first round-the-world flight. Britain, the United States of America, France, Italy and the Soviet Union were the countries most strenuously competing for the prestige of being the first to make all types of pioneering flights. It was the USA that won the laurels for this one.

The decade 1920–30 was a period of rapid advance in long-distance flying. Military pilots and crews were prominent in the field: air forces had suitable aircraft and trained men, and the cost was less than manufacturers and civilian airmen would incur. National standing justified the spending of public money. Since the North and South Atlantic had been flown and the United States crossed non-stop coast to coast, it was time to attempt with confidence a flight round the globe.

On 6 April 1924 four Douglas World Cruisers fitted with interchangeable wheel and float landing gear took off from Seattle. The route took them first to Prince Rupert on the coast of British Columbia. From there they continued in stages to Alaska, where one aeroplane, named *Seattle*, crashed at Dutch Harbour, without injuring the crew. The other three flew on via the Aleutian Islands, Japan, China, Indo-China, Burma, India, Persia, Iraq, Turkey, Romania, Hungary, Germany, France, Britain, Iceland, Greenland and Canada and finally back to where they had started from. The crew in the aircraft called *Boston* had to ditch in the North Atlantic on the way home, but both men aboard were rescued. There was ample sea traffic in those days, and the US Navy was keeping watch and ward for

"It was the USA that won the laurels for this one"

RIGHT: **Three Douglas World Cruisers in floatplane configuration at Seward, Alaska, at an early stage of the flight, attract a gaggle of spectators. One aircraft, *Seattle*, had already been lost.**

RIGHT: The World Cruisers as landplanes, running up their engines at the RAF aerodrome at Drigh Road, Karachi, India.

downed aviators. The two aeroplanes that finished the course bore the names *Chicago* and *New Orleans*. The former was crewed by Captain Lowell H. Smith and Lieutenant Leslie P. Arnold; the latter by Lieutenant Erik H. Nelson and Lieutenant John Harding. The 27,534 miles (44,310km) were covered in 175 days, of which only 15 days, 11 hours and 7 minutes were spent in the air. It was a courageous performance, not least because much of the area they flew over would have been dangerous for a forced landing. The elapsed time was respectable, considering that these middle-sized machines had a maximum speed of 103mph (165kph) and would have been cruising at less than that. ⊙

BELOW: The American airmen pose in front of *Chicago* at Karachi.

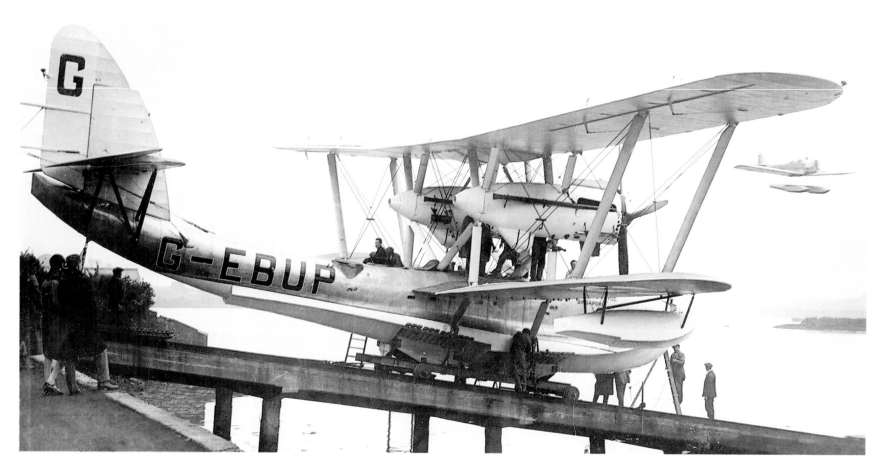

LEFT: The Armstrong Whitworth Siskin IIIA fighters of 32 Squadron, RAF, based at Kenley Aerodrome, Surrey, England, prepare to defend London from a mock attack by bombers during an exercise in the 1930s.

RIGHT: A Junkers-G31de trimotor belonging to Österreichische Luftverkehrs AG awaits its passengers. As well as serving as an airliner, the G31 was also used for heavy freight work in New Guinea by Bulolo Gold Dredging Ltd.

LEFT: This Short Singapore I flying boat, seen on the manufacturer's slipway at Rochester, Kent, England, was flown on a 20,000-mile (32,186km) African Survey Flight by Sir Alan Cobham in 1927–28. It was powered by two 650hp Rolls-Royce Condor IIIA water-cooled inline engines.

RIGHT: A glimpse inside the passenger cabin of a Luft Hansa Junkers G-31, showing an air steward serving food and beverages, an amenity first introduced by the German airline when this aircraft went into service in May 1928.

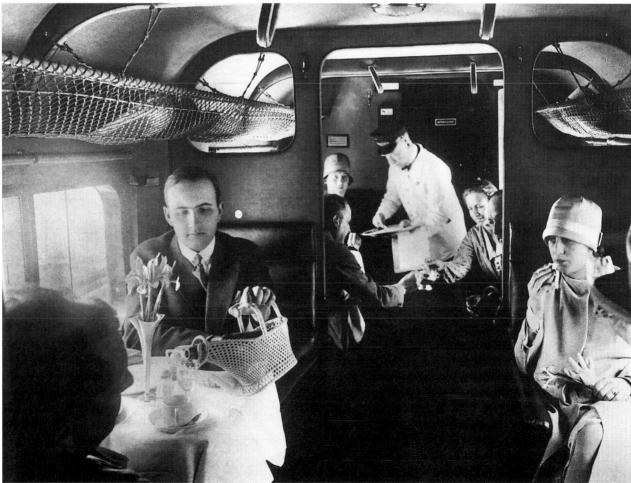

Sir Alan Cobham

In the space of seven years Alan Cobham made a series of outstanding long-distance flights, pioneering the air routes by which Imperial Airways would link the British Empire.

Long-distance flights with all their dangers clearly gave Alan Cobham a simultaneously seductive and menacing challenge. In the 1920s he made more long flights than any other of the pioneer pilots and was the best-known Briton among them.

Cobham began his flying career in the Royal Air Force. After demobilisation he joined the ebullient fraternity of barnstormers in 1919, aged 25: not to hurl an aircraft about the sky, but to give staid joy rides to an eager public. In 1932 he formed a flying circus which gave displays and short flights on what he called his National Aviation Day Campaign, from April to October every year from 1932 to

"He joined the ebullient fraternity of barnstormers"

ABOVE: **Alan Cobham (left) and Henry Seagrave in Selfridges department store, London, after Cobham's return from Cape Town in 1926. Behind is the 4-litre Sunbeam car in which Seagrave broke the world land speed record, and Cobham's Jaguar-engined DH50 biplane.**

1936. It put on over 12,000 performances and carried nearly a million passengers.

His greatest interest was in promoting civil aviation. Between his civilian debut and the outbreak of the Second World War on 3 September 1939 he gave it outstanding service. His main concern was not in speed or altitude records, but to demonstrate that long distances could be flown safely in several stages and that it would be possible to carry passengers to any part of the British Empire if airfields with fuel and servicing facilities were established at suitable intervals along the routes.

In 1921 he made a 5,000-mile (8,047km) circuit of Europe. His shortest international flight, demonstrating the diminutive new de Havilland DH53 Humming Bird in 1923, was from Lymne to Brussels to advertise its economical engine. With his mechanic A. B. Elliott, he took the Director of Civil Aviation, Sir Sefton Brancker, on a survey flight to Rangoon that began on 20 November 1924 and ended on 17 March 1925. On 16 November he was off again, bound for Cape Town 16,100 miles (25,750km) away in a de Havilland DH50 which had been re-engined with a 385hp Armstrong Siddeley Jaguar III, accompanied by Elliott and B. W. Emmott, a photographer. They landed back in England on 13 March 1926.

His next flight, with Elliott, was his most celebrated. The DH50 had been

LEFT: **Readying Cobham's DH50 for its epic 16,000-mile (25,750km) survey flight to the Cape, and back, which began on 16 November 1925 and ended on 13 March 1926.**

"Australia had never seen a seaplane before"

converted to a floatplane. A forced landing on forested or mountainous terrain would have been disastrous, so he had chosen a route along which there was an abundance of sheltered bays and creeks on which to alight. His book about the journey says: "Ninety in every hundred people we met at the various landing places between London [he actually took off, just after dawn, from Rochester on 30 June 1926] and Australia had never seen a seaplane before, and an even greater percentage knew little or nothing about aircraft and what was required for the safe landing, mooring-up and taking off again in a seaplane". He had to depend on the co-operation of the authorities at each landing place, to whom he sent the relevant information and instructions.

After refuelling at Marseilles, Naples was the first overnight stop. The hard work of many weeks' preparation had tired him. Awakened next morning at 4.30am, he postponed departure till 11.00am. Athens was the next stop; and there, "The doctor advised rest, for I was suffering from exhaustion".

Next stop Alexandretta, then Baghdad. They left there before dawn next day and soon met a sandstorm that forced them to fly at 50ft (15m) in a temperature of 110 degrees in the shade. Basra was 100 miles (160km) away when there was a loud explosion and Elliott began to bleed copiously. There was nowhere to land. At Basra he was rushed to hospital, but died that night. He had been hit by a bullet fired from the ground.

ABOVE: **Cobham flies over the Houses of Parliament before landing on the Thames at the end of his 26,000-mile (41,840km) flight to Australia and back in 1926, for which the DH50 was fitted with floats.**

An RAF sergeant who knew the Jaguar engine volunteered to take his place. With five stops on the Indian sub-continent and 11 more in Burma, Malaya and the East Indies, they landed at Port Darwin on 5 August. On 29 August they started back and landed on the Thames near the Houses of Parliament at 2pm on 1 October 1926. Cobham was knighted. In 1927 he flew a flying boat round Africa. ▷

Supermarine Southampton

The longest serving flying boat (excluding the Sunderland) to serve with the Royal Air Force.

SPECIFICATION
Wingspan
75ft 0in (22.86m)

Length
51ft 1in (15.57m)

Height
22ft 4in (6.81m)

Weight
9,000lb (4,082kg) empty
15,200lb (6,895kg) loaded

Engines
Two W-12 cylinder 502hp
Napier Lion V

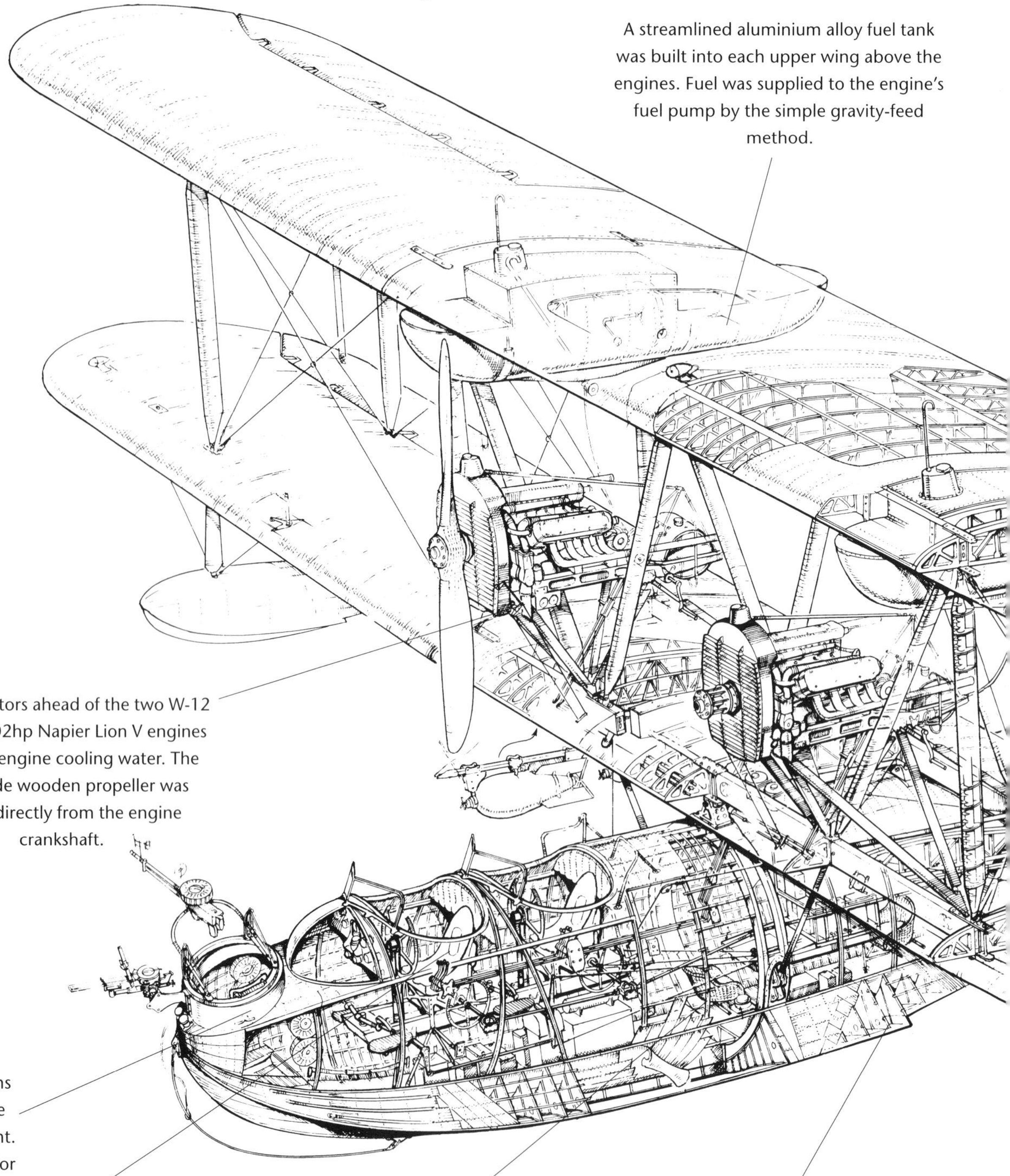

A streamlined aluminium alloy fuel tank was built into each upper wing above the engines. Fuel was supplied to the engine's fuel pump by the simple gravity-feed method.

Large radiators ahead of the two W-12 cylinder 502hp Napier Lion V engines provided engine cooling water. The two-blade wooden propeller was driven directly from the engine crankshaft.

The front gun turret carried two drum-fed .303in Lewis machine guns – one mounted on a Scarff ring, the other on a fixed forward-firing mount. The airgunner was also responsible for handling all mooring lines.

The pilots sat in open tandem cockpits, protected from the elements by small windshields. On the starboard side of the cockpits there was a companion way to enable the crew to move around inside the aircraft's hull.

As part of the crew, the aircraft carried a navigator and also a wireless operator. They and their equipment were positioned in the centre section of the hull.

Early aircrafts' hulls were constructed entirely of wood – one layer of diagonally placed planks; one layer of linen; and finished with one layer of strip planking over a framework of stringers and formers. Later aircraft had aluminium alloy hulls. All wooden hulls were progressively replaced by the alloy type.

Illustration © Frank Munger

KEY FACTS

25 March 1924
The prototype of the Swan flies for the first time. This aircraft is then developed as the Southampton.

March 1925
First flight of the prototype Southampton.

August 1925
Entry into service with No 480 (Coastal Reconnaissance Flight) at Calshot, near Southampton, in southern England.

December 1936
Last of the Southamptons withdrawn from Royal Air Force service.

Rudder and tailplane control surfaces were operated by a system of push-rods and bellcranks. These, in turn, were operated by wire cables from the cockpit.

Wings and tailplane were constructed from pre-assembled ribs and spars. The entire structure was covered in fabric, which was painted. The complete wing section was attached to the fuselage by two massive mounting brackets and supported by four (two each side) struts.

ABOVE: **The Southampton Mk II had a duralumin hull and later, as seen here, the type was given swept-back outer wing panels.**

ABOVE: **The Fairey IIIF general-purpose aircraft, powered by the 570hp Napier Lion XIA water-cooled inline engine, served with the RAF in both landplane and seaplane forms. This one is seen in service with No 8 (Bomber) Squadron at Maala, Aden, in 1929.**

LEFT: **A trio of Boeing F4B-1s of the US Navy. Later members of this famous fighter family were still serving as late as 1941, the F4B-1 having entered service in 1929.**
Wingspan 30ft (9.14m), **length** 20ft 1in (6.10m), **height** 9ft 3in (2.82m), **weight** 2,557lb (1,160kg), **engine** one 500hp Pratt & Whitney Wasp 9-cylinder radial air-cooled, **maximum speed** 169mph (272kph), **range** 371 miles (597km), **crew** 1.

RIGHT: **The French Morane MS138 parasol monoplane of the late 1920s was a two-seat trainer powered by an air-cooled 80hp le Rhône rotary, a rather dated engine type harking back to the First World War.**

ABOVE: A massive Junkers-G38 of Luft Hansa draws the crowds during a visit to Croydon Airport in 1931. As well as accommodating passengers on two levels in its fuselage, the G38 also had cabins in its wing roots.

BELOW: A Focke-Wulf A16d on Luft Hansa's North sea Island route sets off from Wangerooge for Bremen in July 1928. The type had a variety of engines; this variant was powered by a Mercedes 6-cylinder water-cooled inline of 120 or 135hp.

RIGHT: No fewer than 12 engines powered the impressive Dornier Do X flying boat. Originally these were 525hp Siemens Jupiter 9-cylinder air-cooled radials, but it is here seen in 1930 with 600hp Curtiss Conqueror 12-cylinder vee water-cooled engines.

BELOW RIGHT: Lieutenant Monti of Italy prepares to fly his Macchi M-67 racing seaplane in the 1929 Schneider Trophy contest at RAF Calshot, England. That year's contest was won by Britain's Supermarine S6, designed by Reginald J. Mitchell, at an average speed of 328.63mph (528.87kph).

BELOW: The Boeing Model 80A was a refined version of the Model 80 of 1928. Wingspan 80ft (24.38m), length 56ft 6in (17.24m), height 15ft 3in (4.65m), weight 17,500lb (7,938kg), engines three 525hp Pratt & Whitney Hornet 9 cylinder radial air-cooled, cruising speed 125mph (201kph), range 460 miles (740km), crew 2, passengers 18.

Charles Lindbergh

Charles Lindbergh was a professional pilot and skilled navigator who won fame by making the first solo flight across the Atlantic. Several others, six of whom were killed, had tried to fly the northern half of the ocean. It was less difficult for those starting from America than from Europe, as the prevailing wind blows from west to east.

Lindbergh's aircraft, *Spirit of St Louis*, was a high-wing Ryan monoplane. Its engine, the recently developed 237hp Wright Whirlwind J-5-C nine-cylinder radial engine, had a high power-to-weight ratio and was of proven reliability. That was the good news. The bad news was

that extra fuel tanks had to be fitted, which not only added a lot of weight but also obstructed forward visibility. To see where he was going, the pilot had either to peer through the side windows, which afforded only an oblique field of vision, or use the periscope that had been fitted.

His take-off from Long Island at 7.52am on 20 May 1927 in pursuit of the $25,000 prize that success would bring was not auspicious. It had been raining, airfields did not have tarmac or concrete runways in those days, and soft ground was not conducive to a fast take-off run. His route lay across Newfoundland, Ireland, the tip of Cornwall and Cherbourg.

It was a struggle to keep awake. To check wind speed and direction he had frequently to fly low enough to ensure visually that the motion of the waves tallied with the weather forecast. He landed in darkness at Le Bourget at 10.24pm on 21 May, having flown 3,590 miles (5,776km).

After this historic flight Charles Lindburgh made many others over the Caribbean and Central America. In 1931 he and his wife flew a Lockheed Sirius single-engine seaplane to Japan via Alaska, Siberia and the Kuriles surveying possible airline routes. Two years later they flew 30,000 miles around the Atlantic for the same purpose.

RIGHT: **Shortly before the war, Lindbergh paid several visits to Germany to see the nation's growing aerial might. He is seen here at an international flying meeting in Berlin in 1936. The aircraft in the background is a Czechoslovakian Avia BH122 aerobatic aircraft.**

BELOW: **Several replicas of the NYP have been built, of which this is one. It differs from the original in some details. INSET: A candid shot of Charles Lindbergh in the UK in 1937.**

FAR RIGHT: **Lindbergh's Ryan NYP (New York–Paris) monoplane during the tour of the USA following his momentous flight. The lack of forward view for the pilot is evident.**

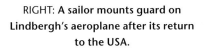

RIGHT: **A sailor mounts guard on Lindbergh's aeroplane after its return to the USA.**

ABOVE: The 1929 Tupolev ANT-9 was produced in both twin- and three-engined forms. The original engines, as seen here, were 230hp Gnome-Rhône Titan 7-cylinder air-cooled radials. The prototype made a goodwill European flight in July and August 1929.

LEFT: One of the RAF's frontline day and night fighters of the late 1920s/early 1930s was the Bristol Bulldog, powered by a 440hp Bristol Jupiter 9-cylinder air-cooled radial engine. These are Bulldog IIs of No 41 Squadron.

ABOVE RIGHT: A Luft Hansa Junkers-G31 undergoing maintenance at Schiphol Airport, Amsterdam, Netherlands. This aircraft had Siemens Jupiter engines.

RIGHT: The Westland Wapiti replaced the DH9 as the RAF's general-purpose workhorse in 1929, and some were still serving in India ten years later. The engine was a 480hp Bristol Jupiter air-cooled radial. This is an aircraft of No 5 Squadron in India.

As aircraft became increasingly sophisticated, so their performance and capabilities improved, pushing back the barriers of speed, range and altitude.

Chapter Five
More Records Fall

It is generally agreed that the greatest of all the long-distance pilots of the 1930s was Wiley Post, an American Indian who had only one eye, and was distinguished for wearing a black patch. He was a famous barnstormer before applying himself to serious aviation. With a navigator, Harold Gatty, he took off from New York on 23 June 1931 and landed back there after making a circuit of the globe in 8 days, 15 hours and 51 minutes. The distance flown was nearly 15,500 miles (24,945km). They had refuelled at Harbor Grace in Newfoundland, Chester in England, Berlin, Moscow, Novosibirsk, Blagovschchenck and Khabarovsk in Siberia – where bad weather delayed them for 14 hours – Fairbanks in Alaska and Edmonton in Canada.

Two years later Wiley Post set off again to repeat the flight, this time on his own and in less time. The aircraft was therefore fitted with an automatic pilot. He took off on 15 July 1933 and made the trip in 7 days, 18hr and 19 min.

In Italy, in 1931, the Air Minister, General Italo Balbo, was only 35 years old. He attracted worldwide attention to himself and his Service in January that year by leading a formation of 10 Savoia S55 twin-hulled flying boats from Portuguese Guinea to Natal (Brazil). On 1 July 1933, he led off a formation of 24 of the same aircraft from Orbetello, in Italy, to Chicago. They flew via Iceland and landed at their destination on the

15th. The formation took off for home on 25 July, lost an aircraft in the Azores, and arrived back in Italy on 12 August.

The first east–west Atlantic crossing was made by Hermann Köhl, Captain J. Fitzmaurice and Baron von Hunefeld in the Junkers-W33 *Bremen* on 12–13 April 1928. James Mollison first attracted public attention when he flew his Puss Moth from England to Australia in under nine days, a record. On 20–21 May 1932 he made the first solo east–west Atlantic crossing, as well as setting a London–Cape Town record. His wife (the renowned Amy Johnson) broke this record later in the year. In July 1933 both Mollisons flew a DH84 Dragon from Pendine, in Wales, to Bridgeport, Connecticut, where they were both injured in a crash landing.

Record flights dominated the aviation scene in the 1930s, and one of the most useful was the flight over Mount Everest on 3 April 1933, because it yielded valuable information about the problems in flying at very high altitude, buffeted by swirling winds. The two aircraft were a Westland PV3, flown by the Marquess of Clydesdale and a Westland Wallace flown by Flight Lieutenant D. F. McIntyre.

AIR RACES

The Schneider Trophy race of 1931 was a welcome antidote, in Europe and the USA, to the Depression that had afflicted the world for the previous two years. Jacques Schneider, a Frenchman born in 1879, was

a racing driver who learned to fly in 1911. In 1913 he instituted a trophy for the winner of a seaplane race – an event that was to have a significant influence over the design of high-speed aircraft. The first contest was held in Monaco in 1913: 28 laps of a 10km (6.2 miles) course. It was won by a Frenchman in a Deperdussin monotype at an average speed of 45.75 mph (73.63kph). The following year a British pilot won with a Sopwith Tabloid at 86.78mph (139.66kph). In 1923 a US Army Air Corps team won at 177mph (285kph). The USA won again in 1925 at Baltimore with 233 mph (375kph). Three

ABOVE: **A pair of Italian Savoia-Marchetti S55X flying boats which took part in General Balbo's second mass Atlantic crossing to visit the 1933 Chicago World's Fair. They were powered by two 850hp Isotta-Fraschini 18-cylinder watercooled inline engines mounted in tandem.**

ABOVE: **The Boeing 247, which first appeared in 1933, was a revolutionary design, being an all-metal monoplane with enclosed accommodation for its passengers and crew, a retractable undercarriage and variable-pitch propellers for its 550hp Pratt & Whitney Wasp radial engines.**

MILESTONES

1928

Hermann Köhl, Captain Fitzmaurice and Baron von Hunefeld make the first east–west Atlantic flight in the Junkers-W33 Bremen.

1930

Amy Johnson makes a record-breaking solo flight from England to Australia.

1931

Flight Lieutenant Boothman wins the Schneider Trophy outright for Great Britain, flying a Supermarine S6B racing seaplane.

wins in succession would gain permanent possession of the trophy. The Americans were regarded as certain winners in 1924, but their competitors were obliged to withdraw and they sportingly cancelled the event.

In 1925 Britain entered a Supermarine S4, designed by R. J. Mitchell and flown by an RAF officer, but it crashed. A Gloster biplane that also competed was easily beaten. The Americans won again. In 1926 Italy won with a Macchi M29. In 1927, at Venice, the RAF team won with Mitchell's Supermarine S5, and again in England in 1929 with the S6. In 1931 the RAF's S6B triumphed at 340.08mph

(547.29kph), flown by Flight Lieutenant J. N. Boothman, thus retaining the trophy in perpetuity. The Rolls-Royce 2,300hp engine was then boosted to 2,550hp and the aircraft set a new world seaplane record of 407.5mph (655.8kph) later that year. Mitchell based the design for the Spitfire on these three seaplanes.

The Italian seaplanes that had competed in the 1929 race had many differences between them. The Macchi M67 had a 1800hp Isotta-Fraschini engine. The Fiat C29 was very small, with a lightweight 1,000hp AS5 engine. Some of the aircraft were quaintly unconventional. The SM65 was a monoplane with twin

floats and twin booms, and had a 1,000hp Isotta-Fraschini engine driving a tractor propeller at the front of the central nacelle and a similar engine at the rear, driving a pusher propeller.

Air races saw increasingly better times set by the competitors, which in turn brought forth faster fighters and bombers. One of the great heroes of military and civil aviation is an American, James (Jimmy) Doolittle. As a fighter pilot, he won the Schneider Trophy in 1925. In 1930 he joined the Shell Company and in 1932 won an annual air race in the USA, the Thomson Trophy, flying a closed circuit around pylons. In the same year

he set a new landplane record of 296.287mph (476.815kph), flying a Gee Bee R-1 Super Sportster. He rejoined the US Army Air Corps in 1940 as a major, flew bombers and rose to lieutenant-general. He also led a hazardous raid on Japan by 16 B-25 Mitchell bombers flying from a carrier in 1942, immortalised by the name, "The Doolittle Raid".

The many annual races held in the USA bred several racing aeroplanes, most of which were one-offs. The Travel Air "Mystery" of 1929 had a top speed of 235mph (378kph). The Wedell-Williams achieved 266.674mph (429.158kph) in 1932. In 1939 the Crosby CR-4 recorded 263mph (423kph) with a 350hp engine.

In Britain the King's Cup Air Race was graced by royal patronage. It was meant to be held annually over a 700–750 mile (1,120–1,200km) course, but the distance was considerably shortened as years went by. The first was flown in 1922, and in

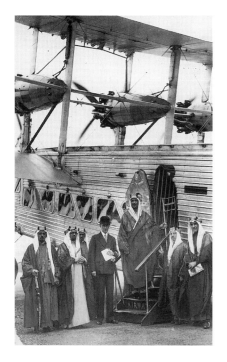

ABOVE: **The Emir Saud, Crown Prince of Saudia Arabia, prepares to enter Imperial Airways' Short Syrinx for a flight over London during his visit to Croydon Aerodrome in June 1935.**

1930 it was won by a woman, Miss Winifred Brown. The race encouraged the design of racing aircraft such as the Mew Gull and Miles Hawk Speed Six.

One of the fastest seaplanes ever built was the Macchi MC72, which in 1934 set a world seaplane record of 440.681mph (709.188kph).

By 1930, military aircraft had attained a streamlined beauty. The Hawker Hart, a two-seater day bomber first delivered to the RAF in January, was both fast and manoeuvrable. Steel structured but fabric covered, its maximum speed was 184mph (296kph), faster than contemporary British fighters. The Hawker Demon two-seat fighter that joined its first squadron three years later was 3mph (5kph) slower. The Hawker Fury single-seat fighter, however, could make 223mph (357kph), and a batch sold to Yugoslavia were 10mph (16kph) faster. The Hawker Hurricane MkI, which first flew in 1935, attained 316mph (509kph); while the Spitfire I of 1937 clocked 355mph (571kph).

In the USA the Boeing P-26A of 1933 achieved 234mph (377kph) and the Curtiss P-36 302mph (486kph). In Germany the pretty Ar 68E flew at 202mph (324kph), and the Messerschmitt Bf 109B-2, 280mph

(450kph). In the USSR the1933 Polikarpov I-15 attained 224mph (360kph), while the 1934 Polikarpov I-16 flew at 362mph (582kph). In Italy the mid-1930s biplane Fiat CR42 had a top speed of 221mph (355kph). In Japan the 1932 Mitsubishi A5M could reach 265mph (426kph).

In 1937 the British company Napier had started development of a 24-cylinder engine, the Sabre, in which high hopes were invested by both the company and the Air Ministry. It turned out to be a compendium of imperfections when installed in the Typhoon fighter a few years later, but one of the lesser-known aeroplane constructors, Heston Aircraft, welcomed it in its early days as the power unit for its Heston Racer, which was judged to be capable of 520mph (837kph). Unluckily for the firm, it suffered an accident on its first flight, and the outbreak of war compelled Heston to abandon it.

In the USA, in a totally different sector of aircraft construction, the design and production of airliners, Douglas, Boeing and Lockheed were all making great strides.

In Europe rapid growth in passenger air traffic spawned a bewildering variety of commercial aeroplanes. The earliest Imperial Airways type to establish itself in the favour of British travellers was the Handley Page HP42, which made its first flight on 17 November 1930. A useful feature was the short take-off and landing run, which enabled it to use relatively small grass airfields. The crew numbered three and there was room for 38 passengers.

One of the most elegant types was an improved version of the DH Dragon, the Dragon Rapide, which accommodated 10 passengers and was first seen in 1934. The RAF bought 521, renamed the type Dominie, and used them for communications and as a radio trainer at Electrical and Wireless Schools.

Some very odd military and civil aircraft were on offer in the 1930s. The Handley Page HP47 general-purpose military monoplane was one, with its pod and boom fuselage that allowed a rear gunner the widest possible field of fire. The Blériot 125 had a twin-boom fuselage, in each of which six passengers were seated, and the two-man crew occupied a cockpit above the fuselage. The British Burnelli monoplane, with its aerofoil-shape fuselage that increased lift and improved efficiency, carried 15 passengers and had two 750hp Perseus engines. This type was also built in the USA.

FLIGHT REFUELLING

Refuelling in flight was of great interest to airlines. In July 1935 two Americans, Al and Fred Key, spent 653hr 34min flying around the airport at Meridian, Mississippi, in a Curtiss Robin that was refuelled in the air. This led to the founding in 1936 of a company in Britain, called Flight Refuelling Ltd, to develop this procedure.

Flight Refuelling Ltd had two Vickers Virginias, an Armstrong Whitworth AW23,

a Handley Page HP51, a Vickers B19/27 and a Boulton Paul Overstrand converted to carry the petrol.

The Imperial Airways technical adviser, Major Robert Mayo, proposed an alternative method to refuelling in flight, in which a small, heavily loaded aeroplane would be placed on top of a big one that would fly it off the ground and release it at cruising height and speed.

In 1938 Imperial Airways agreed to provide a Southampton–New York flying boat service, to be refuelled in the air, after practice had been carried out with a Short C Class flying boat, the *Cambria*. Two Short flying boats, *Cabot* and *Caribou*, were to be refuelled by HP Harrows that had been converted to tankers. *Caribou* took off on the first flight on 5 August 1939, landed at Shannon on the west coast of Ireland to refuel and was refuelled again over the Atlantic by a Harrow. On the return journey the boat was refuelled off Newfoundland.

Transatlantic services also attracted France and Germany, both of which operated over the south Atlantic. Aéropostale flew between Paris and Dakar, in West Africa, and along the South American east coast from Natal to Buenos Aires. Mail was taken only part of the way by air. From Dakar to Natal, Brazil, it was taken by sea. In 1936, after Air France took on the mail, it was flown all the way.

From 1930 to 1932 the German air line Deutsche Luft Hansa was also assisted by ships that took mail from the Canary

LEFT: A classic scene from the 1930s. Handley Page HP42 airliner Hengist of Imperial Airways, ensign flying above its cockpit, taxies on to the Croydon apron, with the airport's distinctive terminal building as a backdrop.

RIGHT: Foreign visitors at Croydon in 1933. Nearest is the Fokker FXX Zilvermeeuw of KLM, powered by three 700hp Wright Cyclone radial engines, and behind are a pair of Air France Wibault 282s with three 350hp Gnome-Rhône Titan Major engines apiece.

BELOW: The Hawker Fury, powered by a water-cooled 525hp Rolls-Royce Kestrel 12-cylinder vee, was the epitome of the elegant, high-speed biplane fighter of the 1930s. These are aircraft of No 1 Squadron, RAF, in 1936.

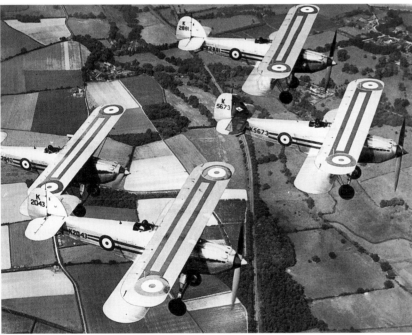

Islands to Fernando do Noronha, in Brazil.

In 1932 a fleet of seaplane/flying boat depot ships made their first appearance and refuelled Dornier Wal flying boats in mid-ocean. The aircraft would alight alongside the steamer, which hoisted it aboard, refuelled and serviced it, then shot it into the air by catapult. As this last ministration imposed a 4.5g acceleration, the method was confined to cargo carriers. Mail flights also crossed the North Atlantic in the same manner, using Heinkel He12 seaplanes launched when 300 miles from New York. Next, Dornier Do18 flying boats replaced them and refuelled alongside a liner, *Schwabenland*, halfway across.

LONG DISTANCES

The year 1934 was a momentous one for flying: it saw the longest air race (England to Australia) ever held before or since. Sir William MacPherson MacRobertson donated the prizes. Two trophies were to be competed for concurrently: an open one for sheer speed and the other a handicap contest. The destination had been chosen to mark the centenary of the Australian city of Melbourne.

Among the entries were three of a new type specially built by de Havilland, the DH88 Comet, a twin-engined, two-seater, long-range, low-wing cantilever mono-

plane. There was no restriction on the number of crew. Every effort had been made to ensure that the race was as safe as possible. Lifebelts and at least three days' provisions had to be taken.

Of the 64 aeroplanes originally entered in the first flush of ambition, only 20 eventually took part. The competitors started from Mildenhall, Suffolk, and were watched by a crowd of 60,000. Numbers had been drawn for starting order and Jim and Amy Mollison were off first. The Mollisons were also the first to reach Baghdad – in 12hr 40min. Next came the two other Comets.

Jim and Amy Mollison arrived at Karachi in record time, 22hr 13min, but had to retire with mechanical problems. C. W. A. Scott and T. Campbell Black won the race in 70hr 54min, a great credit to the Comet's two 230hp Gipsy 6 engines. The handicap winner was a standard Douglas DC2 airliner of KLM.

The Comet inspired many designers to use its shape as a template. The sleek Caudron C41 Typhon high-speed mail plane was one of the derivatives.

Also to put its stamp on the year 1934, with its first flight on 19 June, was an aerial extravaganza that could only have been conceived in Russia – the ANT-20. This was an A. N. Tupolev design built by TSAGI (Central Hydro and Aerodynamic Institute) and named *Maxim Gorki*. It had a crew of 23 and could carry 40 passengers. Illuminated electrical signs and slogans could be displayed under its wings.

The wings and fuselage accommodated a printing press, radio broadcasting unit, and cine equipment for disseminating propaganda leaflets and films. The exterior was equally non-conformist.

Flying a Percival Vega Gull, C. W. A. Scott had another impressive victory in 1936, partnered this time by Giles Guthrie. The event was the Schlesinger race from Portsmouth, England, to Johannesburg, South Africa. They were the only competitors to finish the distance.

Since the Wright brothers had first flown, the proprietors of the *Daily Mail* had been generous and far-sighted in providing financial incentives for the advance of aviation. In 1935 Lord Rothermere, the newspaper's owner, distressed by the British Air Ministry's lack of enterprise, had an aeroplane built for him that he was certain would galvanise the Air Marshals into awareness that the RAF's aircraft were not keeping up with the times.

This handsome monoplane, the Bristol 142, which he named *Britain First*, was a four-passenger executive transport with a top speed of 307mph (494kph). As that was 100mph (161kph) faster than any British fighter, Rothermere's psychological ploy proved successful: the Air Ministry ordered a bomber that would be on much the same lines. In consequence, the Blenheim made its first flight on 25 June 1936 and entered squadron service in 1937. A night fighter variant followed it in December 1938.

Flying Boats

In the 1920s and 1930s the flying boat reached its peak, playing a significant part in the establishment of world-wide intercontinental commercial air routes.

In the infancy of aviation aeroplanes were frequently damaged by heavy landings. It occurred to some pilots and constructors that to alight on water might obviate this. In 1913 an American, Glenn L. Curtiss, accordingly replaced the pontoons on one of his seaplanes by a boat-shaped hull, with which he carried out successful trials. The first European to emulate him was T. O. M. Sopwith with his amphibious Bat Boat, a year later. The First World War accelerated development. In Britain, John Porte, a squadron commander in the Royal Naval Air Service (RNAS), designed flying boats with a V-shaped hull, which was the most important improvement.

For landplanes, increasingly large airfields were needed, with all the expenses of real estate, hangars, terminal buildings and airfield lighting. The overheads for operating flying boats and floatplanes were much lower.

In 1926 the Short Singapore, the first flying boat of metal stressed-skin construction, was launched. The following year the three-engine Short Calcutta began to fly the Mediterranean sector of the Imperial Airways England to India route. The Short Kent followed, and in 1935 the same company began the production of 18 four-engine Empire class boats with four 910hp Bristol Pegasus engines, the first of which flew in July

BELOW: Pan American began operating the Martin M-130, carrying 14 passengers, on transpacific services in 1935. Powered by four 950hp Pratt & Whitney R-1830 Twin Wasp 14-cylinder air-cooled radial engines and spanning 130ft (39.6m), they remained with the airline until 1942.

ABOVE: The Short S23 C-Class Empire flying boats were introduced into service by Imperial Airways in 1936. Four 920hp Bristol Pegasus 9-cylinder air-cooled radial engines gave them a cruising speed of 165mph (265.5kph), and they carried up to 24 passengers. The cockpit is shown in the inset.

ABOVE : A Pan American Sikorsky S-42 Clipper at Foynes, Ireland, after inaugurating an experimental transatlantic service in July 1937. These aircraft had four 700hp Pratt & Whitney Hornet 9-cylinder air-cooled radial engines, which gave them a cruising speed of 170mph (274km/h) and a range of 1,200 miles (1,930km).

"June 1937 Imperial Airways began a Bermuda–New York service"

1936. They carried 24 passengers, who slept aboard, and two tons of mail and freight. Cruising speed was 164mph (264kph), maximum speed 200mph (322kph) and range 810 miles (1,300km). Two years later a daily service was in operation from England to Egypt, four a week were flying from England to India, three to East Africa and two each to South Africa, Malaya and Australia.

When Pan American Airlines decided to introduce a transpacific service, starting from San Francisco, it could be done only by stages via islands. Landing facilities already existed at Honolulu and Manila and two more were created at Guam and Wake Island. The stages were: San Francisco–Hawaii 2,295 miles (3,693km), Hawaii–Wake 2,414 miles (3,885km), Wake–Guam 1,500 miles (2,414km), Guam–Manila 1,594 miles (2,565km). The airline's specification for the necessary aircraft required a flying boat capable of flying 2,500 miles (4,020km) into a

30mph (48kph) headwind while carrying a crew of four and at least 200lb (90kg) of mail. Martin built three M-130 flying boats with four 800/950hp Pratt & Whitney Twin Wasp engines that could carry 41 passengers: but only 14 seats were fitted for the Pacific run. Cruising speed was 157mph (253km) and range 3,200 miles (5,150km) – or 4,000 miles (6,440km) if carrying freight only. The boats were named *China Clipper*, *Philippine Clipper* and *Hawaii Clipper*. The mail service began on 22 November 1935 with a 59hr 40min flight. From 21 October 1936 passengers were also carried.

On 16 June 1937 Imperial Airways began a Bermuda–New York service with the C-class flying boat *Cavalier*, and Pan American followed suit with the Sikorsky S-42 *Clipper III*. On 5–6 July, the long-range class *Caledonia* made Foynes, on the river Shannon in Ireland, to Botwood in Newfoundland, Canada, in 15hr 3min, then on to Montreal; while *Clipper III* flew

in the reverse direction and continued to Southampton. Neither of these aircraft carried enough fuel for commercial services, so, after an experimental air refuelling exercise, C class flying boats were built to take-off with full payload and be refuelled in flight.

The ubiquitous Sunderland was a direct development of the C-class and served throughout the Second World War in the maritime patrol and anti-submarine role.

In 1938 the Boeing 314 Clippers, flagships of Pan American Airlines, began a transatlantic service which was maintained throughout the Second World War.

During the war the development of long-range troop and cargo transport aircraft progressed far ahead of flying boats' performance and the number of airfields increased enormously. These factors, and the fact that not all big cities have expanses of water conveniently near, soon led to the disappearance of large passenger or freight flying boats.

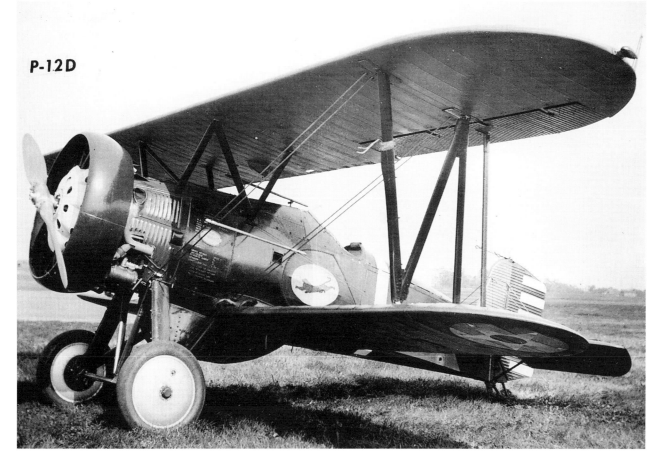

ABOVE: A variety of types at the Paris Aero Show in 1930. In the foreground are three Morane-Saulnier parasol monoplanes; the big flying-boat hull belongs to the Lioré et Olivier H27; the curious double-fuselage monoplane on the right is the Blériot 125; and under its wing are the Blériot 111 and the original cross-Channel Blériot XI of 1909.

LEFT: A classic US Army Air Corps fighter of the 1930s was the Boeing P-12, first flown in 1929. This is a P-12D of 1931. Wingspan 30ft (9.14m), length 20ft 3in (6.17m), height 8ft 8in (2.64m), weight 1,956lb (887kg), engine one 525hp Pratt & Whitney R-1340-17 9-cylinder radial air-cooled, cruising speed 163mph (262kph), range 475 miles (764km), crew 1.

ABOVE: **Jimmy Doolittle poses with Shell Oil's Lockheed 9C Orion Shellightning in 1932.**
Wingspan 42ft 10in (13.05m), **length** 27ft 10in (8.48m), **height** 9ft 8in (2.95m), **weight** 3,325lb (1,508kg), **engine** one 550hp Pratt & Whitney Wasp 9-cylinder radial air-cooled, **cruising speed** 200mph (322kph), **range** 750 miles (1,207km), **crew** 1, **passengers** 6.

LEFT: **Produced by the American Fokker company, the Fokker FXXXII entered service in 1930, but only two were built.**
Wingspan 99ft (30.18m), **length** 69ft 10in (21.3m), **height** 16ft 6in (5.03m), **weight** 14,200lb (6,441kg), **engines** four 575hp Pratt & Whitney R-1690 Hornet 9-cylinder radial air-cooled, **cruising speed** 140mph (225kph), **range** 500 miles (805km), **crew** 2, **passengers** 32.

RIGHT: **The Curtiss Model 53 Condor CO airliner of 1929 was operated by Eastern Air Transport.**
Wingspan 91ft 8in (27.9m), **length** 57ft 6in (17.5m), **height** 16ft 3in (4.95m), **weight** 12,426lb (5,636kg), **engines** two 625hp Curtiss GV-1570 Conqueror V-12 water-cooled, **maximum speed** 145mph (233kph), **crew** 3, **passengers** 18.

ABOVE: **Hawker Hart light day bombers of No 57 Squadron, RAF. The Hart served from 1930 to 1939.**
Wingspan 37ft 3in (11.35m), **length** 29ft 4in (8.9m), **height** 10ft 5in (3.18m), **weight** 2,530lb 1,148kg), **engine** one 525hp Rolls-Royce Kestrel 12-cylinder vee watercooled, **maximum speed** 184mph (296kph), **range** 470 miles (756km), **crew** 2.

RIGHT: **A Supermarine Southampton II is manhandled down the slipway at Felixstowe, Suffolk, England, in 1930.**
Wingspan 75ft (22.9m), **length** 51ft 2in (15.6m), **height** 22ft 5in (6.8m), **weight** 9,000lb (4,082kg), **engines** two 502hp Napier Lion V 8-cylinder arrow water-cooled, **cruising speed** 83mph (133kph), **range** 770 miles (1,240km), **crew** 5.

Women Pioneer Pilots

The first woman pilot to arouse international interest was Britain's Amy Johnson, who took off from Croydon on 5 May 1930 for Australia in a de Havilland Gipsy Moth that she had named *Jason*. The press paid little attention to her until she arrived at Karachi in six days, a new record: thenceforth she was in the headlines and remained there for the rest of her life. On her arrival in Australia on 24 May the *Daily Mail* awarded her £10,000. In the summer of 1931 she flew *Jason II*, a de Havilland Puss Moth, to Tokyo via Moscow.

In 1932 she married Jim Mollison, a world-famous flyer. A year later, between 22 and 24 July 1933, in a twin-engine de Havilland Dragon, they flew from Pendine, in Wales to Bridgeport,

Connecticut – where they crash-landed. The following year they entered a de Havilland DH88 Comet in the Mildenhall–Melbourne race, but retired at Karachi with mechanical trouble.

During the Second World War Amy joined the Air Transport Auxiliary (ATA), which delivered aircraft from factories and maintenance units to squadrons. She crashed fatally, flying an Airspeed Oxford, in foul weather over the Thames estuary in January 1941.

In 1934 Jean Batten, a New Zealander, became the first woman to make a return flight from Australia to England. Such was the general ignorance about flying that when she arrived at Cyprus she found the windsock tied down to its mast to protect it from wind damage. On 11

November 1935, flying a Percival Gull, she made the first South Atlantic crossing by a woman. Between 15 and 16 October 1936, piloting the same aeroplane, she became the first woman to make the flight from Britain to New Zealand. Her time of 11 days and 45 minutes broke the record.

An American, Amelia Earhart, in a Lockheed Vega, was the first woman to fly solo across the Atlantic on 20–21 May 1932. In 1935 she achieved two firsts: Hawaii–California, 11–12 January, a flight of 18 hr 16 min, and Mexico City–New Jersey. In 1937, on a round-the-world attempt in a twin-engine Lockheed Electra, with Fred Noon navigating, they were both lost without trace somewhere over the Pacific.

LEFT **Jean Batten** poses with the Percival Gull Six, powered by a 200hp de Havilland Gipsy Six 6-cylinder inline engine, which was her mount for her record-breaking long-distance flights in the mid-1930s.

LEFT: American aviatrix **Amelia Earhart's** choice for her 1937 attempt on a round-the-world flight was a Lockheed Model 10-E Electra Special with a pair of Pratt & Whitney R-1340 Wasp S3H1s.

RIGHT: **Amy Johnson** flew her de Havilland DH60 Gipsy Moth, *Jason*, from Croydon to Darwin in 1930 to complete the first England–Australia solo flight by a woman.

LEFT: **The Curtiss F9C-2 Sparrowhawk fighter was operated from the American rigid airships *Akron* and *Macon*, being launched from and retrieved on a trapeze. Wingspan 25ft 5in (7.75m), length 20ft 7in (6.25m), height 11ft (3.35m), weight 2,089lb (948kg), engine one 438hp Wright R-975-E3 9-cylinder radial air-cooled, maximum speed 176mph (284kph), range 350 miles (563km), crew 1.**

BELOW: **Used by both the RAF and Fleet Air Arm, the Fairey IIIF was a reliable general-purpose/spotter reconnaissance aircraft. Wingspan 45ft 9in (13.9m), length 34ft 4in (10.46m), height 14ft 3in (4.3m), weight 3,923lb (1,779kg), engine one 570hp Napier Lion XIA 8-cylinder arrow water-cooled, maximum speed 120mph (193kph), endurance 3 to 4 hours, crew 3.**

ABOVE: **Successor to the Hart, the Hawker Hind day bomber first appeared in 1934, and went into RAF service late the following year.**
Wingspan 37ft 3in (11.35m), **length** 29ft 7in (9m), **height** 10ft 7in (3.17m), **weight** 3,251lb (1,475kg), **engine** one 640hp Rolls-Royce Kestrel V 12-cylinder vee water-cooled, **maximum speed** 186mph (299kph), **range** 430 miles (692km), **crew** 2.

RIGHT: **An Imperial Airways Short Scylla taxies out at Croydon Airport in March 1937 despite heavy snow.**
Wingspan 113ft (34.4m), **length** 83ft 10in (25.6m), **height** 31ft 7in (9.6m), **weight** 22,650lb (10,274kg), **engines** four 555hp Bristol Jupiter XFBM 9-cylinder radial air-cooled, **cruising speed** 105mph (169kph), **range** 450 miles (724km), **crew** 5, **passengers** 39.

ABOVE: **This Northrop Gamma 2A was the machine in which Captain Frank Hawks broke a number of speed records.**
Wingspan 48ft (14.63m), **length** 29ft 9in (9.07m), **height** 9ft (2.74m), **weight** 3,500lb (1,588kg), **engine** one 785hp Wright Whirlwind GR-1510 14-cylinder radial air-cooled, **cruising speed** 220mph (354kph), **range** 2,500 miles (4,025km), **crew** 1.

LEFT: **Admiral Byrd flew this float-equipped Curtiss Model AT-32 Condor II airliner, shown here over New York City, to the South Pole in 1933.**
Wingspan 82ft (24.99m), **length** 48ft 7in (14.78m), **height** (on wheels) 16ft 4in (4.95m), **weight** 12,235lb (5,550kg), **engines** two 720hp Wright R-1820F Cyclone 9-cylinder radial air-cooled, **maximum speed** 190mph (305.7kph), **range** 716 miles (1,152km), **crew** 2, **passengers** 12 (sleeper).

RIGHT: Engineers put the finishing touches to the new Fokker FXXXVI monoplane airliner in 1934. **Wingspan** 108ft 3in (33m), **length** 77ft 5in (23.6m), **height** 19ft 8in (6m), **weight** 21,825lb (9,900kg), **engines** four 750hp Wright Cyclone SGR-1820-F2 9-cylinder radial air-cooled, **cruising speed** 149mph (240kph), **range** 839 miles (1,350km), **crew** 4, **passengers** 32.

BELOW: Designed specifically for the 1934 MacRobertson race from England to Australia, the de Havilland DH88 Comet racer took first place. **Wingspan** 44ft (13.4m), **length** 29ft (8.8m), **height** 10ft (3m), **weight** 2,930lb (1,329kg), **engines** two 230hp de Havilland Gipsy Six R 6-cylinder inverted in-line air-cooled, **cruising speed** 220mph (354kph), **range** 2,925 miles (4,707km), **crew** 2.

ABOVE: **A Danish-built Fokker FXII at Kastrup Airport in 1935.** **Wingspan** 75ft 6in (23m), **length** 58ft 5in (17.8m), **height** 15ft 6in (4.73m), **weight** 9,590lb (4,350kg), **engines** three 425hp Pratt & Whitney R-1340 Wasp C 9-cylinder radial air-cooled, **cruising speed** 127mph (204kph), **range** 808 miles (1,300km), **crew** 2, **passengers** 16.

LEFT: **A pair of Junkers Ju86s in front of Luft Hansa's maintenance hangar at Hamburg-Fuhlsbüttel Airport, 1934.** **Wingspan** 73ft 10in (22.5m), **length** 57ft 1in (17.41m), **height** 15ft 5in (4.7m), **weight** 10,935lb (4,960kg), **engines** two 600hp Junkers Jumo 205C heavy-oil (diesel) 12-cylinder vertically opposed liquid-cooled, **cruising speed** 177mph (285kph), **endurance** 5.9hr, **crew** 2, **passengers** 10.

RIGHT: **Gloster Gauntlet fighters of No 19 Squadron, RAF, with Bristol Bulldogs in the background, prepare to defend London during manoeuvres in 1935.** **Wingspan** 32ft 9in (9.98m), **length** 26ft 2in (7.9m), **height** 10ft 4in (3.15m), **weight** 2,775lb (1,259kg), **engine** one 605hp Bristol Mercury VIS2 9-cylinder radial air-cooled, **maximum speed** 230mph (370kph), **range** 460 miles (736km), **crew** 1.

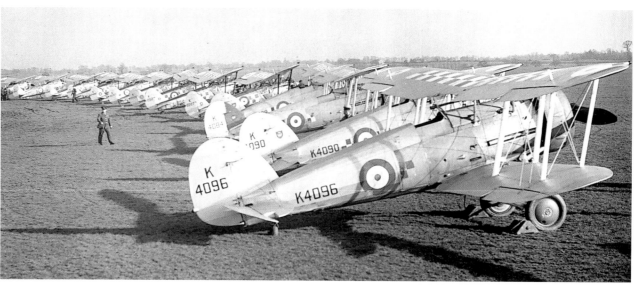

RIGHT: **A Farman F221 bomber at Toussus-le-Noble aerodrome, May 1936.**
Wingspan 118ft (35.9m), **length** 69ft (21m), **height** 17ft (5.18m), **weight** 39,000lb (17,690kg), **engines** four 700hp Gnome-Rhône 14-cylinder radial air-cooled, **maximum speed** 172mph (277kph), **crew** 5.

BELOW: **Grumman's tubby F3F-2 carrier-based fighter entered service with the US Navy in 1938.**
Wingspan 32ft (9.75m), **length** 23ft 1in (7.03m), **height** 10ft 9in (3.27m), **weight** 3,258lb (1,478kg), **engine** one 850hp Wright R-1820-22 9-cylinder radial air-cooled, **cruising speed** 145mph (233kph), **range** 885 miles (1,424km), **crew** 1.

LEFT: An assortment of aircraft line up for the start of the 1938 King's Cup Air Race. Front to rear: de Havilland Technical School TK2, Miles M2L Hawk Speed Six, de Havilland DH88 Comet racer, and two Percival P6 Mew Gulls, the nearer of which won the race.

LEFT: Airmen wearing gasmasks load high-explosive bombs on Fairey Gordon day bombers of 35 Squadron, RAF, during manoeuvres in 1937. **Wingspan** 45ft 9in (13.9m), **length** 36ft 8in (11.18m), **height** 14ft 2in (4.3m), **weight** 3,500lb (1,588kg), **engine** one 525hp Armstrong Siddeley Panther IIA 9-cylinder radial air-cooled, **cruising speed** 110mph (177kph), **range** 600 miles (966km), **crew** 2.

RIGHT: The Morane-Saulnier MS405 fighter first flew in August 1935, and went into service in 1938. **Wingspan** 34ft 9in (10.59m), **length** 26ft 9in (8.15m), **height** 8ft 11in (2.71m), **weight** 5,379lb (2,440kg), **engine** one Hispano-Suiza 12Ycrs 12-cylinder vee liquid-cooled, **maximum speed** 275mph (443kph), **range** 620 miles (1,000km), **crew** 1.

ABOVE: A portent of things to come, the Boeing 307 Stratoliner of 1938 was the first production airliner to have a pressurised passenger cabin. **Wingspan** 107ft 3in (32.69m), **length** 74ft 4in (22.65m), **height** 20ft 9in (6.33m), **weight** 30,000lb (13,610kg), **engines** four 1,100hp Wright Cyclone GR-1820-G102 14-cylinder radial air-cooled, **maximum speed** 241mph (387.8kph), **range** 1,750 miles (2,815km), **crew** 5, **passengers** 38.

The Short-Mayo Composite

In the late 1930s mail between Europe and the American continent went by sea. There was a great demand for an airmail service. Prompted by this, and taking into account the high cost of in-flight refuelling, an ingenious alternative was conceived by Imperial Airways' Technical General Manager, Major Robert Mayo. To avoid the expense of replenishing fuel while airborne and making enough fuel available for a long journey, he suggested that a huge multi-engine flying boat should give a "lift" to a smaller, but heavily laden, seaplane. The engines of both aircraft would combine to produce the power necessary for lift-off and for the initial climb.

Short Brothers designed and built the S.21 flying boat, which had a wingspan of 114ft (34.7m), was 84ft 11in (25.9m) long and was named *Maia*. Its four 920hp Bristol Pegasus nine-cylinder radial engines gave it a maximum speed of 200mph (320kph)

and it had a range of 850 miles (1,360km). *Maia* made its maiden flight on 27 July 1937. The S.20 seaplane, named *Mercury*, which first flew on 5 September the same year, had a 73ft (22.3m) wingspan and was 50ft 11in (15.5m) long. Its engines were four 340hp Napier Rapiers, its maximum speed was 195mph (314mph) and its range 3,900 miles (6,276).

The first composite flight of the two aircraft took place on 20 January 1938 and they made their first in-flight separation on 6 February 1938.

On 21 July 1938 *Mercury*, after becoming airborne by this unorthodox means, made the first transatlantic crossing by an aeroplane whose main cargo was mail and newspapers. *Maia* had taken off, carrying *Mercury*, from Shannon; *Mercury* alighted at Montreal 20 hours and 20 minutes later. From there it flew to Port Washington, New York, but made no more commercial flights. Like many other

good ideas, the innovation proved not to be economically viable.

Three months later *Maia* launched *Mercury* near Dundee to start it on a flight of 6,000 miles (9,656km) to the Orange River in South Africa that set a long-distance record for seaplanes.

BELOW: **A close-up of the superstructure on the flying boat *Maia*, which enabled it to carry the smaller, heavily laden seaplane *Mercury* on its back to assist it into the air.**

BELOW: **The composite at rest at Rochester.** *Maia* **had Bristol Pegasus radial engines, while** *Mercury* **had Napier Rapier inlines.**

130

ABOVE: A dramatic study of *Mercury* leaving Southampton, southern England, for Foynes, Ireland, in July 1938, in readiness for its first transatlantic flight. After the first commercial separation, on 21 July, it flew nonstop to Montreal in 20 hours 20 minutes.

RIGHT: *Mercury* is carefully lowered on to its parent flying boat during airworthiness trials at the Marine Aircraft Experimental Establishment at Felixstowe, Suffolk. The last commercial separations were made on 29 November 1938 and 12 January 1939.

Douglas DC-3

The most widely used air transport in the world, a total of 10,926 DC-3 series had been built by the time production ceased.

Wings constructed by the Douglas cellular multi-web system (3 wing spars, multiple wing ribs and strings), making a very strong, relatively lightweight, longlife component. The aerodynamic design of the wings also gave the DC-3 an immense lifting capability for an aircraft of its size and type.

The cabin was completely sound insulated and was equipped with ventilation and heating systems. Up to 28 passengers could be accommodated in comfortable seating. The DST (Douglas Sleeper Transport) version had sleeping bunks for 14 overnight passengers. At the rear of the cabin there was a galley, and also a toilet compartment.

SPECIFICATION

Wingspan
95ft (28.96m).

Length
64ft 5in (19.66m)

Height
16ft 11in (5.16m)

Weight
16,856lb (7,646kg) empty
25,200lb (11,431kg) loaded

Engines
Two 1,100hp Wright Cyclone or two 1,200hp Wright Cyclone or two 1,200hp Pratt & Whitney Twin-Wasp

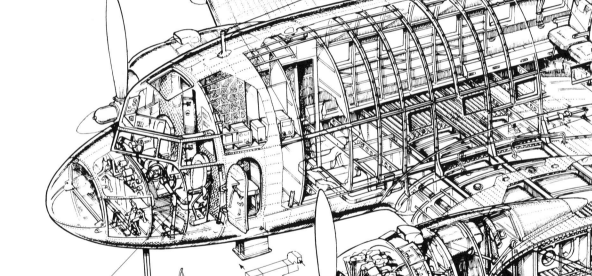

The crew compartment provided comfortable seating for the Captain and his First Officer (co-pilot). It was equipped with Radio Direction Finder (RDF) and blind-flying instruments. Postwar DC-3s were equipped with Instrumental Landing System (ILS).

Three different engine types were fitted to DC-3s. Early types had two 1,100hp nine-cylinder Wright Cyclone GR-1820-G102A air-cooled radial engines or 1,200hp Wright Cyclone GR-1820-G2024s. Later types were fitted with two 14-cylinder 1,200hp Pratt & Whitney Twin-Wasp R-1830-SIC3G air-cooled radial engines. All engine types were supercharged and drove three-bladed Hamilton Standard constant-speed propellers.

Illustration © Frank Munger

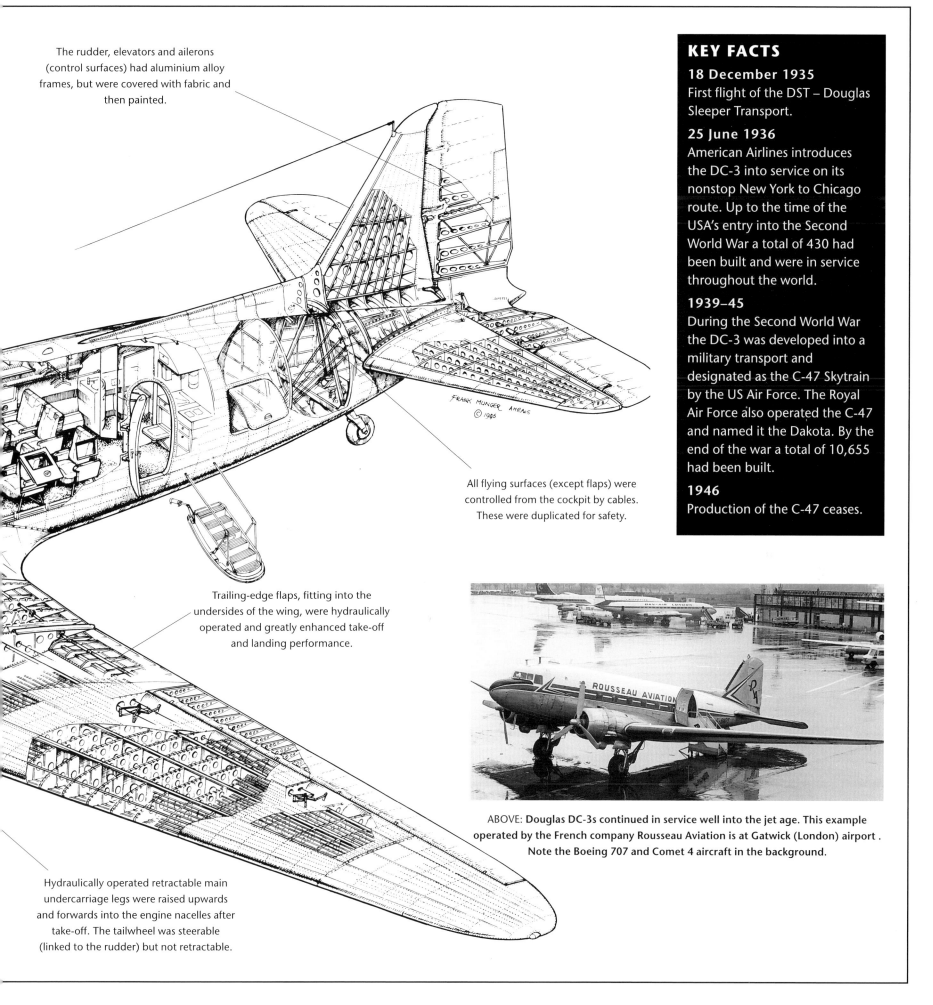

The rudder, elevators and ailerons (control surfaces) had aluminium alloy frames, but were covered with fabric and then painted.

All flying surfaces (except flaps) were controlled from the cockpit by cables. These were duplicated for safety.

Trailing-edge flaps, fitting into the undersides of the wing, were hydraulically operated and greatly enhanced take-off and landing performance.

Hydraulically operated retractable main undercarriage legs were raised upwards and forwards into the engine nacelles after take-off. The tailwheel was steerable (linked to the rudder) but not retractable.

KEY FACTS

18 December 1935
First flight of the DST – Douglas Sleeper Transport.

25 June 1936
American Airlines introduces the DC-3 into service on its nonstop New York to Chicago route. Up to the time of the USA's entry into the Second World War a total of 430 had been built and were in service throughout the world.

1939–45
During the Second World War the DC-3 was developed into a military transport and designated as the C-47 Skytrain by the US Air Force. The Royal Air Force also operated the C-47 and named it the Dakota. By the end of the war a total of 10,655 had been built.

1946
Production of the C-47 ceases.

ABOVE: Douglas DC-3s continued in service well into the jet age. This example operated by the French company Rousseau Aviation is at Gatwick (London) airport . Note the Boeing 707 and Comet 4 aircraft in the background.

133

The aeroplane had changed dramatically by 1939, but the Second World War was to bring another rapid phase of development.

Chapter Six

Defence and Attack

By 3 September 1939, when Britain and France went to war with Germany again, aerial photography, record-breaking long distance flights, air races, and air displays had yielded a substantial amount of information about various nations' commercial aviation and the strength and organisation of their air forces and the mettle of their pilots and crews.

In 1920 the German Defence Ministry set about secretly resuscitating the German air force. In the same year, Professor Hugo Junkers formed an aircraft company to manufacture the all-metal F13 transport and aero engines. In 1922 Ernst Heinkel and in 1924 Heinrich Focke and Georg Wulf founded aircraft manufacturing companies. In 1926 the Bayerische Flugzeugwerke (Bavarian Aircraft Factory) began manufacturing, changing its name in 1938 to Messerschmitt A.G.

A military flying training centre for German officers was established in Russia. In 1926 Germany reactivated its state airline, Deutsche Luft Hansa, with Erhard Milch, an ex-fighter pilot, as chairman. This led to the construction of large airfields that were secretly intended for use also by the embryonic Luftwaffe. Luft Hansa crews later provided training for the newly re-formed air force.

The RAF maintained a higher level of training and a sharper state of operational preparedness than any other air force. It was also unsurpassed in fighting qualities. The Luftwaffe, however, suffered no lack of brave men or skilled senior officers; and some of the aeroplanes it flew were as good as, or better than, the RAF's.

At the outbreak of the Second World War, the Royal Navy's most numerous aircraft was the Fairey Swordfish, a bi-plane torpedo-bomber with the sluggish maximum speed of 138mph (222kph). Entering service in 1934, it was dubbed the "Stringbag", on account of its archaic appearance; but production continued until 1944. Delivery of its successor, the Albacore, only 27mph (43kph) faster, began in December 1939.

The Fleet Air Arm's first victory of the war came on 25 September 1939, when a Blackburn Skua from HMS *Ark Royal* shot down a Dornier Do 18 flying boat on reconnaissance.

The Battle of Britain is the most famous air campaign in history, not only because the numerical odds were heavily in the enemy's favour, but also because it was the crucial victory of the whole war. The simple, direct language of Churchill's touching tribute to the RAF's fighter pilots after the summer-long battle stirred the emotions: "Never, in the field of human conflict, has so much been owed by so many to so few."

That succinctly expressed the essence of the skill and devotion to duty shown by the Spitfire and Hurricane fighter pilots, the air gunners in two-seater Defiants, and the usually forgotten crews of Blenheim night fighters that carried a top secret "black box".

RADAR

The ace up Britain's sleeve in preparation for conflict was radar, installed on the ground and in aircraft. Originally known as "range and direction finding" and shortened to "RDF", the true nature of this facility, invented and developed in Britain, was hidden by its innocuous title: those who were not in on the secret assumed it to be a navigation aid.

When Britain divulged the secret of RDF to the Americans, they renamed it

ABOVE: **The Spitfire's great development potential allowed it to serve throughout the war. This is a clipped-wing Mk XVI of 1944, the last Merlin-powered major production version.**

ABOVE: The crew of a Douglas Boston III bomber of 107 Sqn, RAF, discuss the forthcoming operation, 1943. Powered by a pair of 1,600hp Wright Double-Row Cyclone radial engines, the Boston first entered RAF service in 1941.

MILESTONES

1940

The RAF's eight-gun Hurricane and Spitfire fighters repel Hitler's Luftwaffe in the Battle of Britain.

1941

Japan's surprise attack on Pearl Harbor, Hawaii, brings the USA into the war.

1942

RAF Bomber Command mounts its first "1,000-bomber" raid against a German target.

1944

The Allies return to mainland Europe in D-Day landings on the Normandy coast, with massive air support

"radio direction and ranging" – radar.

The Bristol Blenheim night fighter's "black box" was a radar set known as airborne interception (AI). A derivative of the Bristol 142, the Blenheim began squadron service in March 1937. This marked a huge advance on the RAF's then fastest bomber, the Hawker Hind, a single-engine biplane two-seater with a fixed undercarriage. The Blenheim was a twin-engine monoplane with a retractable undercarriage. AI was first fitted to Mk I Blenheim bombers.

March 1939 saw the Mk IV Blenheim's delivery begin, first to bomber and then to night fighter squadrons. It had a lengthened nose to allow the navigator better

accommodation. When the Blenheim bomber first appeared on the RAF's Order of Battle, it was 13mph (21kph) faster than the RAF's most modern fighter, the Gloster Gladiator, a single-seat biplane with a fixed undercarriage.

The first British monoplane day fighter, the first with a retractable undercarriage and the first to exceed 300mph (482kph) was the Hawker Hurricane. This superb aeroplane entered squadron service in December 1937. In the winter following the Battle of Britain, it was also pressed into use as a night fighter.

The Supermarine Spitfire began its squadron career in 1938, had the same

armament and engine as the Hurricane, but was 40mph (64kph) faster.

DOGFIGHTS

The conflict that would spread around the globe began with Hitler's order to invade Poland. In opposition to the Polish Air Force and the RAF, the Luftwaffe put up an excellent fighter, the Messerschmitt Bf 109. The Bf 109 made its first flight in September 1935 and by September 1939 the 109E was in squadron service. It was faster than the Hurricane and Spitfire, but both could turn inside it, a greater advantage in a dogfight than sheer speed.

A fighter that also took part in the invasion of Poland was the Bf 110 (Me 110), known as the Zerstörer (Destroyer). Originally used as bomber escorts, Bf 110s soon themselves had to be escorted by Bf 109s. However, eventually, fitted with airborne radar, the Bf 110 became a successful night fighter.

In July 1941, RAF pilots on offensive operations over France began to encounter the radial-engined Focke-Wulf Fw 190, whose top speed with boost was 408mph (656kph).

When Germany invaded Poland on 1 September 1939, the spearhead of the air attack was the Junkers Ju 87 dive bomber

ABOVE: **Messerschmitt Bf 109E-1 fighters of 8/JG2 "Richthofen" stand at readiness on a French airfield in May 1940. Powered by a 1,175hp Daimler-Benz DB 601A, this variant had four 7.9mm machine guns.**

(*Sturtzkampfflugzeug*, "Stuka" for short), which first flew in 1936. During the Battle of France in 1940 the Stuka and Bf 109 created havoc on the French roads.

The Polish Air Force faced the might of the Luftwaffe with 12 squadrons of PZL P11c fighters, which were more than 100mph (160kph) slower than the Bf 109 and feebly armed. Nevertheless, the Poles shot down 126 German aircraft for the loss of 114.

The Luftwaffe's most versatile bomber, the Junkers Ju 88, which first flew in December 1936, was made in many versions and used for day and night bombing, torpedo dropping and as a night fighter. In 1940 the Heinkel He 111 bomber became a familiar sight over France and Britain, as did the Dornier Do 17 – known to the British as the "flying pencil".

The best fighter of the French Air Force (l'Armée de l'Air) in the early months of the war was the Bloch MB 152C-1, delivery of which began in December 1939. Of France's 26 combat-ready fighter squadrons on 10 May 1940, when Germany invaded Belgium and Holland and was about to cross the French frontier, 19 flew this type. A better fighter,

which began squadron service on 1 February 1940, was the Dewoitine D520S.

A good French light bomber, the Breguet 693, made its first flight on 25 October 1939. Before France gave up the fight on 22 June 1940, 224 had been delivered to squadrons.

The RAF bomber squadrons based in France had to make do with the Fairey Battle. Introduced to front-line service in May 1937, it was slow and inadequately armed with only two machine guns. The enemy shot Battles down in droves.

RAF Bomber Command also made a valuable contribution to victory in the Battle of Britain. While the fighting over southern England was at its height, Hitler was assembling barges along the French coast in anticipation of winning the air battle and then invading Britain. The barges were bombed almost daily, which not only destroyed great numbers of them but also drew off some of the enemy fighters. Incredibly, in June 1940, when three of the Avro Ansons involved in this task, with their sluggish top speed of 188mph (302kph) and modest armament of two .303 machine guns, were attacked by nine Bf 109s, they shot three of them down.

BOMBING RAIDS

The years 1940–45 were to see the greatest advances in the development of aero engines and aircraft design yet made in so short a period.

Bombers were used both tactically and strategically. At the outbreak of war, the RAF's heaviest bombers were the Hampden, Whitley and Wellington, all with two engines. The first four-engine bomber of this war was the Stirling, which No 7 Squadron began flying in August 1940. Next came the Halifax in March 1941, followed by the Lancaster, which flew its first operation in March 1942. By the time the USA took up Japan's challenge, US Army Air Corps squadrons had been flying the Boeing B-17 for two and a half years and the Consolidated B-24 Liberator for six months.

The other four-engine aircraft was the Shorts Sunderland flying boat, which had been in service with RAF Coastal Command since May 1938. The Luftwaffe called it "The Porcupine", because it was armed with ten machine guns that gave it all-round defensive fire.

The Luftwaffe also had a four-engine

maritime reconnaissance aircraft, the Focke-Wulf Fw 200 Condor, developed from a pre-war airliner that had made record flights to the USA and Japan. The military variant had nine guns and was a menace not only to surface shipping and submarines but also to aircraft.

Surprisingly, Italy, despite its successes in the early Schneider Trophy contests, produced no outstandingly successful fighters. The Savoia-Marchetti SM79 Sparviero (Sparrowhawk) was one of the war's fastest bombers, but its bomb load was not impressive.

NIGHT FIGHTERS

The Bristol Beaufighter, one of the most versatile aircraft of the war, was the first night fighter with a high enough performance to take advantage of AI and was the most heavily armed aircraft in the world at the time. Soon, it was delighting RAF Coastal Command as a formidable anti-shipping strike and torpedo aeroplane with a new type of radar in the nose: ASV (anti-surface vessel), which could pick up motor torpedo boats and even a submarine's periscope if it flew at 450–500ft (140–150m).

Another versatile warplane and regarded as the world's most handsome aircraft, the de Havilland Mosquito was the best of all photographic reconnaissance aircraft in addition to its use as a night fighter, intruder and bomber. It also heralded a

ABOVE: **Ground crew tend to a Boeing B-17E Flying Fortress of the US Eighth Air Force's 414th Bomb Squadron, 97th Bomb Group, at Grafton, Yorkshire, in September 1942.**

ABOVE: **A low-flying Bristol Blenheim I light bomber turns the heads of Army personnel during operations in the Middle East in 1940. Powered by two 840hp Bristol Mercury VIII radial engines, the Blenheim first entered RAF service in March 1937.**

ABOVE: **This Belgian-based Italian Fiat CR42 fighter was shot down by a Hurricane on 11 November 1940, and forced-landed near Orfordness, Suffolk, England. It was repaired and test flown, and now resides in the RAF Museum at Hendon.**

new method of bombing accurately at night. The RAF formed the Pathfinder Force on 11 August 1942 and by early 1943 it comprised five squadrons of Stirlings, Halifaxes, Lancasters and Mosquitoes. Arriving over the target before the main force, they dropped bright, coloured indicators as aiming marks.

USA ENTERS THE WAR

When the USA was propelled into the conflict in December 1941 by Japan's attack on Pearl Harbor, the United States Army Air Force (USAAF) was flying excellent bombers: the twin-engine North American B-25 Mitchell and Douglas DB-7 Havoc (RAF, Boston), soon followed by the Martin B-26 Marauder. The four engine Boeing B-17 Flying Fortress and the Consolidated B-24 Liberator were effective bombers.

Operating by day, the Americans suffered very heavy losses because their own

Lockheed P-38 Lightning fighters, and the RAF's Spitfires, even with long-range tanks, lacked the endurance to escort them all the way to their targets. This changed when the Republic P-47 Thunderbolt and North American P-51 Mustang were able to accompany them.

The campaigns in the Far East and Pacific pitted the Allied air forces against fighters and bombers based mostly on aircraft carriers. The Japanese Mitsubishi A6M, code-named "Zeke", was the first carrier-borne fighter with a better performance than land-based ones. Other good fighters were the Nakajima Ki-43, "Oscar", and the Nakajima Ki-84, "Frank", regarded as Japan's best.

In Europe, from the Normandy landings on 6 June 1944 to Germany's surrender on 7 May 1945, Allied specialist ground-attack fighters became the main air weapon. The star ground-attack type was the sturdy Hawker Typhoon. This, the

RAF's first fighter to fly at over 400mph (644kph), was intended as a response to the Focke-Wulf Fw 190; but, above 15,000ft (4,572m) where the Fw 190 operated, the Typhoon became too slow.

The Hawker Tempest was a development of the Typhoon with elliptical, thin-section wings. Delivery to the first of only seven squadrons began in April 1944. With a top speed of 440mph (708kph), it was the only piston-engined aeroplane fast enough to catch the V1 flying bombs.

The Messerschmitt Me 262A-1a Schwalbe (Swallow) fighter was the first turbojet-powered aircraft to go into action, towards the end of July 1944. The first Me 262 squadron was formed two months later. The bomber variant, Messerschmitt Me 262A-2 Sturmvogel (Stormbird), followed. Their respective maximum speeds were 540mph (869kph) and 470mph (756kph). The Me 163 Komet was the first rocket-propelled aircraft to see action.

RIGHT: Junkers Ju 87 dive bombers – "Stukas" – prepare to take off from a field in Russia. Although the Stuka struck fear into civilian populations, it lacked agility and was easy prey to contemporary fighters.

BELOW: The Gloster Gladiator was the RAF's last biplane fighter. Entering service in 1937, it had largely been replaced in Fighter Command by the outbreak of war, but performed stoically in Norway, Malta, and in early actions in Greece and the Western Desert.

RIGHT: Although it looked somewhat primitive, the Fairey Swordfish torpedo bomber had exceptional handling qualities and served operationally throughout the war. It was powered by a 690hp Bristol Pegasus radial engine.

RIGHT: An extremely rare colour photograph of Hawker Hurricane Is of No 3 Squadron, RAF, at Biggin Hill in 1939.
Wingspan 40ft (12.19m), length 32ft (9.75m), height 13ft 1in (4m), weight 6,600lb (2,994kg), engine one 1,030hp Rolls-Royce Merlin 12-cylinder vee liquid-cooled, maximum cruising speed 318mph(511kph), range 460 miles (740km), crew 1.

ABOVE: **Hurricane IIC nightfighters of 87 Squadron on patrol in 1941. A total of 79 home-based operational squadrons and 66 overseas squadrons were equipped with the type.**

LEFT: **Less successful was the American Bell P-39D Airacobra, which had a tricycle undercarriage, a cannon firing through the propeller boss, and a 1,150hp Allison engine mounted behind the pilot with a long driveshaft to the propeller. The only RAF Squadron to have Airacobras, No 601, soon got rid of them.**

ABOVE: The Messerschmitt Bf 110 proved vulnerable as a long-range strategic fighter, but came into its own as a radar-equipped nightfighter in 1941. These are Bf 110F-1s of SKG 210, powered by Daimler-Benz DB 601Fs.

RIGHT: The 885hp Rolls-Royce Peregrine engines of the Westland Whirlwind single-seat long-range fighter proved troublesome, but it had four 20mm guns in the nose and served usefully as a fighter-bomber from September 1942.

Luftwaffe versus RAF

The Battle of Britain epitomises the contrasting tactics of the RAF and Luftwaffe. To begin with, the British were too nonchalant to call on their 1914–18 allies to join them in enforcing the terms of the Armistice, which forbade Germany to have an air force; and they tolerated politicians who were rabidly pro-disarmament. In contrast, the diligent Germans had set about resuscitating their air force soon after their defeat, with the co-operation of their former enemy, the USSR, which provided them with a training school.

The Luftwaffe hugely outnumbered the RAF and, by sending fighters and bombers to fight on the anti-communist side in the Spanish Civil War, gained valuable experience of battle tactics. Foremost was the discovery that a fighter formation of pairs in echelon, with one pilot covering the other, and multiples of such pairs, was more efficient than the RAF's threes in "V" formation. After the battle, the RAF

adopted this formation, usually in twos, forming a "finger four".

Britain's unique possession of radar stations along her coasts gave the RAF a tactical advantage in early warning of the enemy's approach. Fighter Command's few fighters were able to take off and start climbing sooner than the enemy expected, although there was not always time to do this.

The other great tactical superiority was the control organisation which divided the country into Groups: so if No 11 Group, based in south-east England, could not scramble (the code for take-off) in time, No 12 Group, its neighbour further north, could. This did not always happen, but the sheer fighting spirit of the defending pilots made up for that. The Hurricane and Spitfire could both turn inside the Bf 109 – a huge bonus. Another advantage was the fact that both the latter and the German bombers broke when attacked head-on, a favourite RAF tactic.

BELOW: **The Supermarine Spitfire Mk V began to be delivered to the RAF in February 1941.**
Wingspan 36ft (110.97m), **length** 29ft 11in (9.12m), **height** 11ft 5in (3.46m), **weight** 6,785lb (3,078kg), **engine** one 1,185hp Rolls-Royce Merlin 12-cylinder vee liquid-cooled, **maximum speed** 374mph (602kph), **range** 470 miles (756km), **crew** 1.

BELOW: **While the Bf 109 could outperform the Hurricane and Spitfire in some respects, it could not match their tight turning circles.**

ABOVE: Ground crew push a Bf 109G out of the mud. The need to make the engine easily accessible under battlefield conditions was an important design consideration.
Wingspan 32ft 6½in (9.92m), length 29ft 7½in (9.04m), height 8ft 2½in (2.50m), weight 7,496lb (3,400kg), engine one 1,475hp Daimler-Benz DB605 12-cylinder vee liquid-cooled, maximum speed 385mph (620kph), range 460 miles (740km), crew 1.

LEFT: The Hurricane's structure made it simpler to repair than the Spitfire, but its basic design limited its development potential. Nonetheless, when armed with rockets and 40mm guns it became a formidable ground-attack aircraft.

ABOVE: **The Fiat G50 Freccia (Arrow), which made its maiden flight in 1937, was Italy's first all-metal single-seat fighter monoplane with a retractable undercarriage. It had an 870hp Fiat A 74 RC 38 air-cooled radial engine.**

RIGHT: **Italy's Savoia-Marchetti S81 Pipistrello, powered by three 650-750hp radial engines, was designed as a bomber-transport, being a military version of the S73 airliner.**

RIGHT: Mikoyan & Gurevich MiG-3 fighters of the 12th Fighter Regiment, a component of the Moscow Air Defence forces, in 1942.
Wingspan 33ft 9½in (10.3m), length 27ft ⅞in (8.25m), height 8ft 8⅓in (2.65m), weight 7,456 lb (3,382kg), engine one 1,350hp Mikulin AM-36 12-cylinder vee liquid-cooled, maximum speed 398mph (640kph), range 510 miles (820km), crew 1.

RIGHT: The Ilyushin Il-2 and Il-10 fighter-bombers were produced in larger numbers than any other aircraft, a total of 42,330 being built. Here, Soviet crews prepare to leave East Germany for Russia in 1956.

BELOW: Undoubtedly the most famous Japanese fighter of the war, the redoubtable Mitsubishi A6M Navy Type 0, commonly dubbed the Zero, was deficient in armament and armour but proved an agile and deadly opponent in air combat.

The Mighty Eighth

Until long-range escort fighters, P-47 Thunderbolts and P-51 Mustangs, arrived in Britain, the 8th Air Force suffered appalling losses on daylight bombing missions against targets in Germany.

Maggie's Drawers, *Bomboogie* and the punning *Ascend Charlie* (referring to a tail gunner) were typical names that were cheerfully emblazoned on the noses of United States Army Air Force (USAAF) bombers of the 8th Air Force stationed in England; they reflect the wisecracking and jaunty bravery of their crews. The 8th comprised fighters as well. The P-38 Lightnings, like the Hurricanes and Spitfires, lacked the range to escort bombers to the most distant targets in Germany.

The P-51 Mustang, which had a range of 1,050 miles (1,689km), was the response to a request for a new fighter made by the RAF in April 1940. The Mks I and II with Rolls-Royce engines entered RAF service in July 1942, the USAAF's in December. The III (USAAF P-51B and C) and IV (P-51D) appeared in 1944.

In May 1938 the USA's Chiefs of Staff had decreed that land-based aircraft should be limited to an off-shore radius of 100 miles (161km). It was President Roosevelt who told Congress in January 1939: "Our air forces are so utterly inadequate that they should be immediately strengthened".

On the outbreak of war in Europe it was agreed between Britain and the USA that if the latter entered the conflict her heavy bombers would operate with the RAF from English bases in strategic bombing. RAF day bombers took such heavy casualties that, from late 1940, most bombing was done by night.

The prototype Boeing B-17, the first new USAF bomber, made its maiden flight on 28 July 1935 and the Y1B-17 in January 1937. Delivery of the B-17B began in June 1939. Twenty B17-7s were given to the RAF in return for combat information. Reports told that the Browning guns froze, the Norden bombsight had defects and enemy fighters attacked from a blind area astern. Corrective action was duly taken. The four-engine Consolidated B-24 Liberator was delivered to American squadrons in March 1942.

> ## " *The tables were turned on the Luftwaffe's fighters* "

The USAF's introduction to combat came on 4 July 1942, when six crews borrowed Douglas Boston III bombers from the RAF for a raid on Holland. Two of them were shot down. In August 1942 it was agreed that the 8th AF and the RAF would co-ordinate a day and night offensive. On 17 August General Ira C. Eaker, Commander of the 8th, led 12 B-17Es, escorted by Spitfires, against the Rouen–Sotteville marshalling yards without casualties.

The following day 326th Bombardment Squadron, flying B-17Fs arrived to join the 92nd Bomb Group. Three heavy Bomb Groups were now in place, and there was one squadron of Boston IIIs. A fourth Bomb Group joined them from November 1942 to May 1943. In November 1942 two Groups went to North Africa.

There were two Fighter Groups with P-38s and two with Spitfire Vs. A raid on an engineering factory in Belgium and railway works at Lille, escorted by RAF and USAF fighters, showed the B-24s' defects: of 24, 10 returned prematurely with various faults. Only three aircraft were lost, but 36 B-17s and 10 B-24s were damaged.

By March 1943 the 8th's average bombing accuracy had risen from 15 per cent to 75 per cent.

LEFT: When provided with long-range underwing drop tanks, North American's superb P-51D Mustang could escort 8th Air Force bombers all the way to Berlin and back from their UK bases. A 1,450hp V-1650-7 Merlin engine provided the power.

ABOVE: **Four 1,200hp Wright R-1820-65 air-cooled radial engines gave the immortal Boeing B-17 a maximum speed of 317mph (510kph) at 25,000ft (7,620m).**

On 24 July 324 B-17s crossed the North Sea. One target was a nitrate factory at Heroya; others were the harbours at Bergen and Trondheim and a nearby aluminium and magnesium plant. In one week that month the Luftwaffe lost 40 fighters, the 8th lost 128 B-17s.

On 17 August 1943 an attack on the ballbearing works at Schweinfurt was met by 200 enemy fighters from bases in Germany, France and Belgium. A total of 36 B-17s and 374 lives were lost. After this General Arnold ordered that the P-38s' and P-51s' priority would be to give cover.

The tables were turned on the Luftwaffe's fighters, but ahead lay many more devastating raids and battles.

RIGHT: **A USAAF 8th Air Force fighter pilot poses with his mount, a Republic P-47D Thunderbolt powered by a 2,000hp Pratt & Whitney R-2800 radial engine. Its top speed was 433mph (696kph) at 30,000ft (9,144m).**

Hawker Typhoon

Although a failure as an interceptor, it became <u>the</u> fighter bomber of the Second World War.

SPECIFICATION
Wingspan
41ft 7in (12.67m)

Length
31ft 11in (9.73m)

Height
15ft 3in (4.65m)

Weight
8,800lb (3,992kg) empty
13,250lb (6,010kg) loaded

Engine
24-cylinder flat-H 2200hp Napier Sabre IIB sleeve-valve liquid-cooled

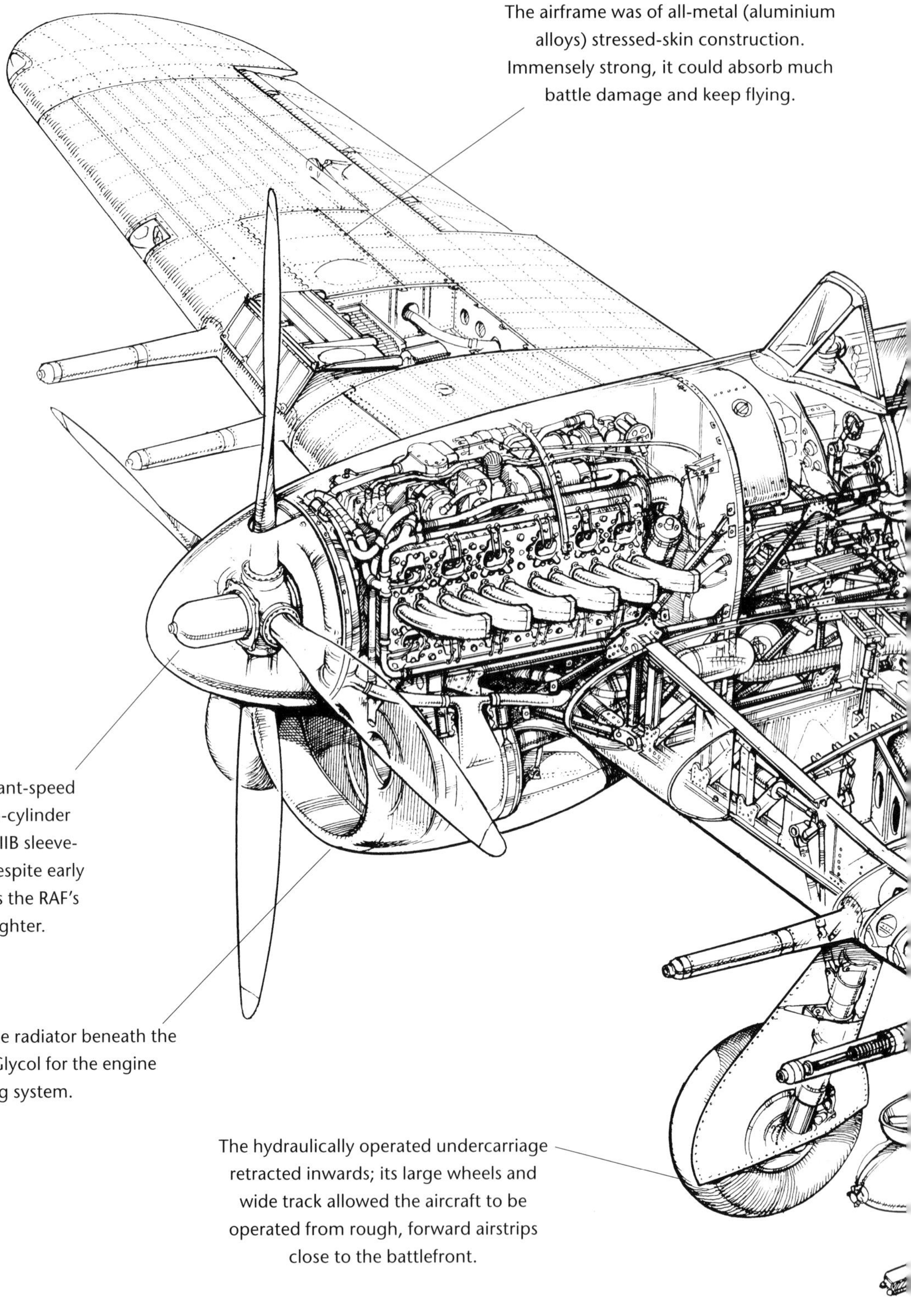

The airframe was of all-metal (aluminium alloys) stressed-skin construction. Immensely strong, it could absorb much battle damage and keep flying.

The large four-bladed, constant-speed propeller was driven by a 24-cylinder flat-H 2,200hp Napier Sabre IIB sleeve-valve liquid-cooled engine. Despite early unreliability the Typhoon was the RAF's first 400mph (644kph) fighter.

A large "beard"-type radiator beneath the nose contained Glycol for the engine cooling system.

The hydraulically operated undercarriage retracted inwards; its large wheels and wide track allowed the aircraft to be operated from rough, forward airstrips close to the battlefront.

In the battlefield support role, two 1,000lb (454kg) bombs or eight 60lb (27kg) rocket projectiles were carried on special racks under the wings.

Illustration © Frank Munger

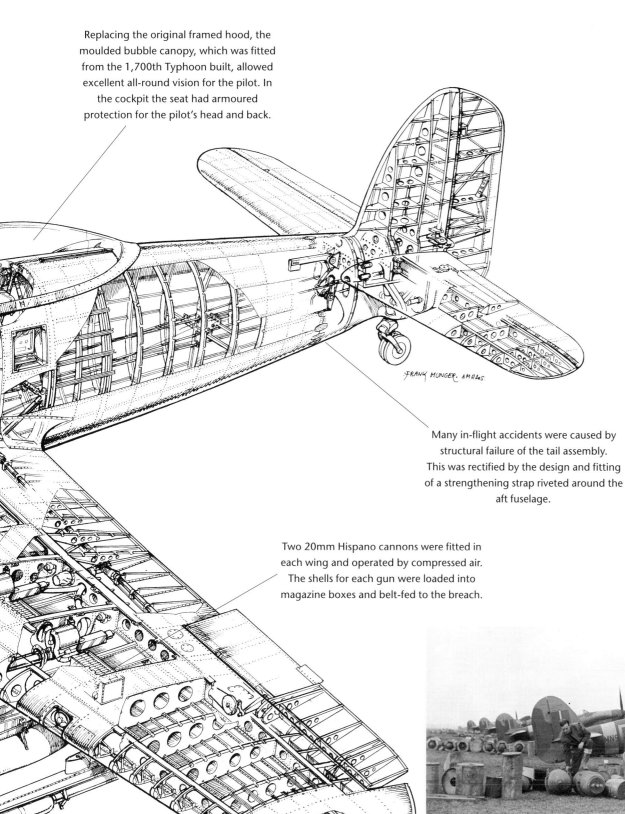

Replacing the original framed hood, the moulded bubble canopy, which was fitted from the 1,700th Typhoon built, allowed excellent all-round vision for the pilot. In the cockpit the seat had armoured protection for the pilot's head and back.

FRANK MUNGER. AMRaeS.

Many in-flight accidents were caused by structural failure of the tail assembly. This was rectified by the design and fitting of a strengthening strap riveted around the aft fuselage.

Two 20mm Hispano cannons were fitted in each wing and operated by compressed air. The shells for each gun were loaded into magazine boxes and belt-fed to the breach.

KEY FACTS

February 1940
First flight of prototype.

May 1941
First flight of production model.

August 1941
Deliveries to the Royal Air Force begin.

September 1941
No 56 Squadron based at Duxford, Cambridgeshire, are the first to be equipped with the Typhoon.

June 1944
In preparation for D-Day landings 26 Squadrons of the 2nd Tactical Air Force are equipped with Typhoons.

November 1945
The last aircraft is delivered after 3,317 had been built. By the end of 1945 no Typhoons remained in RAF service.

ABOVE: **Hawker Typhoon IBs of 193 Squadron, RAF, with the 2nd Tactical Air Force in Holland, are bombed up with 1,000lb bombs at a forward airfield in readiness for a mission.**

ABOVE: An Avro Lancaster Mk I of 50 Squadron, RAF Bomber Command, displays the lines of this classic Second World War heavy bomber. Its four 1,280hp Rolls-Royce Merlin liquid-cooled 12-cylinder vee engines gave the Lancaster a maximum speed of 287mph (462kph) at 11,500ft (3,505m).

LEFT: The Douglas A-20 was known as the Havoc in US service and as the Boston in the RAF. Originally designed as a bomber, it was modified for the attack role, as seen here, with the bomb-aimer's nose transparency replaced by a "solid" nose filled with guns.

ABOVE: The most versatile aeroplane of the war was de Havilland's Mosquito, which was adapted to perform almost every role from unarmed high-speed bombing to photographic reconnaissance and night fighting. A range of marks of the ubiquitous Rolls-Royce Merlin provided the power.

RIGHT: The Kawasaki Ki-45 Toryu (Dragon Killer) two-seat fighter equipped Japanese Army units, this one belonging to the 53rd Sentai (Group). The engines were Army Type 1 (Mitsubishi Ha-102) 14-cylinder air-cooled radials producing 1,050hp at 9,185ft (2,800m).

LEFT: Another of Bomber Command's "heavies" was the Handley Page Halifax. This is a Mk VI, which had four 1,800hp Bristol Hercules 100 air-cooled radial engines and additional fuel tankage to extend its range to 1,260 miles (2027m) with a 13,000lb (5,897kg) maximum bomb load.

RIGHT: Known to the Japanese ground forces as "whispering death" owing to the relative quietness of its 1,770hp Bristol Hercules air-cooled radial engines, the Bristol Beaufighter made a formidable anti-shipping aircraft in its Mk X form, seen here, armed with a torpedo, bombs or rockets.

BELOW: Another twin-engine bomber which served with both the USAAF and RAF was the North American B-25 Mitchell. This is a Mitchell II of No 180 Squadron, RAF, powered by two 1,350hp Wright Double-Row Cyclones. In the RAF the Mitchell served mainly as a day bomber.

BELOW: The outstanding German fighter of the later war years was the Focke-Wulf Fw 190, represented here by an early Fw 190A development aircraft with an auxiliary underfuselage fuel tank.

Battle of Midway

Japan's surprise attack on Pearl Harbor by 360 aircraft launched from six carriers on 7 December 1941 gave her control of the Pacific: four out of eight American battleships were sunk and one beached. The USA's intended strategy in the expectation of Japanese aggression had therefore to be changed. The US Navy's three aircraft carriers, which were far away on exercises, remained intact and it was on them that the counterattack would be based. Japan possessed 10 carriers.

On the following day there were Japanese air raids on Guam and Wake Islands and Midway Island was bombarded by two destroyers.

On 18 April 16 B-25 Mitchell bombers aboard the aircraft carrier *Hornet* attacked Tokyo, Nagoya and Kobe. The Japanese at once brought fighters back from sea to strengthen home defence and immediately aimed to expand their perimeter. The Battles of the Coral Sea and Midway were direct consequences. On 27 May the carriers *Akagi*, *Kaga*, *Soryu* and *Hiryu*, and transports carrying 5,000 troops, escorted by two battleships, many cruisers and destroyers set sail for Midway. Admiral Yamamoto, Supreme Commander of the Japanese Navy, believed that the fall of

Midway would bring the US fleet down upon it and he would win the ensuing battle, and the war, before the USA could make up her losses.

On 28 May a US task force comprising *Enterprise* and *Hornet* sailed with escorts. On 4 June 108 Japanese aircraft attacked Midway. Defending fighters went up to meet them while bombers set about the enemy carriers: both formations suffered

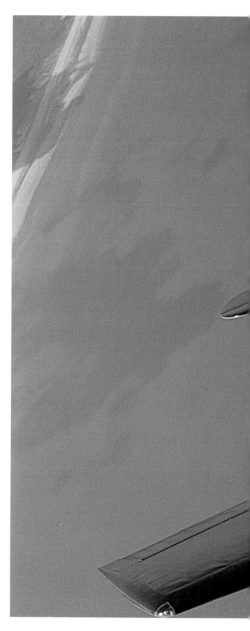

heavily. At about 9.30pm American aircraft took off from their carriers and made 41 attacks. They scored no hits and 35 were shot down. An hour later US dive bombers damaged all four enemy carriers so badly that they were sunk or scuttled within 24 hours.

The Japanese not only lost valuable equipment but also many experienced pilots in the battle.

ABOVE **and** BELOW: **Japan's formidable Mitsubishi Zero fighter first flew in 1939, and well over 10,000 were built. The advent of more advanced Allied fighters such as the Lightning and Corsair caused heavy losses among the now outclassed Zeros.**

ABOVE: **Grumman's sturdy F6F Hellcat carrier-based fighter first saw combat in the Pacific in August 1943. Wingspan** 42ft 10in (13.05m), **length** 33ft 7in (10.20m), **height** 13ft 1in (3.99m), **weight** 12,186lb (5,527kg), **engine** one 2,000hp Pratt & Whitney R-2800-10 Double Wasp 18-cylinder radial air-cooled, **maximum speed** 376mph (605kph), **range** 1,085 miles (1,746km), **crew** 1.

RIGHT: **The Consolidated PBY Catalina long-range patrol bomber flying-boat and amphibian served with both the US Navy and RAF Coastal Command. With a pair of 1,200hp Pratt & Whitney Twin Wasp R-1830s it had a range of 4,000 miles (6,437km) and an endurance of over 17 hours.**

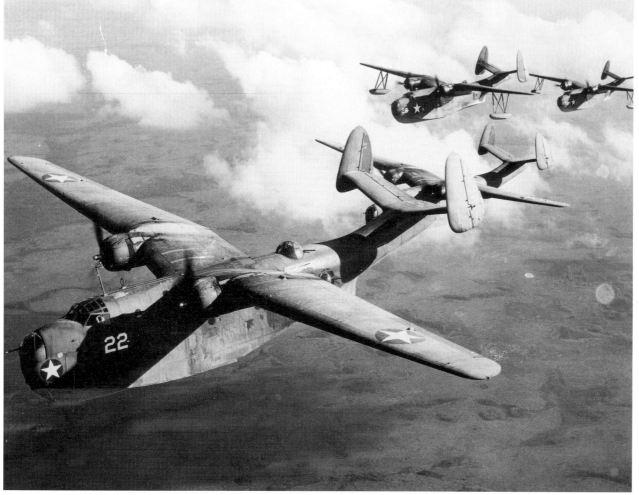

ABOVE: One of the war's most extraordinary aircraft was the Messerschmitt Me 323 Gigant military transport, powered by six 1,140hp Gnome-Rhône 14N air-cooled radial engines. The Me 323D-6 production aircraft could carry 130 troops in addition to its five-man crew, but many more could be accommodated *in extremis.*

LEFT: Martin PBM Mariner patrol flying boats of the US Navy, powered by two 1,700hp Wright R-2600 air-cooled radial engines. The two nearest aircraft are PBM-1s with retractable underwing floats, while the other two are PBM-3s, with fixed, strut-braced floats.

RIGHT: A de Havilland Mosquito NF XVII nightfighter formates on a captured Messerschmitt Me 410A-3 reconnaissance aircraft during comparative trials in Britain. The Me 410 Hornisse (Hornet) was also used in light bomber and "destroyer" roles.

BELOW: One of the foremost Russian fighters was the Yakovlev Yak-9, powered by a 1,260hp M-105PF-1 inline engine, which entered service in 1942. These are aircraft of a Guards Regiment over Sevastopol in the Crimea in the early summer of 1944.

ABOVE: Boeing's B-29 Superfortress heavy bomber achieved dubious fame as the deliverer of the two atomic bombs on Hiroshima and Nagasaki. First flown in 1942, it was powered by four 2,200hp Wright R-3350 air-cooled radial engines.

ABOVE: A Vought F4U Corsair fighter-bomber of the US Navy displays the distinctive cranked wing that allowed a short undercarriage while providing sufficient ground clearance for the large three-bladed propeller of its Pratt & Whitney R-2800 Wasp radial engine.

ABOVE: Supermarine Spitfire Mk VIIIs of 136 Squadron, RAF, South East Asia Command, lined up on an airstrip in the Cocos Islands in 1945.

ABOVE LEFT: The Lockheed P-38 Lightning single-seat fighter and long-range escort was easily recognised by the twin booms.
Wingspan 52ft (15.85m), **length** 37ft 10in (11.53m), **height** 9ft 10in (3.01m), **weight** 21,600lb (9,798kg), **engine** two 1,425hp Allison V-1710 12-cylinder vee liquid-cooled, **maximum speed** 360mph (579kph), **range** 2,260 miles (3,637km), **crew** 1.

RIGHT: A Vought F4U Corsair keeps close company with a Grumman TBM Avenger torpedo bomber. Powered by a 1,700hp Wright R-2600-8 radial and carrying a crew of three, the Avenger entered service in 1942.

LEFT and FAR LEFT: **The Arado 234 Blitz** was the world's first jet bomber. Seen in these two shots is one of the early prototypes, which took off on a three-wheeled trolley and landed on a central skid. Junkers 004B-0 turbojets of 1,848lb (838kg) thrust provided the power.

RIGHT: **The Bachem Ba 349 Natter** (Viper) semi-expendable, vertically launched piloted missile was intended as a fast-climbing interceptor. It had a Walter 109-509A-2 rocket motor in the rear fuselage and four external Schmidding booster rockets to assist launch, and its nose was loaded with 24 Föhn 73mm unguided rockets.

ABOVE: Another bomber interceptor was the Messerschmitt Me 163 Komet, which had a Walter 109-509A-2 rocket motor. This Me 163B-1a, seen at Bad Zwischenahn in 1943, had a maxiumum speed of 596mph (959kph) at 9,840ft (3,000m) and a powered endurance of 8 minutes.

LEFT: Surrendered by a defecting company test pilot on its maiden flight in 1945, this Messerschmitt Me 262A-1a single-seat interceptor had two 1,980lb-thrust Jumo 004B turbojets which gave it a top speed of 540mph (869kph) at 19,685ft (6,000m).

The advent of the jet engine, just as piston-engined aircraft were approaching their performance limits, brought major advances in the aeroplane's development.

Chapter Seven

The Jet Era Begins

The early jet aircraft were either experimental or, in keeping with the mood of the times, fighters. The first was of the former kind, the Heinkel He 178, which made a short hop on 24 August 1939 and a circuit of the airfield three days later. On 1 November it was demonstrated to General Udet, head of the Luftwaffe Technical Department, and General Milch, head of the Air Ministry, but neither showed interest. It was in the Berlin Air Museum when an air raid in 1943 destroyed it. The next was the Heinkel He 280 fighter, the world's first combat jet aircraft and first twin-engine jet, which made its maiden powered flight on 2 April 1941.

Britain's first jet aircraft, the experimental Gloster E28/39, made its maiden flight on 15 May 1941 powered by an 860lb (390kg) thrust Whittle W1 turbojet. The first and only Allied jet fighter to go into action in the Second World War was the Gloster Meteor F1. Its design, to Air Ministry specification F9/40, had begun in 1940. The twin-engine configuration was forced on the designers because the jet engines of the day lacked the thrust to give a single-engine type the required performance. The first Meteor to be completed had two Rover-built W2B turbojets: these failed to develop more than 1,000lb (454kg) of thrust each, so the aeroplane was limited to taxying trials. The first Meteor to fly was the fifth proto-type, with two 1,500lb (680kg) thrust Halford H1 turbojets. Twenty Mk 1 Meteors were built, of which 16 were received by the RAF. Delivery to 616 Squadron began on 12 July 1944, and its first success was the destruction of a V1 flying bomb 15 days later by toppling it with a wingtip when the guns jammed.

In the USA, the Bell P-59 Airacomet was the world's first jet to undergo Service trials, which began in 1944. Its General Electric turbojet engine was based on the Whittle engine. In all, 66 P-59s were built but, not being combat worthy, were used only as trainers.

The Messerschmitt Me262 made its first flight on 25 March 1942, an abortive event because the engine flamed out and the pilot barely completed a circuit. After further vicissitudes, the first production Me262A-1a were delivered to the test unit in April 1944. In July they shot down two P-38 Lightnings and a Mosquito. The first regular Me262A-1a squadron was formed in November 1944. Me262s shot down 427 Allied aeroplanes, among them 300 four-engine bombers. In October the Me262A-2a was declared operational.

THE COLD WAR

The return to what was euphemistically called peacetime did not lessen the recently warring nations' interest in the development of military aircraft. There was growing tension between the Soviet Bloc and the Western Allies. The Soviet block-ade of Berlin that began on 25 June 1948 enabled Britain and the USA to demonstrate their readiness to defy their potential enemy. RAF and civilian Dakotas and Yorks and the USAF's C-54 Skymasters began to fly in the food and fuel necessary to feed the inhabitants. It was a total success and the disgruntled Soviets reopened the supply routes on 11 May 1949. Britain and the USA remained on the brink of an armed confrontation with the USSR that cast a shadow over the next four decades.

The greatest attention was being paid to rapid evolution of the jet engine. The early turbojet engines were of two types,

ABOVE: **The Heinkel He 280, the world's first twin-engine jet aircraft, comes in to land at the end of its first powered flight, on 2 April 1941. Its two 1,290lb (585kg) thrust HeS 8A engines were uncowled at the time.**

ABOVE: The Gloster-Whittle E28/39 takes off from Farnborough during its test programme under the power of its 1,760lb (798kg) thrust Power Jets W2/500 turbojet. It originally had an 860lb (390kg) thrust Power Jets W1 (inset).

MILESTONES

1939

The Heinkel He 178 makes the first flight of a turbojet-powered aeroplane.

1941

Britain's first turbojet-powered aircraft, the Gloster-Whittle E28/39 makes its maiden flight.

1944

The first operational jet aircraft, the Messerschmitt Me 262 and the Gloster Meteor, enter service.

axial flow and centrifugal flow. In the first of these, which Germany pioneered, air sucked into the engine is compressed longitudinally as it flows through a series of axial compressors before entering the combustion chamber. In the second type, which Britain was the first to build, the air is compressed radially by a centrifugal compressor, then turned again through a right angle before entering the combustion chambers arranged around the back of the engine casing. Before long the British engineers perceived that their method produced a much bulkier engine, so resorted to axial flow.

The next step was the addition of re-heat, or afterburning, to give increased thrust. This is done by mixing additional fuel with the exhaust gases in a jet pipe extension to the gas turbine engine. In order to ignite the fuel and gases in the reheat process, extremely high temperatures are necessary. One system, which is known as the "hot shot unit", acts as a miniature rocket motor to produce a stream of already heated fuel to be fed into the jet pipe.

The attention of designers was focused not only on the engine: to give maximum aerodynamic efficiency attention to the aircraft's shape was equally essential. At very high speed, the air meeting the wings and fuselage was compressed around the leading edges and other areas, which caused turbulence, buffeting and drag. German scientists' solution to the problem was to sweep the wings back, out of the line of the shock wave.

In Britain, the Meteor was followed by another fighter, the de Havilland Vampire, first known by the grotesque name Spider Crab. There were night and day variants of both aircraft types.

During the war, Britain and the USA had been under pressure to manufacture large numbers of aircraft, with no time to spare on development. In Germany, on the contrary, scientists working in gov-

ernment and university research institutes were allowed time to experiment, building and testing in wind tunnels or flight. At the war's end the relevant designs were seized by the Allies, but the USA and USSR made more dynamic use of them than Britain. During the next five years France and Sweden also made remarkable progress. The former introduced the Dassault MD-450 Ouragan, and the latter the Saab J29A Tunnan.

The greatest achievement of the late 1940s was supersonic flight. On 14 October 1947, Captain Charles "Chuck" Yeager of the renamed United States Air Force (USAF), flying a rocket-powered Bell X-1, exceeded the speed of sound.

WAR IN KOREA

In the first week of the Korean War in June 1950, four Lockheed F-80Cs fought eight Lavochkin La-11 piston-engine fighters and shot down four. Close-support aircraft were the most urgently needed, and the P-51 Mustang had to be resorted to. The USAF were flying the Lockheed F-80 Shooting Star, Republic F-84 Thunderjet

LEFT: **The USA's first jet fighter design was the XFJ-1, later the FJ-1 Fury, produced for the US Navy. Powered by a 3,820lb (1,733kg) thrust General Electric J35-GE-2 engine, the XFJ-1 made its maiden flight on 27 November 1946.**

To reassure the public, airline advertisements depicted rock-jawed aircraft captains and pretty stewardesses.

When not fighting one another with weapons, nations are in commercial competition that is no less fierce. The end of world war was the starting pistol for a scramble after rich prizes in the aviation world: not only among aircraft manufacturers but also air carriers. The major airlines were solidly established before the war: British Overseas Airways Corporation (BOAC), Pan American, Air France, Lufthansa, Alitalia, Swiss Air, Sabena, and KLM among them. Now there was a new category of operators, the charter firms, which offered cheaper fares than the airline companies. As standards of living rose in developed countries, people who had never been able to afford foreign travel were beginning to take holidays abroad for granted. This did not mean a sudden boom in the sale of new aeroplanes, for many small companies made do by buying secondhand from the major ones.

Manufacturers turned their attention to the requirements of those operating on short-haul routes with a small number of passengers or light cargo.

The first big airliner to make an impact was the Lockheed Constellation. It had first flown in 1943 and began life in military livery as the C-69. In 1946 it entered service with Pan American Airways.

Britain's first postwar airliner was the Vickers Viking, with room for 36 passengers. Several Vikings were still at work for airlines and charter firms in the early 1960s. Other aircraft competing for sales to airlines were the French Breguet 761 Provence (Deux-Ponts) and the Languedoc. Despite its small population, Sweden too was more than keeping pace; its Saab Scandia 36-seater was built both there and also in the Netherlands in small numbers.

Some of the early postwar passenger aeroplanes appear to have fulfilled eccentric fantasies. One of these, designed originally for the military, was the Hughes Hercules flying boat, intended to carry 700 passengers. On 2 November 1947 Howard

LEFT: **Italy's Caproni-Campini N-1, first flown on 28 August 1940, was not a true jet aircraft. A 900hp Isotta-Fraschini 12-cylinder piston engine drove a compressor with three stages of variable-pitch blading to blow air out of its tail nozzle. Its performance was inferior to that of a similarly powered propeller-driven two-seater.**

PASSENGER AEROPLANES

Between 1939 and 1945 hundreds of thousands of military personnel became used to trooping all over the world by air instead of sea, and returned to civilian life with no qualms about safe air travel. They were to pass this confidence on to their families and friends. In the 1960s fear of flying was still a strong deterrent.

and North American F-86 Sabre, while the US Navy flew the Grumman F-9F Panther and McDonnell F-2H Banshee. Boeing B-29s based in Japan were able to carry out strategic bombing.

China, almost as formidable a country as the USSR, sprang a surprise on South

Korea's allies by coming briskly to support North Korea with vast numbers of ground troops and swept-wing MiG-15 fighters supplied by the USSR. On 7 November 1950 the first combat ever between two jet fighters brought victory to an F-80C, which shot down a MiG-15.

RIGHT: **An intimate look inside the flight deck of a Lockheed Constellation 749 airliner, with the pilot on the left, copilot on the right and the engineer nearest the camera, facing the banks of instruments for the four 2,200hp Wright Cyclones.**

Hughes himself flew it on its only flight, which was about a mile long – a poor return for the $25 million it had cost.

Of similar capricious concept was the Bristol Brabazon. This originated in 1943 when a committee sponsored by the British government authorised the Bristol Aeroplane Company to design and build an aircraft of large capacity that would be able to fly the Atlantic nonstop. Construction began in 1945 and the first aircraft was completed five years later. A special hangar had been built to accommodate it. The wingspan was 230ft (70m) and length 177ft (54m). Eight Bristol Centaurus engines coupled in pairs drove contra-rotating propellers. The Brabazon accumulated only 400 flying hours before being scrapped because it was so expensive.

A disappointment in 1952 was the Saunders-Roe Princess flying boat. In 1943 the company began designing it to meet BOAC's requirement for a long-range aircraft to operate on the Southampton–New York route. The Princess had a maximum cruising speed of 360mph (579kph). She could carry a crew of six and 105 passengers. The maiden flight on 22 August 1952 was at least five years too late, for by then BOAC, like all the other international carriers, was seeking faster and even bigger landplanes.

SCHEDULED SERVICES

The year 1952, however, also saw compensating triumph. On 2 May BOAC introduced the world's first scheduled jet passenger service with the 36-passenger DH Comet 1, which had a maximum cruising speed of 480mph (772kph). Many other airlines wanted to add Comets to their fleets, until, on 2 May 1953, one crashed on take-off at Calcutta and everyone aboard was killed. On 12 January 1954 another Comet dived into the sea near Italy and again there were no survivors. On 8 April 1954 yet another broke up in the air with total fatalities.

All Comets were grounded. From studying pieces of wreckage it was decided that metal fatigue around a window had been caused by the constant increase and decrease of pressure in the cabin.

Some redesign of the fuselage was done and heavier gauge metal was used. The Comet 4, with seats for 81 passengers, first flew in 1958 and the type proved a success. BOAC ordered 19 and on 4 October 1958 one of these flew the first ever North Atlantic jet service: London to New York in 10hr 22min.

The second European turbojet airliner to enter service was the Sud-Aviation Caravelle, which first flew on 22 May 1955, and had its two turbojets mounted on each side of the rear fuselage.

Five years after the pure-jet Comet began operating in the BOAC livery, the company introduced the 90-seat Bristol Britannia, which had four Bristol Proteus turboprop engines. It made its debut on the London–Johannesburg route on 19 December 1957 and was the first turboprop airliner to cross the North Atlantic. British European Airways (BEA) also flew another turboprop, the 139-seat Vickers-Armstrongs Vanguard, which had four Rolls-Royce Tyne engines. The only USA-built turboprop, the Lockheed Electra, began service in January 1959 with American Airlines. Its four engines were Alison 501s. In October 1955 Pan American Airways ordered 20 of Boeing's 707-120 four-engined jet airliners. The first of the type made its maiden flight on 20 December 1957. In the following year, on 26 October 1958, Pan American operated the first 707 route, from New York to Paris, across the North Atlantic.

LEFT: The USA's first jet aeroplane, the Bell P-59 Airacomet, made its maiden flight on 1 October 1942. The unreliable 1,300lb (590kg) thrust General Electric I-A turbojets were succeeded by 1,650lb (748kg) thrust I-16s (later J31). This is a YP-59A on Service trials.

BELOW: Typical of the early Russian jets was the Yakovlev Yak-23, initially powered by a 3,500lb (1,588kg) thrust Rolls-Royce Derwent engine given to the USSR, and later by a copy, the RD-500. First flown on 17 June 1947, the Yak-23 served with several Eastern Bloc air forces.

RIGHT: The Gloster Meteor F4 entered service with first-line fighter squadrons in 1948, and also equipped the RAF High-Speed Flight, being used to set two world air speed records of 606 and 616mph (975 and 991kph) in 1945 and 1946. The powerplant was two 3,500lb (1,588kg) thrust Rolls-Royce Derwent 5 turbojets.

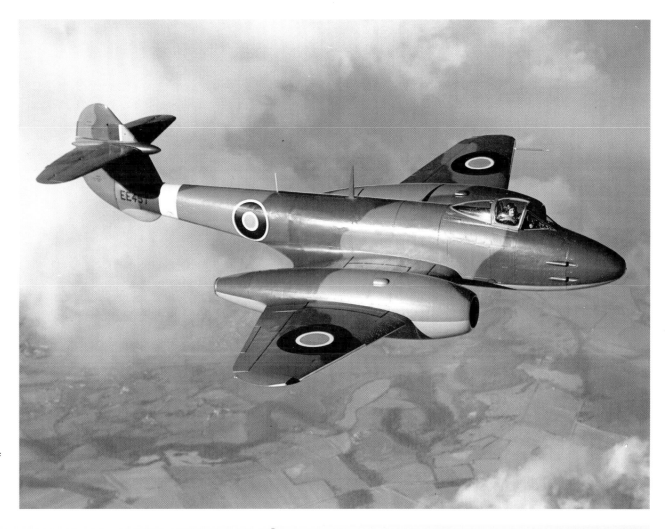

BELOW: Chance Vought's XF6U-1 Pirate, first flown on 2 October 1946, had a 3,000lb (1,360kg) thrust Westinghouse J34-WE-22. The US Navy took delivery of three prototypes and 30 production F6U-1s, but cancelled an order for a further 35.

LEFT: Boeing's fully pressurised Model 377 Stratocruiser, with its distinctive "double-bubble" fuselage carrying up to 112 passengers, heralded a new era in commercial air transport. Wingspan 141ft 3in (43.05m), length 110ft 4in (33.62m) height 38ft (11.58m), weight 145,800lb (66,133kg), engines four 3,500hp Pratt & Whitney R-4360-B6 Wasp Major 28-cylinder radial air-cooled, maximum speed 375mph (603kph), range 4,600 miles (7,402km), crew 5, passengers 112.

BELOW: The Douglas DC-4 was a civilian version of the C-54 Skymaster military transport. Carrying 44 passengers, it had four 1,450hp Pratt & Whitney R-2000 Twin Wasp 14-cylinder air-cooled radial engines.

RIGHT: In the early postwar years British airlines had to make do with converted bombers, of which the Avro 691 Lancastrian, a Lancaster conversion, was typical. Powered by four 1,635hp Rolls-Royce Merlins, the Lancastrian could carry from 9 to 13 passengers and cruised at 230mph (370kph).

BOTTOM LEFT: First flown in 1947, Lockheed's elegant L-749 Constellation originated from a 1939 TWA specification, but initially flew as the C-69 military transport. This is an L-749A, powered by four 2,200hp Wright R-3350-C18-BA1 18-cylinder air-cooled radials and seating 43 passengers.

LEFT: This study of Heathrow Airport in the immediate postwar period shows just how makeshift things were, with converted bombers plying their trade amid widespread construction work. The aircraft is a civil-registered black and yellow Lancaster III belonging to Flight Refuelling Ltd and still retaining the bomb-aimer's nose transparency. The receiver nozzle for the hose from the tanker aircraft can be seen beneath the rear fuselage.

Chuck Yeager

After a distinguished war career, General Charles "Chuck" Yeager became a USAF test pilot based at Muroc in California. He was testing the new generation of jet-powered fighters when asked to fly the rocket-powered Bell X-1 research aeroplane.

"We were hell-raising fighter jocks with plenty of swagger", said Charles "Chuck" Yeager. There was a lot more in his character – immense bravery and an exemplary sense of responsibility.

Aged 18, he volunteered for the US Army Air Force in 1942. His career almost ended prematurely on 23 October 1943 when, flying a P-39 Airacobra in a mock attack on a bomber formation, there was an explosion. "Fire came out from under my seat and the airplane flew apart in different directions." He baled out. "When the chute opened I was knocked unconscious." He was taken to hospital: "My back was fractured and it hurt like hell."

His squadron was posted to England. Over France on 5 March 1944 the P-51 Mustang he was flying on escort to B-24s was hit and set alight by an Fw 190's cannon shells. Suddenly, "I'm a wounded twenty-one-year-old American fighter pilot, shot down and on the run". He parachuted into a pine wood. Wounded in the feet, hands and leg, he spent the night there. At dawn a woodcutter appeared, who Yeager stopped with a drawn pistol. The Frenchman fetched help and Yeager was led to a Maquis group. He returned to England in mid-May. Shot-down air crew who evaded the enemy were sent home lest they be downed again, captured and tortured into betraying their helpers. After the Normandy landings the Resistance emerged from hiding; so Captain Yeager claimed there was now no need for secrecy. After an interview with General Eisenhower the order was rescinded. He flew his last operation on 15 January 1945 after 17 victories.

Home again, he flew his first jet, a Lockheed P-80 Shooting Star, and in 1946 qualified as a test pilot. Next, he was selected to be the principal pilot to fly the Bell X-1 in an attempt to break the sound barrier. In power dives an aeroplane experiences severe buffeting called compressibility, which prompted a belief in a sound barrier – an invisible wall of air that would cause any aircraft that tried to penetrate it at the speed of sound (Mach 1) to disintegrate. Discouragingly, a British test pilot, Geoffrey de Havilland, flying the DH108 Swallow swept-wing research aircraft, was killed in September 1946 when it broke up over the Thames Estuary.

When Yeager flew a P-84 Thunderjet straight and level at Mach .82 it began to shake violently and its nose pitched up. "It was hard to believe that there wasn't a wall out there."

The X-1 pilot, Chalmers "Slick" Goodlin, a civilian research pilot, received risk bonuses. It was considered unfair for military pilots to run that type of risk for much lower pay. Goodlin's contract required him to take the X-1 to Mach .8, which he had done. He was negotiating a further sum for going to Mach 1.1, but it took so long that the USAAF moved in.

"I never knew when I might be taking my last ride."

LEFT: Chuck Yeager poses alongside *Glamorous Glennis*, the bright orange Bell X-1 in which he exceeded the speed of sound for the first time on 14 October 1947, attaining a speed of Mach 1.06 at 40,000ft (12,192m).

" That first Mach 1 ride launched the era of supersonic flight."

During May 1947 fighter test pilots were asked to volunteer to replace him. Yeager applied, and was chosen.

On his first flights the X-1 would be dropped from 25,000ft (7,620m) with no fuel and would glide to earth. He would not be able to bale out, because he would probably hit the starboard wing. He made the first powered flight on 29 August 1947 and, after many vicissitudes and modifications to the aircraft, on 14 October 1947 (his ninth flight) Yeager finally broke the sound barrier. His stupendous feat was the first step towards space flight.

In 1966, a colonel now, he was given command of a wing comprising five squadrons operating over Vietnam. Flying a B-57 Canberra, he led 127 missions. In 1975 he retired as a Brigadier General. He could have earned one more promotion, but that would have meant a desk job – anathema to a man born to fly.

TOP: **The Bell X-1 was powered by a four-chamber Reaction Motors XLR-11RM3 rocket motor, which delivered a maximum thrust of 6,000lb (2,722kg) at sea level for five minutes, using liquid oxygen and diluted ethyl alcohol for fuel.**

ABOVE: **The compact cockpit of the Bell X-1A**

LEFT: **Developed from the X-1, the X-1A married the earlier aircraft's wings, tailplane and powerplant to a completely new fuselage with increased fuel capacity. Yeager took this aircraft beyond Mach 2.**

ABOVE: **First flown in 1946, Convair's massive B-36 bomber began life with six 3,500hp Pratt & Whitney 4360 engines, but later variants also had four General Electric J47-GE-19 jet engines in podded pairs under each wing, making it a ten-engined aircraft.**

LEFT: **Northrop's unconventional XB-35 flying-wing bomber made its maiden flight on 25 June 1946.**
Wingspan 172ft (52.43m), **length** 53ft 1in (16.18in), **height** 20ft 1in (6.12m), **weight** 162,000lb (73,482kg), **engines** four 3,000hp Pratt & Whitney (two R-4360-17 two R-4360-21) Wasp Major 28-cylinder radial air-cooled, **cruising speed** 391mph (629kph), **range** 10,000 miles (16,100km), **crew** 7.

RIGHT: The Lancaster's peacetime successor was the Avro Lincoln long-range bomber, which first flew on 9 June 1944 but did not go into service until August 1945. This is a Lincoln B2, powered by four Rolls-Royce Merlin 86 liquid-cooled 12-cylinder vee engines.

BELOW: From the Boeing B-29 was evolved the B-50 Superfortress, capable of carrying 5 tons of bombs 6,000 miles (9,656km) without refuelling. An early B-50A made the first nonstop flight round the world, using flight refuelling, in 1949. Four 3,500hp Pratt & Whitney Wasp Majors provided the power.

ABOVE: Russian-built MiG-15 jet fighters provided tough opposition for Western fighters over Korea. This one was the first to be evaluated by the USAF. Powered by a 5,005lb (2,270kg) thrust RD-45F and armed with one 37mm and two 23mm cannon, the MiG-15 saw wide service with Eastern Bloc countries, more than 16,000 being built.

LEFT: One opponent of the MiG-15 was the Hawker Sea Fury, the last piston-engined fighter to serve in first-line Fleet Air Arm squadrons. In the Korean War they were used chiefly for ground-attack, but did successfully engage the Russian jets. A 2,480hp Bristol Centaurus radial engine gave the Sea Fury a maximum speed of 460mph (740kph).

TOP: The West's counterpart to the MiG-15 was the North American F-86 Sabre, powered by a 5,200lb (2,359 kg) thrust General Electric J47 turbojet. It went to Korea in December 1950, where war had begun a month earlier. Initial versions were inferior to the Russian fighter in combat, but later marks gained the upper hand.

ABOVE: The US Navy had the F9F Panther, Grumman's first jet fighter, powered by the 6,520lb (2,957kg) thrust Pratt & Whitney J48 turbojet. These are F9F-2s, one of which became the first US Navy jet to shoot down a jet aircraft in combat, on 9 November 1950.

ABOVE RIGHT: Republic's F-84 Thunder-jet was the last subsonic, straight-wing fighter-bomber to see operational service with the USAF. This version, the F-84E, was the first of the type to arrive in Korea. It was powered by the 5,000lb (2,268kg) thrust Allison J35-A-17D.

RIGHT: A star of the war in the Pacific, the Vought F4U Corsair also saw service in Korea with the US Marines in its low-altitude AU-1 variant, with additional armour, increased underwing load-carrying ability and a Pratt & Whitney 2,300hp R-2800-83W engine. This one wears the markings of France's Aeronavale.

LEFT: Produced by the Group Technique de Cannes, the SO.30P Bretagne was a 30 or 37-passenger transport aircraft powered by two 1,620hp Pratt & Whitney R-2800-B43 air-cooled radial engines. It first flew on 11 December 1947. Some of the 45 production aircraft were supplied to the French air force and navy, and also to the national airline, Air France.

LEFT: One of the most elegant piston-engined airliners ever designed, the medium-range Airspeed Ambassador first appeared in 1947. Its two 2,625hp Bristol Centaurus 661 18-cylinder sleeve-valve radial engines enabled it to carry 47 to 60 passengers at a cruising speed of 272mph (438kph) over a range of 1,550 miles (2,494km).

RIGHT: SAAB of Sweden produced the functional Scandia, destined to be the first airliner of Swedish design to go into regular commercial service, which it did in 1950. Unfortunately the market was flooded with surplus DC-3s, and only 18 Scandias were built. A pair of 1,800hp Pratt & Whitney R-2180-E1 Twin Wasp radials provided the power.

LEFT: The Convair CV-340 was one of a family of short-haul passenger transports that emerged from this US manufacturer. First flown in 1951, the 340 had two 2,400hp Pratt & Whitney R-2800-CB16 Double Wasp 18-cylinder radial engines and could carry up to 52 passengers.

BELOW: Another US manufacturer, Glenn Martin, produced the 4-0-4 short-haul pressurised passenger transport, again powered by two 2,400hp Pratt & Whitney R-2800-CB16 Double Wasps. Seating up to 40 passengers, the 4-0-4 first flew on 21 October 1950.

Comet and Viscount

On 29 July 1950 British European Airways (BEA) inaugurated the world's first scheduled passenger service by turboprop airliner. Turbine engines, which greatly reduced both vibration and cabin noise, made a welcome improvement in passenger comfort. They also greatly reduced flight times. This first flight of the V630 in BEA livery carried 14 fare-paying passengers and 12 guests from Northolt to Le Bourget, with seats for six more aboard. From 13 to 23 August the same aircraft operated on the London to Edinburgh route – the world's first turbo-engine domestic service.

The power of the four Rolls-Royce Dart engines was increased, which raised the Viscount's passenger capacity to 60. This variant was the V700, of which BEA ordered 20. On 18 April 1953 it began to fly the London–Rome–Athens–Nicosia route. Altogether 438 Viscounts in various ver-

sions were built and sold to many countries, among them the USA and China.

The next innovative civil airliner to make its maiden passenger-carrying flight was the de Havilland Comet I on 2 May 1952. BOAC had taken delivery of 10 to provide the world's first jet operation for passengers, starting with the London–Johannesburg service. The next two jet services were London–Singapore and London–Tokyo. All made great time savings: for example, the journey to Tokyo was reduced from 86 to $33^{1}/_{4}$ hours.

Aircraft constructors in the USA were much perturbed. They had not yet produced even turbojets: their customers were operating piston-engine 100-seaters at less than 300mph (483kph), while the Comet flew at almost 500mph (805kph).

Several airlines ordered Comets, but a year later three crashes with total loss of life halted production of the aircraft. The

cause of the accidents was discovered to be metal fatigue around the square window apertures in the fuselage.

BOAC began to operate a duly modified Comet in 1958, but it was too late: the Boeing 707 jet had appeared.

ABOVE: **The prototype de Havilland DH106 Comet on flight test following its maiden flight on 27 July 1949, powered by four 4,450lb (2019kg) thrust de Havilland Ghost 50 turbojets. Its already graceful lines were further enhanced when the nose was stretched in later marks.**

LEFT: **Vickers Viscount V802s under construction at Weybridge in the mid-1950s. This version had a lengthened fuselage accommodating 65 passengers, compared with 47 in the V700 Series, and was powered by four 1,742shp Rolls-Royce Dart R.Da.6 turboprop engines.**

RIGHT: De Havilland Comet prototype G-ALVG on display in BOAC livery at the Farnborough Air Show in September 1950. By this time it had undertaken a number of fast overseas flights to measure fuel consumption under airline conditions, starting with a return flight to Castel Benito in Libya on 25 October 1949, when it averaged 448mph (721kph).

BELOW: A fine in-flight study of a BEA Viscount V701. Large windows and a spacious cabin made the Viscount popular with passengers. This version had 1,540shp Rolls-Royce Dart R.Da.3 engines, which gave it a cruising speed of 316mph (508kph).

LEFT: SAAB's rotund J29A fighter, nicknamed the Tunnan (flying barrel), first flew on 1 September 1948 and deliveries to the Swedish Air Force began in May 1951. Its 5,000lb (2,268kg) thrust de Havilland Ghost turbojet gave it a top speed of 643mph (1,035kph). The type was also operated by the Austrian Air Force.

RIGHT: One of the great classic jet fighters of the 1950s, the Hawker Hunter appeared in many variants and in many national colours. Seen here are Hunter F6s of No 208 Squadron, RAF, shortly before leaving Tangmere for their base in Nicosia, Cyprus, in 1958. The F6 was powered by a 10,000lb (4,536kg) thrust Rolls-Royce Avon 203 turbojet.

BELOW RIGHT: A brace of Tupolev Tu-16 bombers, powered by 19,180lb (8,700kg) thrust RD-3M-200s. Some 2,000 of these aircraft served the Soviet Air Force for 40 years, owing to their serviceability and ruggedness. The Tu-16A had a maximum speed of 628mph (1,010kph).

LEFT: Lockheed's P-80 Shooting Star was the first jet aircraft accepted for operational service by the USAF. Its maiden flight took place on 10 June 1944, and service entry came in December 1945. These P-80B-5s are from the famous 94th Fighter Squadron, based at Ladd Field, Fairbanks, Alaska, in 1947.

ABOVE: The Sud-Ouest SO.4050 Vautour was designed to perform the roles of all-weather fighter, close support, light bomber and reconnaissance. This is a single-seat SO.4050-003, prototype of the tactical support version, powered by two 6,170lb (2,799kg) thrust Atar 101C turbojets.

ABOVE: Britain's first jet bomber, the English Electric Canberra, first flew on 13 May 1949. This one began life in 1954 as a B2 bomber, set a world altitude record of 70,310ft (21,430m) on 28 August 1957, with the assistance of a Napier Double Scorpion rocket motor in its bomb bay. It was later modified to B6 standard.

LEFT: The Douglas RB-66 Destroyer tactical light bomber and reconnaissance aircraft entered service with the USAF in 1956. This is an RB-66C, designed for electronic reconnaissance, with small radomes at its wingtips and a shallow radome beneath the rear fuselage. Power was provided by a pair of 10,000lb (4,536kg) thrust Allison J71-A-13 turbojets.

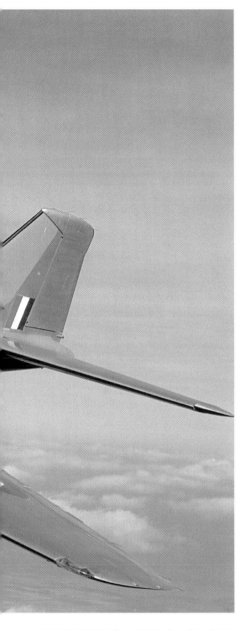

ABOVE RIGHT: **The USSR's Ilyushin Il-28 tactical bomber first flew on 8 July 1948 and subsequently appeared in a range of variants. These are Czechoslovak-built B-228s. Two VK-1 turbojets gave the Il-28 a maximum speed of 559mph (899kph).**

RIGHT: **Designed as a carrier-based attack bomber for the US Navy, the Douglas A3D Skywarrior first flew on 28 October 1952. This aircraft formed the basis for the USAF's RB-66. Wingspan** 72ft 6in (22.10m), **length** 76ft 4in (23.30m), **height** 23ft 6in (7.16m), **weight** 82,000lb (37,195kg), **engines** two 12,400lb (5,625kg) Pratt & Whitney J-57 turbojets, **maximum speed** 630mph (1,014kph), **range** 2,880 miles (4,630km), **crew** 3.

Lockheed 1049 Super Constellation

The first four-engined airline from Lockheed was successful in civilian airline service, until the introduction of jet airliners.

SPECIFICATION:
Wingspan
123ft (37.49m)

Length
113ft 7in (34.62m)

Height
24ft 9in (7.54)

Weight
69,000lb
(31,298kg) empty
120,000lb
(54,432kg) loaded

Engines
Four 3250hp Wright Turbo-Cyclone 972TC18DA1

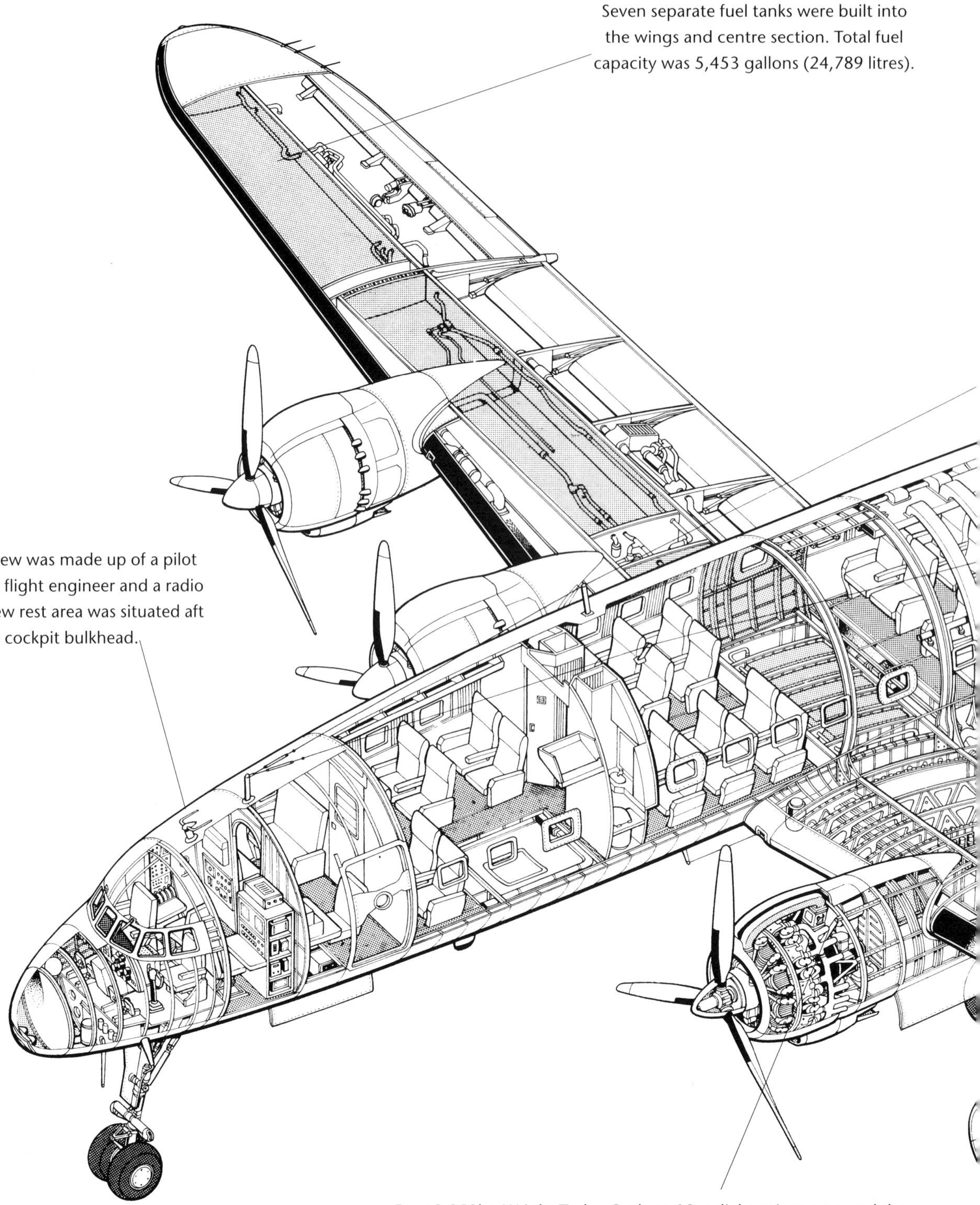

Seven separate fuel tanks were built into the wings and centre section. Total fuel capacity was 5,453 gallons (24,789 litres).

Flight-deck crew was made up of a pilot and co-pilot, a flight engineer and a radio operator. A crew rest area was situated aft of the cockpit bulkhead.

Four 3,350hp Wright Turbo-Cyclone 18 radial engines powered the 1049C. Each engine has 18 cylinders, arranged in two rows, and three exhaust-driven turbochargers. The propeller, Hamilton Standard Hydromatic three-bladed, reversible, was driven via an engine-mounted reduction gearbox.

Illustration © Mike Badrocke

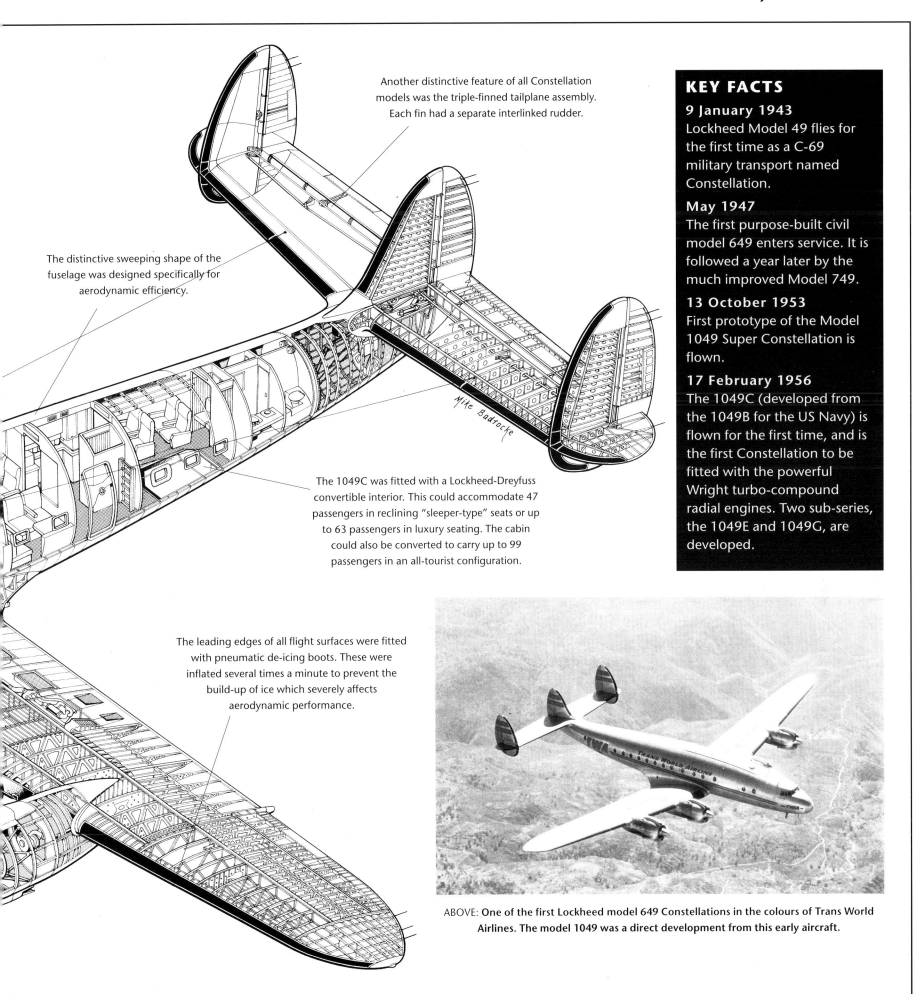

Another distinctive feature of all Constellation models was the triple-finned tailplane assembly. Each fin had a separate interlinked rudder.

The distinctive sweeping shape of the fuselage was designed specifically for aerodynamic efficiency.

Mike Badrocke

The 1049C was fitted with a Lockheed-Dreyfuss convertible interior. This could accommodate 47 passengers in reclining "sleeper-type" seats or up to 63 passengers in luxury seating. The cabin could also be converted to carry up to 99 passengers in an all-tourist configuration.

The leading edges of all flight surfaces were fitted with pneumatic de-icing boots. These were inflated several times a minute to prevent the build-up of ice which severely affects aerodynamic performance.

KEY FACTS

9 January 1943
Lockheed Model 49 flies for the first time as a C-69 military transport named Constellation.

May 1947
The first purpose-built civil model 649 enters service. It is followed a year later by the much improved Model 749.

13 October 1953
First prototype of the Model 1049 Super Constellation is flown.

17 February 1956
The 1049C (developed from the 1049B for the US Navy) is flown for the first time, and is the first Constellation to be fitted with the powerful Wright turbo-compound radial engines. Two sub-series, the 1049E and 1049G, are developed.

ABOVE: One of the first Lockheed model 649 Constellations in the colours of Trans World Airlines. The model 1049 was a direct development from this early aircraft.

LEFT: The Convair F-106 Delta Dart, a much modified version of the F-102 Delta Dagger, first flew in December 1956 and entered USAF service in July 1959, remaining in production until July 1961. Its 17,200lb (7,802kg) thrust Pratt & Whitney J 75-P-17 turbojet gave it a maximum speed of 1,327 mph (2,135kph) at 35,000 ft (10,668m). Armament comprised one Genie unguided air rocket and four Falcon air-to-air missiles, stowed internally.

BELOW: Known for obvious reasons as "the missile with a man in it", the Lockheed F-104 Starfighter was the first operational interceptor able to fly at Mach 2 for sustained periods. First flown on 7 February 1954, it entered service in 1958, powered by the 10,000lb (4,536kg) thrust General Electric J79 turbojet. Seen here are CF-104s of the Royal Canadian Air Force.

RIGHT: Not only was the North American F-100 Super Sabre the first of the USAF's "Century Series" fighters, but it was also the world's first operational fighter capable of supersonic speed in level flight.
Wingspan 38ft 9⅓in (11.82m), length 47ft 4⅔in (14.44m), height 16ft 2⅔in (4.94m), weight 21,847lb (9,910kg), engine one 16,905lb (7,675kg) thrust Pratt & Whitney J-57 turbojet with afterburner, maximum speed 891mph (1,434kph), range 1,150 miles (1,840km), crew 18.

BELOW RIGHT: The McDonnell F-101 Voodoo interceptor and fighter-bomber was the heaviest single-seat fighter in service when it was introduced into the USAF in May 1957. This is an F-101B two-seat long-range interceptor, which carried an observer behind the pilot. Powered by a pair of 10,700lb (4,854kg) thrust Pratt & Whitney J57-P-55s, it carried two Falcon air-to-air missiles under its fuselage and two Genie missiles in its internal bomb bay.

LEFT: The Sud-Aviation SE210 Caravelle, with two turbojet engines in rear-mounted nacelles, first flew on 27 May 1955. The prototype is seen here, powered by 10,500lb (4,763kg) thrust Rolls-Royce Avon RA.29 engines, taking off for a demonstration during the Paris Air Show at le Bourget, France.

BELOW: Based on the Tu-20 bomber, Tupolev's massive Tu-114 Rossiya was powered by four 14,795shp Kuznetsov NK-12M turboprops driving 18ft 4in (5.59m) diameter eight-blade contrarotating reverse-pitch propellers. Between 170 and 220 passengers could be carried at a cruising speed of 460mph (740kph). A number of international records were established by the type in the early 1960s.

RIGHT: **First flown on 20 December 1955, the Douglas DC-7C was developed to meet a Pan Am requirement for an aircraft able to fly transatlantic services in either direction, and was therefore the world's first true long-range commercial transport. Wingspan** 127 ft 6in (38.86m), **length** 112ft 3in (34.21m), **height** 31ft 10in (9.7m), **weight** 143,000lb (6,4863kg), **engines** four 3,400hp Wright R-3350 Turbo-Compound 18-cylinder radial air-cooled, **cruising speed** 355mph (571kph), **range** 4,605 miles (7,410km), **crew** 4, **passengers** 105.

BELOW RIGHT: **Tupolev Tu-104 airliners of Aeroflot at a Moscow airport in the 1960s. Incorporating the wings, tail unit, undercarriage, engine installation and nose of the Tu-16 bomber, the Tu-104 was for a period in the 1950s the only turbojet-powered transport in regular airline service.**

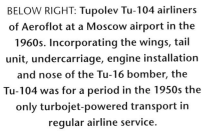

Technological advances
bring rapid progress in
aeronautical research,
air defence and
air transport.

Chapter Eight

Defending the Peace

It is a paradox that, in order to conduct a peaceful life, a nation must be so well prepared for war that potential adversaries will not dare to challenge it. The end of the Second World War was the beginning of an era in which the USSR regarded the USA, Britain and soon the other NATO nations with deep suspicion. Possessed of the world's largest strategic bomber force, and the most destructive weapons ever invented, the USA felt totally secure. But the nuclear age had dawned, and the deadly threat of wind-blown nuclear contamination had not been fully appreciated.

The 1950s saw a resurgence of making ready to attack as well as defend if the USSR's threatening posture developed into global war. By the middle of the decade the USA had about 300 nuclear weapons, and approximately 840 bombers capable of delivering them. Western intelligence estimated that at this time the USSR had about 24 nuclear weapons and 200 suitable bombers. A nuclear war appeared to be a distinct possibility.

The tension was enhanced by the jet age. The piston-engined Boeing B-29 Superfortress or its Russian counterpart, the Tupolev Tu-4, could carry nuclear weapons at 300mph (483kph) at 30,000ft (9,144m). The new breed of jet bomber, exemplified by the Boeing B-52 Stratofortress, first flown in April 1952, had eight engines, allowing it to carry a huge nuclear weapons load from one continent to another at speeds up to 660mph (1,062kph) at 40,000ft (12,192m). When the Boeing engineers designed the B-52 in the late 1940s they could have had no idea that the giant bomber, following a massive structural rebuild programme and other technical equipment upgrades, would still be in service over 45 years later.

AUTOMATED INTERCEPTION

The next move was to supersonic bombers, capable of Mach 2 and above, such as the Convair B-58 Hustler and the North American XB-70 Valkyrie (which never entered service), which would make fighter interception problematical. Given the destructive capability of nuclear-armed bombers, not one could be allowed to slip through defences. High speeds, coupled with the restricted manoeuvrability at high altitudes, reduced the value of the traditional interception from astern, so more effective interception procedures, and weapons, would have to be devised. The necessity of manoeuvring for position could be avoided by a collision course attack from the front quarter. The interceptor could be vectored towards its target, lock its radar on the target, and arm the weapon system. Its computer would then launch the weapons automatically when the target came within range.

Guns would be totally inadequate for this task. They were first replaced by batteries of unguided rockets, then later by homing missiles. Automated interception reached its zenith with the Convair F-106 Delta Dart, which had a fire control system and autopilot tied to ground control via a data link. The interception could thus be guided from the ground, with the pilot reduced to the status of system manager. The Soviet equivalent was the MiG-25 Foxbat, of similar concept but with even higher performance.

From 1958, long-range, high-altitude surface-to-air missiles (SAMs) entered service, with an anticipated kill probability of around 90 per cent. Against this, the high-speed, high-altitude bomber did not look

ABOVE: **On 10 March 1956 test pilot Peter Twiss set a new world absolute air speed record of 1,131.76mph (1,821kph) in the elegant Fairey Delta 2, powered by a Rolls-Royce Avon turbojet.**

MILESTONES

1956

The Fairey Delta 2 sets the first world speed record in excess of 1,000mph (1,609kph), breaking the previous record by nearly 310mph (499kph).

1959

First flight of the North American X-15, destined to become the fastest and highest-climbing aircraft ever built.

1969

The Hawker Siddeley Harrier becomes the first vertical-take-off combat aircraft in the world to enter regular squadron service.

ABOVE: **The pilot of a North American X-15 rocket-powered research aircraft prepares to be launched from beneath the wing of the parent Boeing B-52 bomber that carried his machine aloft.**

such a good option. The response was to switch to low-level, subsonic penetration, under the defender's radar.

Such factors also affected the development of another important military aircraft at the time: strategic reconnaissance. The most significant of such aircraft was the Lockheed U-2, the first aircraft to be designed specifically for obtaining reconnaissance photographs by illegal overflights, in other words by boldly flying across hostile territory without permission in order to locate military or strategically interesting installations. The U-2 was followed by a second-generation reconnaissance aircraft, the Lockheed SR-71 Blackbird, able to fly not only as high (above 85,000ft/25,908m) but almost five times faster (2,100mph/3,380kph). Because of the huge cost of such aircraft, and the fact that they would be vulnerable during the penetration of defended airspace, it is generally accepted that strategic reconnaissance is best left to space-orbiting satellites.

With such threat and counter-threat developments, huge sums of money were being spent by the USSR and the NATO allies on increasing the performance of aeroplanes and their weapon capabilities. For the Western nations it was as much to obtain commercial advantage as in anticipation of a war against the Communist Bloc. Manufacturers also pursued the sale not only of military aircraft but also of civil variants and aero engines. For the airlines, passenger fares were the motivation as well as, perhaps more than, safety. For the USSR, which would impose its aircraft and powerplants on the Communist bloc countries, the prime purpose of development was to be one step ahead of NATO and the USA in the event of another war.

OVERTAKING SOUND

When Captain (now General) Charles "Chuck" Yeager became the first person to exceed the speed of sound on 14 October 1947, he attained 670mph (1,078kph), Mach 1.105, at 42,000ft (12,802m). On 12 December 1953, in the Bell X-1A, he set a new record of Mach 2.42. At very high speed, heat generated by the friction between the aircraft's skin and molecules of air becomes a great danger, because it not only degrades the strength of the structure but can cause the fuel to boil. Bell built an experimental aircraft, the X-2, with sweptback wings to minimise these problems. This was to be air-launched from a modified Boeing B-50 Superfortress and, in 1956, attained a speed of 2,094mph (3,369kph), Mach 3.2.

In France, the Sud-Ouest SO 9000 Trident, which had two wingtip-mounted turbojet engines and a booster rocket in the fuselage, reached Mach 1.6 in 1953.

some respects, having studied German aerodynamic research into the benefits of sweepback as a way of delaying the drag created by compressibility. Their engine technology was derived from the Jumo 004B axial-flow turbojet. They also employed many German engineers who had worked on jet aircraft development in the Second World War.

The Mikoyan-Gurevich MiG-15, which had first flown on 30 December 1947 with a 5,000lb (2,268kg) thrust Kimov RD-45F turbojet engine, attained a maximum speed of 665mph (1,070kph). It owed little to original Russian inspiration, for it was the product of wartime German research in aerodynamics and British Rolls-Royce jet-engine technology. The USSR repaid the British Government's trust by copying the Nene engine without having a licence production agreement. The first Russian fighter to break the sound barrier in level flight was the twin-engine MiG-19, which entered service in 1955.

When Britain's first jet bomber, the English Electric Canberra, entered squadron service in May 1951, few were aware that the first jet bomber to fly in combat was the German Arado Ar234B Blitz, a twin-jet single-seater, which began flights over Britain in September 1944. In the last winter of the war, Ar234s operated over the Normandy battlefields. Remarkably, an ejector seat was fitted; and even more unusually, although a single-seater, it was equipped with an automatic pilot.

On 22 February 1957 the RAF's latest bomber, the first in the world with a delta-wing planform, the Avro Vulcan B1, entered squadron service. It was powered by four 17,000lb (7,711kg), thrust Bristol Siddeley Olympus 201 engines and had a maximum speed of 620mph (998kph).

While preparations for future wars were in hand, the USSR introduced a jet airliner. It was a development of the Tupolev Tu-16 ("Badger") medium bomber, and the timing of its first appearance was well judged: the Comet was grounded as a result of three fatal mid-air accidents. The Tupolev Tu-104, which had two 21,385lb (9,700kg) Mikulin turbojets, first flew on 17 June 1955, and had a maximum cruising speed of 560mph (901kph). It could carry 50 passengers and transformed the USSR's medium-range services, but proved uneconomical. Later it was replaced by the 70-seat Tu-104A and then the Tu-104B, which carried 100 passengers. From 1956 to 1958

ABOVE: **An English Electric Lightning F6 of 74 Squadron, RAF, fitted with overwing fuel tanks for long-range ferrying, refuels from a Handley Page Victor tanker over Scotland in 1967.**

On 3 August 1954 another French aircraft, the delta-winged SFECMAS (Nord) Gerfaut (Gyrfalcon), became the first European aircraft to exceed Mach 1 in level flight without the assistance of a rocket or afterburner. Three years later, the mixed turbojet/ramjet-powered Nord 1500 Griffon (Griffin) reached Mach 1.85.

In 1957 the next US project was decided upon. The end product, to be built by North American Aviation, would be capable of flying at almost Mach 7 – 4,500mph (7,240kph) – and to an altitude of over 250,000ft (76,200m). This meant that the airframe would have to withstand a temperature of 1,200° F (649°C). Designated the X-15, it was powered by a Reaction Motors XLR 99-RM-2 liquid fuel rocket motor that could deliver 60,000–70,000lb (27,216–31,752kg) thrust for just 84 seconds. The span of its trapezoidal-shaped wings was only 22ft (6.7m). Three were ordered and two Boeing B-52 Stratofortress bombers were modified as launch aircraft.

On 17 September 1959 the X-15 made its first powered flight. It reached Mach 2.3 in a shallow climb to 50,000ft (15,240m) but was powered on this flight by two LR11-RM-5 engines that gave a combined thrust of 12,000lb (5,443kg), because construction of the proposed XLR-99 engine had been delayed by technical problems. In 1961 Mach 3 was attained and in October 1967 an X-15 reached 4,534mph (7,297kph) – Mach 6.7 – at an altitude of 100,000ft (30,480m).

The Soviets were ahead of the West in

LEFT: **A Dassault Super Etendard shipboard strike fighter of France's Aeronavale, powered by a SNECMA Atar 8K 50 turbojet, is launched from a carrier's catapult in 1977.**

ABOVE: **A pilot of F10 Wing of the Royal Swedish Air Force prepares to fly his Saab J35 Draken fighter, armed with two Rb24 (Sidewinder) infrared homing missiles.**

the Tu-104 was the world's only operational jet airliner.

THE VIETNAM WAR

The Vietnam War, never formally declared, was a civilian war between South Vietnam and the Viet Cong (Communist guerrillas) operating from the north, ultimately aided by and allied with the North Vietnamese Army (NVA). It was a war in which the USA became increasingly heavily embroiled for more than 10 years. It spilled over into Vietnam's neighbouring states, and involved, to varying degrees, many other nations, if not directly in the hostilities then in the supply of weapons systems and training. In 1961 US Army helicopter squadrons were sent there to help the South Vietnamese Air Force. Four years later the Viet Cong began to receive help from the NVA. In February 1965 the American base at Pleiku, where fighter-bomber and medium bomber squadrons had been based since the previous year, was attacked. The USAF therefore considered itself free to retaliate.

The war dragged on. The USSR provided the North Vietnamese and the Viet Cong with surface-to-air guided missiles (SAMs), and by the end of 1967 the US

forces had lost approximately 3,000 aircraft. Apart from having long-range bombers (B-52s), other fixed-wing US aircraft that were used on operations were the Republic F-105 Thunderchief, the Douglas A-1 Skyraider, the McDonnell F-4 Phantom, the Douglas A-4 Skyhawk, the Grumman A-6 Intruder, which could hit targets by night or in bad weather, and the Vought A-7 Corsair II. Transport aircraft in the campaign were the Lockheed C-141 Starlifter and the Lockheed C-130 Hercules. The nature of the terrain and the US forces' strategy and tactics made this mostly a helicopter war, however.

By contrast, the North Vietnamese Air Force (NVAF) was comparatively small, operating Soviet-built MiG-17s and MiG-21s. In the last two years of the war the NVAF operated the Shenyang J-6, a Chinese-produced version of the MiG-19. The NVAF was trained by Soviet instructors, and its aircraft operated under Soviet-style close ground control. Too weak even to think of inflicting a decisive defeat on the US forces, it settled for a policy of air deniability, remaining in being as an effective force and thus making the US waste a lot of resources in providing fighter escort and electronic countermeasures for their strikes. Nevertheless, in December 1972, when the USAF made an all-out attack, and the North Vietnamese failed to shoot down a US aircraft, SAMs accounted for the loss of 17 B-52 Stratofortresses.

In April 1973 the US forces were evacuated, and the North Vietnamese marched into Saigon two years later.

ABOVE: **Soviet Air Force MiG-21F Mach 2 fighters armed with underwing rocket pods. More than 10,000 MiG-21s were built in the USSR for no fewer than 56 customer air forces.**

FREIGHTERS

Meanwhile, the competition among manufacturers of transport aircraft, for both civil and military use, was growing, and the active life of the aircraft born out of this became stretched. The market for short- and medium-haul types was as important as for long-haul aircraft, and the demand for freighters grew and continues to do so.

Airframes had to be built that were more versatile. The adaptation of airliners as military versions continues: the Boeing 707 was adapted to carry radar and other equipment that provided an airborne warning and control system (AWACS). Now the Boeing 747 is being fitted out as an advanced airborne command post. It will be succeeded by the 767 airborne warning and command post.

On the other side of the Atlantic, the 1970s saw the emergence of credible competition to the might of the US airline industry. The Airbus Industrie consortium brought together France, Britain, Germany and Spain to produce a wide-bodied airliner, the Airbus A300 (first flown on 28 October 1978). It was followed by the A310 (1982), intended to compete with the USA's 737, and then the A320 (1987) and the similar but shorter A319 and the stretched version, the A321. The ultra long-range A340, four-engined airliner entered service in 1996.

Antonov builds the An-226 Mriya, the world's largest aeroplane, in the Ukraine. It has six turbofans and can carry 60–70 passengers, with freight.

Seldom are civil aircraft built with components totally indigenous to one country. For example, in Sweden, the Saab 2000 short-haul regional transport, which seats 50–58 passengers, has twin Allison turboprops from the USA. International cooperation, and competition, are the order of the day.

LEFT: Nigeria Airways was one of 73 operators of the Fokker F27 Friendship, powered by two Rolls-Royce Dart turboprops. The F27, first flown in January 1957, was also built under licence by Fairchild in the USA.

BELOW: The Vickers-Armstrongs Vanguard prototype takes off from a wet Brooklands airfield in Surrey, England, for its maiden flight on 20 January 1959. Designed as a Viscount replacement, the Vanguard, powered by four 5,545shp Rolls-Royce Tyne RTy.11 turboprops, achieved only limited success.

RIGHT: The portly Breguet 761 Deux-Ponts passenger and cargo carrier first flew in February 1949. This is a 761S pre-series aircraft under trial with Air Algérie. It was developed into the 763, powered by four 2,100hp Pratt & Whitney R-2800-CA18 air-cooled radial engines, of which 12 were operated by Air France in the 1950s.

BELOW RIGHT: Lockheed's L-188 Electra, first flown in 1957, was the only large American airliner to be developed with turboprop engines, being powered by four 3,750shp Allison 501-D13s. Up to 99 passengers could be carried at a cruising speed of 405mph (652kph).

BOTTOM RIGHT: The first purpose-designed turbine-powered Russian airliner was the Ilyushin Il-18, which made its maiden flight in 1957. Production aircraft, powered by four 4,250shp Ivchenko AI-20s, could carry from 75 to 122 passengers at a cruising speed of 404mph (650kph).

Strategic Air Command

The Boeing B-47 was the first bomber to benefit from research on swept wings carried out in Germany during the war. The prototype first flew on 17 December 1947. The aircraft was designed in response to the USAF's requirement for a jet-engined bomber. The B-47's six engines were pylon-mounted, beneath the wings in nacelles: there were two inboard and one outboard on each side. The thin wing obviated storage of the main landing gear and the aircraft had tandem main gear retracting into the fuselage instead, with outrigger wheels retracting into the inboard engine nacelles.

The all-US designed and produced axial-flow turbojets produced adequate perormance, but for take-off at maximum weight additional thrust was provided by 18 booster rockets. Thrust reversers did not exist, so a brake parachute was fitted. The final version, the B-47E, first flew on 30 January 1953.

The eight-engine Boeing B-52 Stratofortress is regarded as *the* classic bomber, and the mainstay of Strategic Air Command for over two decades. The aircraft was first delivered to the USAF on 29 June 1955. During the Vietnam War it operated against targets in the North from bases in Guam, Okinawa and Thailand. Designed to operate at 40,000ft (12,192m), the B-52 later became a "ground-hugger", on low-level penetration using radar navigation.

The Convair B-58A Hustler, with four General Electric J79 turbojet engines, was the first supersonic strategic bomber in service. Designed to perform at high altitude, it was unique in carrying a nuclear bomb in a pod under the fuselage. It could exceed Mach 2, had a range of 5,000 miles (8,045km) without refuelling and was in squadron service from 1960 to 1970. During that time it set 19 world records and received five major aviation trophies for outstanding flights.

ABOVE: **Convair's delta-winged B-58 Hustler was the first supersonic bomber to enter production for the USAF, its four 15,600lb (7,076kg) thrust General Electric J79-GE-5 turbojets giving it a maximum speed of 1,385mph (2,228kph) at 40,000ft (12,192m). First flown in 1956, it served with the USAF from 1960 to 1970. The large external pod contained fuel for the outward journey and a nuclear weapon.**

LEFT: **The Boeing B-47 Stratojet was the first swept-wing bomber built in quantity for any air force, entering service with the USAF in 1950. Wingspan** 116ft (35.36m), **length** 108ft (32.92m), **height** 28ft (8.53m), **weight** 220,000lb (99,790 kg), **engines** six 5,800lb (2,631 kg) thrust General Electric J-47 turbojets, **maximum speed** 606mph (975kph), **range** 3,600 miles (5,794km), **crew** 3.

RIGHT: A Convair RB-36D intercontinental reconnaissance bomber displays its six 3,500hp Pratt & Whitney R-4360-41 piston engines and four podded 5,200lb (2,359kg) thrust General Electric J47-GE-19 jets. The B-36 was the biggest bomber to go into USAF service, spanning 230ft (70m).

BELOW: A Boeing B-52G Stratofortress takes fuel from a Boeing KC-135 Stratotanker. Powered by eight 13,750lb (6,237kg) thrust Pratt & Whitney J57-P-43WB turbojets, the 185ft (56m) -span B-52G had a range of 7,500 miles (12,070km) without refuelling. It entered USAF service in 1959.

ABOVE: By housing the VC10's four 21,000lb (9,526kg) thrust Rolls-Royce Conway 42 turbofans in pods on the rear fuselage, Vickers gave the airliner a "clean" wing and a relatively quiet passenger cabin. First flown in 1962, the design was later stretched to produce the Super VC10, with higher capacity and transatlantic range, but only 54 of both types were built.

RIGHT: When its Model 880 failed to sell in the face of competition from Boeing and Douglas, Convair produced the 990 Coronado, with distinctive trailing-edge wing fairings to minimise transonic drag and house extra fuel. Four 16,050lb (7,280kg) thrust General Electric CJ-805-23C aft-fan turbofans were fitted, but initial failures to meet performance guarantees resulted in only 37 being built.

RIGHT: The Ilyushin Il-62 was the Soviet Union's first true long-range four-engined jet transport. First flown in 1963, it entered service with Aeroflot in 1967, and was powered by four 23,150lb (10,500kg) thrust Kuznetsov NK-8-4 turbofans. Poor operating economics led to the installation of 23,353lb (10,593kg) thrust Soloviev D-30KUs on the Il-62M.

RIGHT: First flown in 1971, the Dassault Mercure medium-range high-capacity airliner initially suffered performance and handling problems, but production went ahead with only ten on order, for Air Inter, destined to be the type's sole operator.
Wingspan 100ft 2½in (30.50m), length 114ft 3½in (34.84m), height 37ft 3in (11.35m), weight 124,560lb (56,500kg), engines two 15,500lb (7,030kg) thrust Pratt & Whitney turbojets, cruising speed 575mph (925kph), range 1,295 miles (2,084km), crew 2, passengers 162.

RIGHT: The British Aircraft Corporation's BAC One-Eleven was Britain's most successful pure-jet civil aircraft. Powered by a pair of rear-mounted Rolls-Royce Spey turbofans, it was developed through a series of variants and production eventually transferred to Romania. The 500 series could accommodate up to 119 passengers and cruised at 540mph (869kph).

ABOVE: The first prototype Handley Page Victor first flew on 24 December 1952, and is seen here landing at the Farnborough Air Show in September 1953. Powered by four 11,050lb (5,012kg) thrust Armstrong Siddeley Sapphire turbojets, the Victor B1 entered operational service with RAF Bomber Command in April 1958.

LEFT: France's nuclear bomber was the Dassault Mirage IVA, powered by two 10,362lb (4,700kg) thrust SNECMA Atar 9K turbojets, which gave it a maximum speed of 1,454mph (2,340kph) (Mach 2.2) at 40,000ft (12,192m). It first flew in June 1959, entering service with the Commandement des Forces Aériennes Stratégiques in 1964.

ABOVE: First flown in August 1952, the Avro Vulcan entered service in 1956, with the Blue Steel stand-off bomb as its prime weapon. This was essentially a tactical weapon, so in 1960 plans were made for Britain to buy the long-range Douglas Skybolt air-launched ballistic missile; dummies are seen here in a trial installation on Vulcan B2 XH537. The plans were suddenly cancelled in December 1962.

RIGHT: All three of Britain's V-bombers in formation. Front to rear: Vickers Valiant B1 XD869, Avro Vulcan B1 XA904 and Handley Page Victor B1 XA931. The Valiant, powered by four 10,050lb (4,559kg) thrust Rolls-Royce Avon 204 turbojets, was first to enter squadron service, doing so in January 1955.

LEFT: **Russia's Yakovlev Yak-38 vertical/short take-off fighter first flew in 1970, and was serving on Soviet Navy carriers from the mid 1970s.** Wingspan 24ft (7.32m), **length** 50ft 10in (15.52m), **height** 14ft 4in (4.37m), **weight** 25,795lb (11,700 kg), **engines** one 15,300lb (6,934kg) thrust Turmansky R-27 turbojet and two 6,725lb (3,050kg) thrust Koliesov RD-36 liftjets, **maximum speed** 628mph (1,010kph), **range** 460 miles (740km), **crew** 1.

BELOW: **The Hawker Siddeley Trident was damned at birth by a misguided BEA specification that limited both capacity and range and therefore rendered it inferior to Boeing's 727.** Powered by three 9,850lb (4,468kg) thrust Rolls-Royce Spey turbofans, the Trident 1 entered service with British European Airways in 1964.

ABOVE: **One of the greatest successes in the history of commercial aircraft is the Boeing 727 short/medium-range jet, first flown in February 1963. This is the 727-200, with a considerably stretched fuselage.**
Wingspan 108ft (32.92m), **length** 153ft 2in (41.51m), **height** 34ft (10.36m), **weight** 207,500lb (94,112kg), **engines** three 14,500lb (6,577kg) thrust Pratt & Whitney JT-8D turbofans, **cruising speed** 599mph (964kph), **range** 2,880 miles (4,635km), **crew** 3, **passengers** 189.

RIGHT: Designed to operate from grass airfields, as a replacement for the ageing piston-engined twins in use in the USSR, the Yakovlev Yak-40 was a straight-winged trijet powered by three 3,300lb (1,497kg) thrust Ivchenko AI-25 turbofans and seating up to 33 passengers. It first flew in October 1966.

ABOVE: First flown on 15 July 1954, the Boeing 707 quickly established itself as one of the greats in air transport history, serving with countless airlines in a wide number of variants. This aircraft, N707PA, was the first 707-100 delivered to Pan American, the launch customer. It had four 12,500lb (5,670kg) thrust Pratt & Whitney JT3C-6 turbojets.

BELOW: Boeing's 747 revolutionised the air transport business. This is a 747-246B of Japan Airlines. With four Pratt & Whitney JT9D-74R4G2 turbofans of 54,750lb (24,835kg) thrust, the 747-200 has a maximum speed of 610mph (981kph) and can carry 442 passengers.

RIGHT: The 737 prototype, seen here, made its maiden flight on April 1967, powered by two 14,000lb (6,350kg) thrust Pratt & Whitney JT8D-7 turbofans. The type's passenger capacity has risen from 99–107 to 146–170 in the -400 version.

Vertical Take-Off (VTOL)

While the advantages of vertical take-off and landing capabilities for aeroplanes have long been realised, the struggle to develop practical systems has been long and expensive, with many failures on the way.

Frank Whittle's invention, the world's first turbojet engine, first run on 12 April 1937, set off a revolution in aircraft design, though full development of the engine did not occur until the war ended. As autogyros and helicopters were past the initial stages of development before the war, engineers throughout the aviation industry must surely have been thinking already of a means of obtaining vertical take-off and landing (VTOL) with this new type of engine, which could develop a thrust of higher value than its own weight.

By 1953 the Rolls-Royce Nene engine had developed a thrust of 4,000lb (1,814kg), which was approximately twice its weight, and could therefore easily lift the structure on which it would be mounted. The first feasibility trial was made with two Nene engines, the tailpipes modified so that the efflux blew vertically down, mounted horizontally on a four-legged framework. To study the attitude control system when hovering, air was bled through four nozzles from the engines' compressors: one nozzle blew forward, one astern, one on each side downward. When publicly demonstrated at Farnborough, England, this rig became known as the "Flying Bedstead".

Rolls-Royce now concentrated on designing engines with very high power-to-weight ratios. That of the first, the RB108, was 8:1. Short Brothers & Harland used it for their SC-1, the first-ever fixed-wing VTOL aircraft. It made its first vertical take-off in 1958, and first transition from hover to wingborne flight in 1960. The four lift engines could be swivelled aft slightly to add to the thrust of the forward-propulsion unit. They could also be swivelled forward to help as brakes.

Meanwhile Bristol Siddeley (later Rolls-Royce) had developed a vectored thrust turbofan engine, the BS53 Pegasus. Hawker Siddeley Aircraft were approached to design an airframe to suit the engine. The result was the P1127, later named Kestrel, and evaluated as a prototype strike and reconnaisance fighter by a tripartite squadron assembled from British, US and German aircrew. In 1964 it flew at supersonic speed in a shallow dive. Not judged adequate for squadron service, it was developed into the Harrier.

In France Marcel Dassault began flight trials in 1962 using a Bristol Siddeley Orpheus to adapt a Mirage fighter to VTOL. This version, the Balzac V-001 with eight Rolls-Royce RB162 jets and a SNECMA TF306 with afterburner, was abandoned after many accidents.

"The brilliant and long-lived Harrier entered squadron service in June 1969"

BELOW: **The grandfather of jet lift was the Rolls-Royce "Flying Bedstead", which sat on the efflux from two Nene jet engines while the pilot kept it steady by means of four nozzles from the engines' compressors.**

LEFT: **Seen here during an air show at Domodedovo, Moscow, in 1967, Yakovlev's experimental Yak-36 made its first free hovering flight in September 1964. The long nose boom housed a reaction control nozzle; there were others in the wingtips and tail.**

In Germany a research group of Bolkow, Heinkel and Messerschmitt in collaboration with Vereinigte Flugtechnische Werke (VFW) was formed in 1960. Using two banks of four Rolls-Royce RB162s and two Bristol Siddeley Pegasus 5s, flight trials of a prototype high-wing monoplane transport, the Dornier Do31E, with an intended cruising speed of 466mph (750kph), started in 1967 but came to an end in 1971. There was no further development. Bolkow, Heinkel and Messerschmitt also formed a research group in 1960 to develop the VJ-101C small high-wing monoplane, using six Rolls-Royce RB108 lift jets. Flight trials began in 1963, and stopped in 1964. Also in Germany VFW-Fokker flew the VAK-191 in November 1970 but this was not a success.

In the USA, Lockheed built and flew the XV-4A Humming Bird VTOL fighter prototype with two Pratt & Whitney JT12A-3 turbojets. The intended maximum speed of 520mph (837kph) was not reached, so work on the aircraft ceased.

Between 1950 and 1970 Ryan Aeronautical, Boeing Vertol and Canadair experimented with various concepts including tilting propellers.

ABOVE: **Dornier's Do31E was the first and, so far, the only VTOL jet transport. It proved highly successful, if excessively noisy, and established several world records in its class. It spanned 59ft 3in (18m) and had a cruising speed of 400mph (644kph) at 19,685ft (6,000m).**

The world's first VTOL strike and reconnaissance fighter, the brilliant and long-lived Hawker Siddeley Harrier, developed from the Kestrel, entered squadron service with the RAF in June 1969. Vertical lift is achieved by four rotatable nozzles, two on each side, which point down for lift and are then gradually rotated rearward to give forward propulsion.

No successful civilian use for VTOL has yet been achieved. ⊘

RIGHT: **Early attempts to produce VTOL aircraft are typified by the Convair XFY-1 "Pogo" of 1954, powered by a specially developed 5,850shp Allison YT40-A-14 turboprop. Successful transitions were made, but the return to earth in a "backwards" descent was a delicate manoeuvre.**

Harrier II

The original "Jump Jet" VTOL fighter bomber, designed by Hawker Aircraft, developed by McDonnell Douglas and British Aerospace.

SPECIFICATION:

Wingspan
30ft 4in
(9.25m)

Length overall
46ft 4in
(14.12m)

Height
11ft 8in
(3.56m)

Weight
13,086lb (5,936kg)
empty
31,000lb (14,062kg)
loaded

Engine:
Rolls-Royce Pegasus
Mk105
(F402-RR-406A)
23,800lb thrust

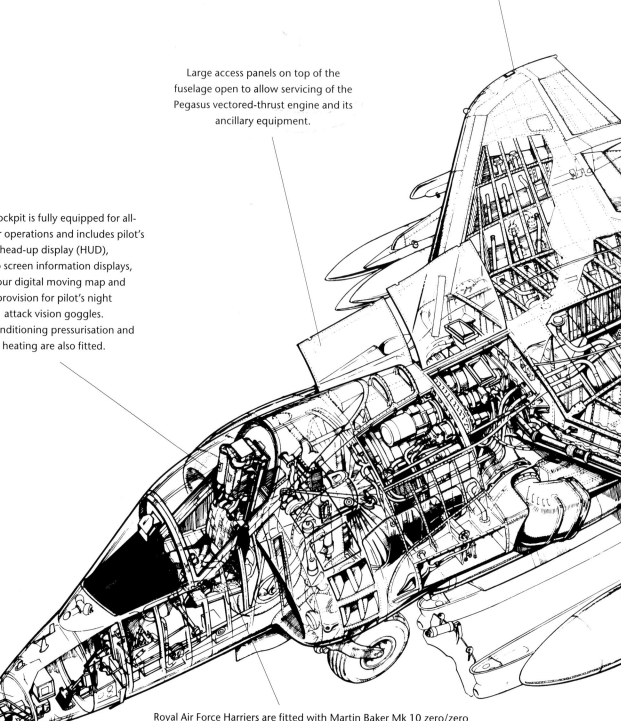

Puffer jets at each wing tip, nose and tail supplied with air from the engines' compressor, balance the Harrier while hovering

Large access panels on top of the fuselage open to allow servicing of the Pegasus vectored-thrust engine and its ancillary equipment.

The cockpit is fully equipped for all-weather operations and includes pilot's head-up display (HUD), video screen information displays, colour digital moving map and provision for pilot's night attack vision goggles. Air conditioning pressurisation and heating are also fitted.

Weapons delivery sensor system mounted in the nose is an Angle Rate Bombing set comprising a dual mode (laser and TV) target seeker and tracker.

Royal Air Force Harriers are fitted with Martin Baker Mk 10 zero/zero rocket ejection seats. Those for the US Marine Corps are fitted with UPC/Stencel seats of the same capability.

Illustration © Quadrant

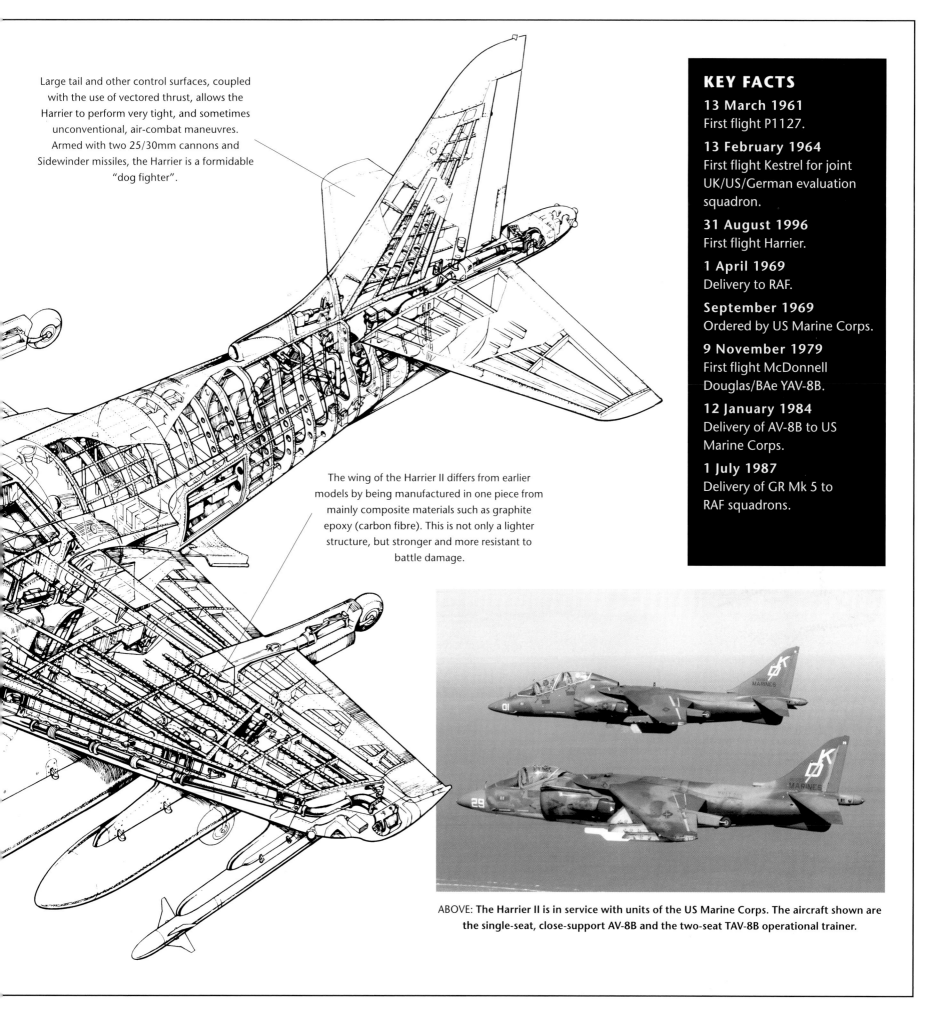

Large tail and other control surfaces, coupled with the use of vectored thrust, allows the Harrier to perform very tight, and sometimes unconventional, air-combat maneuvres. Armed with two 25/30mm cannons and Sidewinder missiles, the Harrier is a formidable "dog fighter".

The wing of the Harrier II differs from earlier models by being manufactured in one piece from mainly composite materials such as graphite epoxy (carbon fibre). This is not only a lighter structure, but stronger and more resistant to battle damage.

KEY FACTS

13 March 1961
First flight P1127.

13 February 1964
First flight Kestrel for joint UK/US/German evaluation squadron.

31 August 1996
First flight Harrier.

1 April 1969
Delivery to RAF.

September 1969
Ordered by US Marine Corps.

9 November 1979
First flight McDonnell Douglas/BAe YAV-8B.

12 January 1984
Delivery of AV-8B to US Marine Corps.

1 July 1987
Delivery of GR Mk 5 to RAF squadrons.

ABOVE: **The Harrier II is in service with units of the US Marine Corps. The aircraft shown are the single-seat, close-support AV-8B and the two-seat TAV-8B operational trainer.**

LEFT: A Douglas DC-9-15 of Ozark Airlines, USA. The last civil transport designed exclusively by Douglas Aircraft Corporation, the DC-9 short to medium-range airliner proved a bestseller, and has undergone several stretches since this early model appeared in the mid-1960s, powered by two 12,000lb (5,443kg) thrust Pratt & Whitney JT8D-5 turbofans.

BELOW: The McDonnell Douglas DC-10 series 10 flew for the first time on 29 August 1970. Northwest Orient Airlines operated the series 40, a more powerful version of the series 30, on extended-range intercontinental routes. Wingspan 165ft 4⅛in (47.34m), length 182ft 4in (55.50m), height 58ft 1in (17.70m), weight 572,000lb (259,459kg), engines three 49,000lb (22,226kg) thrust General Electric CF6 turbofans, cruising speed 574mph (924kph), range 4,690 miles (7,550km), crew 4, passengers 380.

ABOVE: A McDonnell Douglas Phantom FG1 of No 43 Squadron RAF, based at Leuchars in Scotland, intercepts a Soviet Tupolev Tu-20 long-range reconnaissance aircraft over the North Sea in 1973. Such encounters were commonplace during the Cold War era, the Soviets constantly testing the responses of NATO's defences.

RIGHT: Two Lockheed L-1011-100 TriStars of Middle East airline Saudia, powered by three 42,000lb (19,051kg) or 43,500lb (19,732kg) thrust Rolls-Royce RB211-22 turbofan engines, at London Heathrow Airport in 1976. The TriStar first flew in November 1970 and deliveries began in April 1972.

New materials, new systems and continuing progress in aerodynamics have brought exciting developments in the decades leading to the new century.

Chapter Nine

Advanced Technology

The year 1970 was a figurative watershed. Until then, flying was a novelty for most people; thenceforward it increasingly became the norm, due largely to package holidays that encouraged people to go abroad and to do so cheaply. In the 1970s many aircraft that had been in service during the previous decade were still holding their market share in terms of passengers carried, but there was as great a need for small and medium-sized passenger aeroplanes as for the biggest.

Although not intended for, and not affordable by, package-holiday goers, the aeroplane most esteemed among the whole array was, and still is, that joint venture of the British Aircraft Corporation (BAC) and Aérospatiale – Concorde, the fastest civil aircraft in the world, and the most expensive in which to travel. BAC and Aérospatiale were responsible for the airframe, while Rolls-Royce and SNECMA produced the engines. One of the requirements of the aircraft was that it would be capable of cruising at more than Mach 2, say about 1,332mph (2,143kph). The outcome was a slim, delta-wing shape with four 38,050lb (17,260kg) thrust Olympus 593 turbojets, capable of crossing the Atlantic in under four hours. It made its first flight on 2 March 1969 and began service with British Airways and Air France on 24 May 1976. Concorde had a rival that proved to be no threat

– the Tupolev Tu-144 supersonic airliner, which has much the same configuration (the aircraft is referred to as "Concorde-ski"). Although it beat Concorde into the air, on 31 December 1968, it did not start a passenger service until 1977, and this ceased in 1978 after an aircraft was lost in flight. It was recently dusted off and re-engined as the Tu-144LL in a joint US–Russian research project.

A short-haul airliner that could accommodate 40 passengers was the Yakovlev Yak-40, which first flew on 21 October 1966. Three AI-25 turbofan engines give it a maximum cruising speed of 342mph (550kph). Since its first flight on 21 October 1966, several hundred have been built.

Progress in the performance of military aircraft during the last 35 years or so has been no less impressive. One constant demand is that today's military aircraft have to be versatile. The days of specialised interception or ground-attack fighters and bombers are, generally speaking, at an end.

The warplanes of the last two decades of the 20th century have had to be built such that versions can fire missiles that can be guided against targets in the air or on the surface, and they are exorbitantly expensive to build.

Among the more interesting have been Russia's MiG family of fighters and fighter-bombers. The MiG-23/MiG-27 "Flogger" was the first to employ variable-geometry swing-wings (with three sweep angles), and it has a hinged ventral tailfin that can

be folded sideways to avoid scraping it on the ground when taking off or landing. It enjoys a combination of good short-field performance with acceleration and high speed, but it turns relatively poorly, which is a disadvantage in air combat.

The MiG-29 "Fulcrum", first flown in October 1977, was designed as an agile air combat fighter to counter the USA's McDonnell Douglas F-16 and General Dynamics F-18. One of its most remarkable features was its helmet-mounted sight, which allowed missiles to be launched at high (45-degree) off-boresight angles. The MiG-31 "Foxhound" is a two-seater interceptor. Developed from the MiG-25, it is

ABOVE: **The Grumman F-14 Tomcat variable-sweep, carrier-borne air-superiority fighter for the US Navy, powered by two 20,900lb (9,480kg) thrust Pratt & Whitney TF30 turbofans, made its first flight in December 1970.**

ABOVE: **The Airbus A310-300 is an extended-range version of the A310, carrying 220 passengers over a range of 5,000-6,000 miles (8,045–9,654km) with either General Electric or Pratt & Whitney engines.**

MILESTONES

1979

Gossamer Albatross, designed by Dr Paul MacReady of the USA, wins the £100,000 Kremer Prize for the first flight across the Channel by a human-powered aircraft.

1982

An RAF Vulcan bomber operation against Port Stanley during the Falklands conflict is the longest operational sortie ever flown.

1988

The Antonov An-225 Mriya transport aircraft, the world's largest aeroplane, makes its maiden flight from Kiev.

AIR STRIKES

specifically designed to counter cruise missiles. Operational from 1982, it has a multiple-target kill capability and its radar is claimed by the Russians to be able to detect Stealth aircraft.

Another Russian family of fighter aircraft, designed by Sukhoi, include some extremely useful types. The Su-27 "Flanker" is huge, long-range, very capable and carries up to 10 air-to-air missiles (AAMs). Developments of it, the Su-35 and Su-37 (fitted with thrust-vectoring engine nozzles), have displayed amazing manoeuvrability at recent air shows, making Western fighter designers stop and think. Not that the West has been slow in introducing

highly capable and often unusual warplanes. Sweden's Saab J37 Viggen, for example, first flown in 1967, is a canard aircraft and has interesting features that enable it to operate from short stretches of highway and assume many roles: strike, reconnaissance, interception or training. Using reverse thrusters, its landing run needs only 1,700ft (518m).

Like the MiG-23/MiG-27, the Grumman F-14A Tomcat is a variable-sweep aircraft, and is used mainly as a fleet air defence interceptor by the US Navy. Its radar can detect targets at over 230 miles (370km) and can track up to 24 targets and guide missiles at six targets

simultaneously. It is also a formidable opponent in close combat.

Another variable-sweep combat aircraft is the Panavia Tornado, produced during the 1970s by a European consortium of Britain, Germany and Italy. One version is optimised for the interdiction strike role, in which it is capable of blind, first-pass attack at over 920mph (1,480kph) at sea level, and another is an interceptor combining high speed with long endurance, capable of operating autonomously far away from base in the teeth of electronic jamming. It represents not only a shift to all-round aircraft but also to joint design and manufacture.

Both versions of the Tornado took part in the Gulf War of 1991, when a coalition of Western and Arab forces joined ranks to liberate Kuwait from an invasion by its neighbour, Iraq. Against an estimated 7,000 SAMs and 9,000–10,000 anti-aircraft guns, as well as the Iraqi Air Force, the coalition sent wave after wave of land- and carrier-based attack aircraft, which were escorted by fighters and assisted by dedicated radar jamming and SAM suppression warplanes. Within 72 hours the Iraqi defence system was rendered almost completely impotent.

Prominent among the carrier-based aircraft were Sea Harriers, a variant of the first short take-off and vertical landing (STOVL) type to enter service with any air

213

LEFT: In September 1992 the world's largest aircraft, Antonov's An-225 Mriya, cast its shadow over the Farnborough Air Show, England. Designed to carry a Buran spacecraft on its back, the Mriya had a maximum take-off weight of 1,322,750lb (600,000kg) and was powered by six 51,660lb (23,433kg) thrust Lotarev D-18T three-shaft turbofans.

force in the world. The first production Harrier made its maiden flight on 31 August 1967. Sea Harriers had their combat debut in 1982, when a British task force was sent by sea to the South Atlantic to recover the Falkland Islands. The Harrier can perform unconventional manoeuvres with thrust-vectoring, but this was never used. However, the ability of the Sea Harriers to land vertically allowed them to operate in weather conditions that grounded other carrier aircraft. Armed with the latest AIM-9L Sidewinder air-to-air missiles, the Sea Harrier performed superlatively. The Sea Harriers of the British task force had an overwhelming victory.

Other Western warplanes that witnessed combat during the latter part of the 20th century include the ubiquitous McDonnell Douglas F-4 Phantom, the F-15 Eagle and F-18 Hornet from the same US company and the Lockheed Martin (formerly General Dynamics) F-16 Fighting Falcon. The Phantom, originally a carrier-fighter but later developed into a multi-role combat aircraft, fought against a variety of MiGs in the Arab-Israeli Wars and also in the skies over Southeast Asia.

Ageing now, it was a fast two-seater (with a weapons systems operator in the back seat), could carry an enormous weapons load externally, and incorporated a weapons system that was better, because it was more flexible, than any other war-plane of its era. Although the Phantom first flew in May 1958, the F-4G Wild Weasel version hunted for and killed SAM radars in the 1991 Gulf War.

Alongside it in that conflict flew the F-15 Eagle, whose combat debut came, however, while in service with the Israeli Air Force, against Syrian MiG-21s in June 1979. Later it was responsible for the first ever defeat of a MiG-25 interceptor. The Eagle has proved a superlative air combat fighter that for years far outclassed anything in the Russian stable in both performance and manoeuvrability.

Also engaged in both conflicts in the Middle East was the F-16, a small single-engined, lightweight and much cheaper fighter of unparalleled agility, with com-puterised fly-by-wire avionics and capable of sustaining a 9g turn in close combat. As with other aircraft, versions of the F-16 have also carried out bombing raids, testament

once again to the much-needed versatility of modern combat aircraft.

When the F-16 was first developed it was in competition for the role of new lightweight fighter. The loser, the Northrop F-17, was adopted by the US Navy as a multi-role fighter to supplement the Tomcat and replace the Phantom and the also-ageing A-4 Corsair in the attack role. Having been navalised by McDonnell Douglas, it emerged eventually as the F/A-18 Hornet, which was more carrier-capable than the F-16, offered greater development potential and, for operations far out over the ocean, twin-engined safety. It was also the first of the advanced "glass-cockpit" fighters, in which the old-fashioned dial instruments were replaced by screens on which all relevant information could be called up at the touch of a button. As such, it set the trend for all future fighter cockpits. The F-18 went into combat in the Gulf, launched from US Navy carriers.

STEALTH TECHNOLOGY

The Gulf War also saw the operational value of stealth technology, which

includes careful airframe shaping, internal carriage of all fuel and weapons, curved inlet ducts to shield the compressor face of the engine, the extensive use of radar-absorbent materials, minimum active radar emissions, and the reduction of the heat signature from the engines. The angular black Lockheed F-117 Nighthawk made its combat debut over Panama in 1989. In the Gulf just over a year later it made precision attacks against targets in Baghdad against modern air defence systems. Practically the first the Iraqis knew of its presence was when the bombs hit the targets.

Stealth will exert a decisive influence on future air warfare for those few nations able to afford it. The Northrop B-2A Spirit stealth bomber has a weird, all-wing shape, and its tiny radar signature and diffuse exhaust make it difficult to detect by conventional means, and almost impossible to intercept. Stealth concepts are included in many other warplanes, including the Lockheed F-22 Raptor. Called the fighter of the future, it combines stealth with supercruise and thrust-vectoring, making it as good in beyond-visual-range combat as it is in the close dogfight.

In Europe, the latest co-operative type, the Eurofighter, is being produced by Britain, Germany, Italy and Spain. It will reach Mach 2 and climb to 35,000ft (10,668m) in 2min 30sec. One of these has been carrying out flight trials to assess air-frame characteristics at supersonic speeds, and has completed over 100 sorties. The Eurofighter project is the largest procurement programme Britain's Ministry of Defence has ever supported, it having invested £15 billion in the scheme and ordered 232 of these fighters.

Meanwhile, the world's biggest airliner, the Boeing 777-300, which is more than 33ft (10m) longer than the 777-200, was rolled out in October 1997 and began a seven-month flight test programme. It will seat between 368 and 550 passengers.

RIGHT: **Continuing a long family line, the Dassault Mirage 2000 can be used for air-superiority/defence, long-range strike, multi-role, reconnaissance and electronic warfare duties. Seen here are the 2000B operational trainer (nearest) and two 2000C single-seat air defence versions. Both have the SNECMA M53 12,230/14,455lb (5,548/6,557kg) thrust engine.**

Military transport aircraft are as important as passenger-carriers. The frequency of minor wars in the past four decades has necessitated the speedy movement of troops, usually from the USA or a former colonialist continental European country. In consequence, huge carriers of soldiers and cargo, including tanks, other vehicles and artillery, have been in demand.

NATO has to be the world's police, able quickly to staunch the outbreaks of minor wars. During the Gulf War, for example, the Coalition effort was underpinned by the biggest strategic airlift in history.

The requirement is for aeroplanes big enough to carry up to 400 troops or a vast amount of cargo, or smaller numbers and quantities of both. Typical cargoes would comprise motor vehicles, tanks, artillery and even small helicopters. They must cruise at no less than Mach 0.75 and have a range of at least 2,500 miles (4,022km). Loading and unloading has to be quick. A high wing and low-slung fuselage are essential in order to give clearance for moving cargo in and out. Unlike civil aircraft, they need missile jammers and radar warning sensors.

SPEED AND MOBILITY

For the oncoming years the major NATO countries need a strategy that will focus on member nations' military strengths and enable them to be ready to move anywhere to meet any challenge. Speed of reaction and instant mobility are the touchstones. Taking Britain as an example, one possibility could be a carrier-based air group comprising Fleet Air Arm Sea Harriers and RAF Harrier 7s, escorted by nuclear-powered submarines armed with Tomahawk cruise missiles. Another expeditionary force could comprise troops and tanks backed by air power and some form of anti-ballistic missile protection. For this, strategic lift aircraft such as the American

McDonnell Douglas C-17 Globemaster II, able to carry heavy armoured vehicles, would be necessary.

In air combat, perhaps the future lies with the Unmanned Combat Air Vehicle (UCAV). This would have a new air-breathing engine, a third, steering, wing at the front to increase manoeuvrability, and reach a speed of Mach 15. Its acceleration would be 20g, which is twice that of any present aircraft, and it would be guided towards targets by the global satellite positioning system (GPS). It could enter service by 2005. A second, smaller version under development could be launched from current bombers, which would increase the UCAV's range.

BIGGER JUMBOS

Since 1918 nobody has been certain whether another major war would interrupt the pursuits of peace. When, in the last two decades, international collaboration in a new aircraft, whether military or civil, has been considered, the contrivances and artful manipulation to gain desired ends has taken as long as the ultimate engineering work from design to production. That Concorde came to fruition and the Eurofighter is at last on its way to the same happy conclusion are victories against the odds. Now, under the aegis of Airbus Industrie, based at Toulouse in France, the European aerospace industry is negotiating over a fitting commercial flagship for its most prominent members – a £5 billion project, the Airbus A3XXX.

When built, it would be the world's biggest commercial aircraft, with a maximum capacity of more than 800 passengers on certain "sardine" routes, such as the Japanese short-haul ones, and is planned to enter service in 2003. In it lies the future of "jumbo" jets.

The A3XXX could be the template for the future of the European defence, as well as the aerospace, industry. The expectant participants feel that growing bigger in aerospace and in defence electronics is the only option, given the competitors being formed in the USA (the merger of Boeing and McDonnell Douglas, for example), as well as the need for efficiencies of scale as post-Cold War budgets keep shrinking. The French and German governments

have told their companies "to rationalise or die" and Britain has followed suit.

The restructuring of Airbus Industrie into a single company is being considered. If this occurs, the French, German and British partners will be pressed to add their integrated defence aerospace activities, to form one European aerospace company.

One means by which a single European aerospace company could be formed would be by turning the four participants in the Eurofighter consortium into a single company. The partners' non-European defence activities could then be injected into the new company, added to France's Dassault, and the whole lot then merged with Airbus.

At this point, where commercial interest overrides the technical aspects, there is an even greater problem to face, a political one: workers would have to be made redundant in France and Germany, where unemployment is already high.

Despite all the difficulties, the odds are in favour of a satisfactory agreement, which would enable a new Airbus to compete successfully against the USA's vast defence industry.

ABOVE: **In RAF service the Boeing E-3A Airborne Warning and Control System (AWACS) is known as the Sentry AEW1. The wingtip pods carry electronic support measures (ESM). The 707-derived aircraft, which has served with NATO since 1983, is powered by four 24,000lb (10,886kg) thrust General Electric/SNECMA CFM-56 turbofans.**

LEFT: Sweden's Saab AJ37 Viggen (Thunderbolt) canard delta, seen here with a large underfuselage drop tank, is powered by a 26,000lb (11,794kg) thrust Flygmotor RM8 bypass engine, a unique afterburner-equipped supersonic engine developed from the Pratt & Whitney JT8D, originally designed for subsonic airliners.

TOP RIGHT: Northrop's F-5F was rolled out in 1974. Powered by two 3,500lb (1,588kg) thrust General Electric J85-GE-21 engines, it was armed with a 20mm cannon and two AIM-9 Sidewinder air-to-air missiles.

RIGHT: Panavia Tornado GR1s of No 9 Squadron, RAF, refuel from an Italian Air Force Boeing KC-135R. While Britain prefers the probe-and-drogue system, other forces have the US-developed flying boom system, so a hybrid version is used for compatability.

LEFT: Powered by a pair of 11,200lb (5,080kg) thrust Rolls-Royce Spey Mk101 turbojets, the Hawker Siddeley Buccaneer S2 initially entered service with the Royal Navy in 1965 as a carrier-borne low-level-strike aircraft, but in 1970 the type was also adopted by the RAF; hence the variety of markings in this formation. It was finally retired from the RAF in 1994.

BELOW: A formidable close-support attack aircraft, the Fairchild Republic A-10A Thunderbolt II first entered service with the USAF's Tactical Air Command in 1976. In addition to the 30mm General Electric GAU-8A Avenger multi-barrel cannon in its nose, it can carry 16,000lb (7,258kg) of bombs and missiles on eleven external stores stations.

RIGHT: Performing the same role as the USAF's A-10A, the Soviet Air Force's Sukhoi Su-25 close-support aircraft entered service in 1980. Claimed to be the world's most difficult aircraft to shoot down, the heavily armoured Su-25 is powered by two 9,037lb (4,099kg) thrust R-95Sh engines, and can carry a maximum external load of 9,548lb (4,330kg).

BELOW: Lockheed's C-5A Galaxy long-range logistics transport entered service with the USAF's Military Airlift Command in 1969.
Wingspan 222ft 8½in (67.88m), length 247ft 10in (75.54m) height 65ft 1½in (19.85m), weight 769,000lb (348,810kg), engines four 41,100lb (18,642kg) General Electric TF-39 turbofans, maximum speed 571mph (919kph), range 3,749 miles (6,033km), crew 5.

Concorde

The design, construction and long commercial service of the world's first successful supersonic transport aeroplane is a story of great technological achievement and outstanding international co-operation, with regard to both the airframe and its mighty Olympus engines.

"The first supersonic passenger service began on 21 January 1976"

What is the predominant factor that sells an airline's tickets in preference to its competitors'? It is not the superior comfort of the seating, quality of on-board meals, film shows or piped music. It is speed: passengers give priority to the service that will take them to their destination most quickly. About Concorde, one has to add "if they can afford it".

By the mid-1960s the time for a supersonic airliner had arrived. Aircraft constructors and airlines had to decide first whether people would want to travel at such a phenomenal speed – going superfast suggests danger to the general public when associated with cars, motorcycles and fighter aircraft.

Would the huge selling price occasioned by the high development and production costs make it impossible for airlines to operate supersonic services profitably? Finally, a slender delta wing is built for speed and needs a long runway for high-speed take-off and landing, adding another consideration. The decision was taken to go ahead.

Bristol Aircraft, which was absorbed by the new British Aircraft Corporation (BAC) in 1960, and Sud-Aviation, which became Aérospatiale, began their studies and both decided on a slim, delta-wing design with a passenger capacity of about 100. Both also recognised that their Governments were unlikely to subsidise research and construction of the aircraft. The obvious answer was collaboration.

On 29 November 1962 the two essential agreements were signed: the British and French Governments would put up the money; and four companies, British Aircraft Corporation, Rolls-Royce, Sud-Aviation and the Société National d'Etude et de Construction de Moteurs d'Aviation (SNECMA), would jointly attend to engine and airframe design and development. The following year a basic design for a Mach 2.2 (1,332mph/2,144kph) aeroplane cruising at 63,000 ft (19,202m) was decided on. At that speed, new special and expensive alloys would not be needed for the high temperatures generated if it was designed for Mach 3 operations.

The first prototype Concorde flew on 2 March 1969. The first supersonic passenger service began on 21 January 1976, with Air France on the Paris–Dakar–Rio de Janeiro service and British Airways on the London–Bahrain route. Air France next launched Concorde on the Paris–Caracas route.

On 27 May two Concordes, one aircraft displaying British Airways livery and the other that of Air France, arrived together at Dulles Airport, Washington DC, making the inaugural supersonic debut on the London–Washington and Paris–Washington services.

"The sonic boom has not wrought destruction"

LEFT: With its nose drooped and visor lowered, a British Airways Concorde touches down at Bournemouth (Hurn) Airport in southern England in 1996. Its extraordinary low-speed aerodynamics give it a relatively short landing run.

ABOVE: **Two world-famous aviation spectacles in one. An impressive study of Concorde leading the RAF's famous Red Arrows aerobatic team in a formation flight.**

Concorde's operations have been amply rewarded, all flights being filled to between 80 per cent and 85 per cent capacity. At the end of the first year's operation the London–Washington service achieved a 90 per cent load factor. Concorde's payload/range performance has been better than expected, but its maximum cruising speed has proved to be Mach 2.02.

Before the aircraft was even built, dire predictions about its adverse effects on the environment were made: its sonic boom would cause buildings to fall; pollution of the upper atmosphere would further increase the Earth's temperature and contribute to global warming, melting the polar ice. The facts are that aircraft produce less pollution than any other form of transport, and the sonic boom has not wrought destruction. Concorde is also an easy and pleasant aircraft for its pilots to handle. ⟩

ABOVE: **Although it bore a close superficial resemblance to Concorde, Russia's Tupolev Tu-144 was both aerodynamically and technologically inferior, and saw only limited service.**

LEFT: **Concorde 002, the British-built prototype, approaches completion at the British Aircraft Corporation's works at Filton, Bristol, in 1968. First flown in April 1969, this aircraft is now preserved at the Fleet Air Arm Museum, Yeovilton, Somerset, as part of the Science Museum's Air Transport Collection.**

ABOVE: A McDonnell Douglas F/A-18 Hornet strike fighter of the US Marine Corps over desert terrain in the western USA. The Hornet's night-strike capability enables it to mount continuous sorties by day and night, and it has found buyers worldwide. Two 16,000lb (7,258kg) thrust General Electric F404-GE-400 turbofans give it a maximum speed of 1,190mph (1,915kph) at 45,000ft (13,716m).

LEFT: A Dassault Super Etendard transonic shipboard strike fighter of Flottille 11F, operating from the French carrier *Foch* in the late 1970s. Powered by an 11,025lb (5,000kg) thrust SNECMA Atar 8K-50 turbojet, the first Super Etendard, a converted Etendard IVM, flew in October 1974.

CENTRE RIGHT: A McDonnell Douglas F-15 Eagle of the 5th Fighter Interceptor Squadron, USAF, based at Minot Air Force Base, North Dakota, USA, displays its tail colours. It has AIM-9 Sidewinder missiles underwing and four AIM-7 Sparrows on its fuselage flanks.

RIGHT: The four-man crew of the US Navy's Grumman EA-6B Prowler carrier-borne electronic warfare aircraft comprised a pilot and three operators for its electronic countermeasures equipment. It was powered by a pair of 11,200lb (5,080kg) thrust Pratt & Whitney J52-P-408 turbojets, which gave it a maximum speed of 610mph (981kph) at sea level.

LEFT: This General Dynamics F-16A Fighting Falcon of the USAF's 496 Tactical Fighter Squadron, 50th Tactical Fighter Wing, is carrying two long-range tanks instead of some of the great variety of weaponry it would usually carry on its underwing pylons. Its 14,670lb (6,654kg) thrust Pratt & Whitney F100-PW-200 turbofan gives the F-16 a maximum speed of 1,350mph (2,172kph) at 40,000ft (12,192m).

ABOVE: Developed from the Lockheed U-2, the TR-1A high-altitude reconnaissance and stand-off battlefield surveillance aircraft first flew in August 1981, powered by a 17,000lb (7,711kg) thrust Pratt & Whitney J75-P-13B turbojet. It carried a sensing system to locate and identify hostile radar sites and direct strike aircraft or missiles against them.

RIGHT: Lockheed's U-2R was designed to carry nearly two tons of sensors or experiments in interchangeable noses, wing pods and bays for high-altitude strategic or weather reconnaissance. Heavier and of greater span than the earlier U-2s, it retained the 17,000lb (7,711kg) thrust Pratt & Whitney J-75-P-13B engine.

LEFT: The ultimate high-performance strategic reconnaissance aircraft was the Lockheed SR-71, the first Mach 3 aeroplane to enter service with the USAF. Able to operate for sustained periods at Mach 3.5 at 85,000ft (25,908m), it first flew in December 1964, entering service in January 1966.

LEFT: The Airbus A310, represented here by an aircraft of Air Niugini, is a short/medium-range widebody airliner typically accommodating 220 passengers in a two-class layout. First flown in April 1982, it began commercial operations a year later. It can be powered by 52,000 or 56,000lb (23,587 or 25,401kg) thrust Pratt & Whitney, or 53,500 or 59,000lb (24,268 or 26,762 kg) thrust General Electric, turbofans.

BELOW LEFT: Sukhoi's extraordinarily agile Su-27 long-range air-superiority fighter was designed to be inherently unstable, and is controlled via a quadruple redundant analogue fly-by-wire control system. Its two 17,857lb (8,100kg) thrust Lyulka AL-31F turbofans give it a top speed of 1,550mph (2,494kph) at 39,370ft (12,000m).

RIGHT: The futuristic Beech Model 2000 Starship executive transport, powered by a pair of 1,200shp Pratt & Whitney Canada PT6A-67 propeller-turbines driving pusher propellers, made its maiden flight in February 1986. **Wingspan** 54ft 4¼in (16.58m), **length** 46ft 1in (14.05m), **height** 13ft (3.96m), **weight** 14,400lb (6,531kg), **engines** two 1,200hp Pratt & Whitney Canada PT6 turboprops, **cruising speed** 350mph (563kph), **range** 1,865 miles (3,001km), **crew** 2, **passengers** 8.

BELOW: The USSR's Tupolev Tu-160, the heaviest and most powerful combat aircraft of all time, was a response to the USAF Rockwell B-1. It was powered by four 30,843lb (13,990kg) thrust Kuznetsov NK-321 three-shaft turbofans, the most powerful military engine in history. Almost twice as fast as the B-1B at high altitude, the Tu-160 had a maximum speed of 1,243mph (2000kph), or Mach 1.88.

LEFT: Boeing's 747-400, seen here in the colours of Garuda Indonesia, is a greatly improved variant of the -300, with a significant saving in weight and increased-span wings with 6ft (1.8m) high winglets at their tips. **Wingspan** 211ft (64.31m), **length** 231ft 10in (70.66m), **height** 63ft 5in (19.33m), **weight** 836,000lb (379,201kg), **engines** four 58,000lb (26,308kg) thrust class TRS Rolls-Royce RB-211-524 or Pratt & Whitney PW4056 or SNECMA/General Electric CF6-80 turbofans, **maximum speed** 612 mph (985kph), **range** 8,406 miles (13,528km), **crew** 2, **passengers** 412.

ABOVE RIGHT: **First flown in August 1984, the ATR 42 regional airliner or cargo transport was the product of Avions de Transport Régional, formed by Aérospatiale of France and Alenia of Italy. In its basic version it accommodates 48 passengers, and is powered by a pair of 2,000shp Pratt & Whitney Canada PW120 turboprops.**

RIGHT: Embraer of Brazil first flew its EMB-120 Brasilia regional airliner and cargo transport in July 1983, and it went into service in August 1985. Powered by two Pratt & Whitney Canada PW118 turboprops, it can carry 30 passengers at a maximum cruising speed of 340mph (547kph).

LEFT: The Airbus A300-600R extended-range airliner has a range of 4,050nm with 266 passengers under the power of two Pratt & Whitney or General Electric turbofans. This variant has a 6,150-litre fuel tank in the tailplane, with a computerised fuel-transfer system to provide active centre-of-gravity control.

Stealth

Stealth, with its implications of furtive malfeasance, guile and general ill-purpose, is a stunningly appropriate choice of name for the aircraft that bears it, the Lockheed F-117 Nighthawk. Its design has an instantly intimidating impact on the eye; and rightly so, for here is an aircraft that is able to penetrate hostile airspace where no other has been able to do so. Its fuselage and wings, all plane surfaces set at cunningly calculated angles, form a carapace of material that deflects radar beams in a way that renders it invisible. Not only can it venture into hostile areas without fear of detection, but if it encounters defending fighters it can also engage them.

Doing the unexpected is the essence of victory in war. Without betraying its presence, the Northrop B2 Stealth bomber could drop a nuclear bomb capable of destruction vastly out of proportion to the size of the aircraft.

Stealth's successor, the Unmanned Combat Air Vehicle (UCAV), is already under development. Its surfaces of the same material, instead of being angular, might be rounded and equally baffling to radar. Real-time datalinks between operators on the ground and the weapon system enable it to attack without risking air crews' lives. It will be able to make deep strikes into enemy territory with impunity.

A second, smaller variant is envisaged for launching from current conventionally crewed bombers. Once it is over a hostile area, a constantly updated map of known defences will be used to pinpoint targets. Virtual-reality technology and even holographic displays are foreseen as means for operators on the ground to control it. When it has launched its payload, it will be brought back to base and landed. A feature of pilotless aircraft that seems incongruously humanitarian in the context of savage future action against an enemy is that a stealth aeroplane's performance will not have to be reduced in order to save a pilot's life.

INSET, RIGHT: **The Nighthawk looks far from elegant on the ground. Note the screened engine intakes and the glazed panels coated with gold to conduct radar energy into the airframe. Official public unveiling of the bomber did not take place until 21 April 1990.**

BELOW: **The Northrop B-2A is the result of many years research by that company into the feasibility of "flying wings". Built as a stealth bomber the advanced aerodynamic airframe is constructed mainly of carbon fibre and other composite materials. It is powered by four General Electric F118-GE-1110 turbofans, carries a crew of two and is armed with conventional, laser-guided and nuclear weapons.**

RIGHT: **The F-117's fuselage and wings are shaped from a combination of multi-faceted plain surfaces to dissipate radar energy away from its source. The entire airframe is sprayed with radar-absorbent material, and regular resprays ensure that the coating is kept in top condition.**

ABOVE: Saab's contender for the regional airliner market is the 2000, seating 50–58 passengers and powered by a pair of 4,152shp Allison AE 2100A turboprops driving six-blade composite propellers. It first flew in March 1992, entering service two years later.

LEFT: Embraer's 50-passenger EMB145 regional twin-jet made its maiden flight in August 1995, and it entered service with launch customer Continental Express in April 1997 as the RJ-145. Two 7,040lb (3,193kg) thrust Allison Ae3007A-1 turbofans give it a cruising speed of 507mph (815kph) at 35,000ft (10,668m).

ABOVE: Indonesia's IPTN N-250 regional airliner has a pair of 3,271shp Allison AE2100C turboprops driving six-blade composite propellers, cruises at 380mph (611kph) and carries 64–68 passengers over a range of 920 miles (1,480km). It first flew on 10 August 1995.

RIGHT: A mid-size corporation jet and crew trainer, the sleek Learjet 45 was rolled out in September 1995. Powered by a pair of 3,500lb (1,588kg) thrust Allied Signal TFE731-20 turbofans, it has accommodation for ten passengers and a maximum cruising speed of 534mph (859kph).

Lockheed Martin F-22A Raptor

The USAF Advanced Technical Fighter (ATF) has been developed and built by Lockheed-Martin and Boeing.

SPECIFICATION
Wingspan
44ft 6in (13.56m)

Length
62ft 6in (19.05m)

Height
17ft 9in (5.41m)

Weight
*33,000lb
(14,969kg) empty
55,000lb
(24,948kg) loaded*

Engines
*Two Pratt & Whitney
F119-100 turbofan
with afterburner*

Although a sophisticated missile-equipped "stealth" fighter, the F-22 is fitted with an M61A2 Vulcan 20mm cannon for air combat and ground attack.

The pilot is seated on a McDonnell/Douglas ACES II zero-zero ejection seat under a single-piece canopy. A sidestick control, on the right-hand side of the cockpit, operates the computer-controlled "fly-by-wire" flight systems. All flight information is displayed to the pilot on six liquid-crystal multi-function display screens.

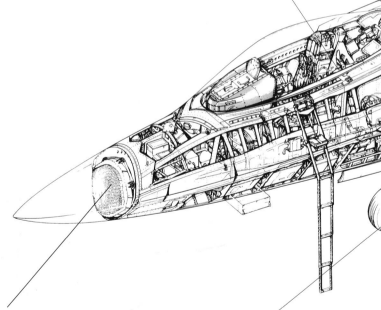

A side bay on each side of the fuselage houses an AIM-9M Sidewinder missile. The main bay, in the underside of the fuselage, houses four AIM-120A advanced range air-to-air missiles (ARAAM).

The nose cone houses a multimode radar scanner, and the rest of the nose section, ahead of the cockpit, contains highly sophisticated electronic equipment.

The engine air intakes are shaped to deflect radar waves without reducing engine efficiency. The edges of the intakes are manufactured from carbon fibre composite to enhance the "stealth" effect.

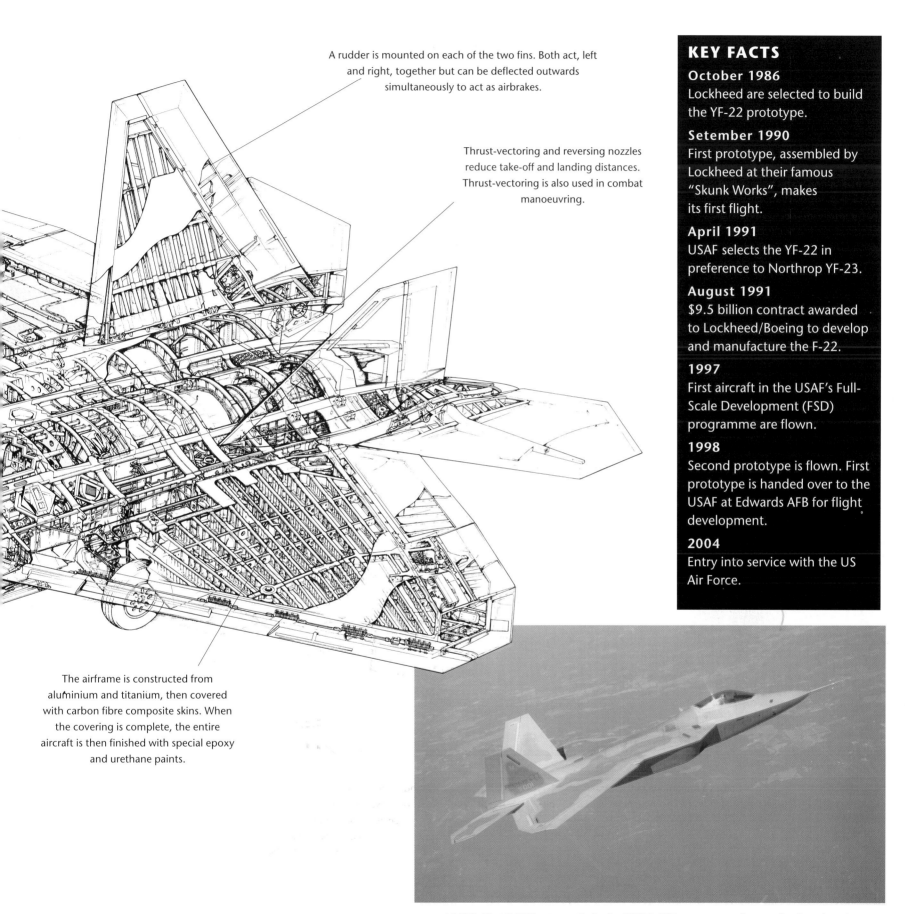

A rudder is mounted on each of the two fins. Both act, left and right, together but can be deflected outwards simultaneously to act as airbrakes.

Thrust-vectoring and reversing nozzles reduce take-off and landing distances. Thrust-vectoring is also used in combat manoeuvring.

The airframe is constructed from aluminium and titanium, then covered with carbon fibre composite skins. When the covering is complete, the entire aircraft is then finished with special epoxy and urethane paints.

KEY FACTS

October 1986
Lockheed are selected to build the YF-22 prototype.

Setember 1990
First prototype, assembled by Lockheed at their famous "Skunk Works", makes its first flight.

April 1991
USAF selects the YF-22 in preference to Northrop YF-23.

August 1991
$9.5 billion contract awarded to Lockheed/Boeing to develop and manufacture the F-22.

1997
First aircraft in the USAF's Full-Scale Development (FSD) programme are flown.

1998
Second prototype is flown. First prototype is handed over to the USAF at Edwards AFB for flight development.

2004
Entry into service with the US Air Force.

ABOVE: **First F-22 Raptor to fly in the USAF's FSD programme is a production aircraft.**

LEFT: Sweden's Industrigruppen JAS was founded in 1981 to develop and produce the JAS 39 Gripen lightweight multirole fighter, maritime or ground-attack and reconnaissance aircraft, powered by a 12,140lb (5,507kg) thrust Volvo RM12 turbofan. The prototype first flew on 9 December 1988.

ABOVE: The Sukhoi Su-37 is the designation of the strike variant for export of the Su-35/Su-27M advanced air-superiority fighter. A pair of 30,865lb (14,000kg) thrust Saturn AL-31FM turbofans give it a maximum speed of 1,553mph (2,499kph).

ABOVE: British Aerospace produced the Experimental Aircraft Programme (EAP) demonstrator to prove the advanced technology of the Eurofighter EF2000, meeting NATO's requirement for an agile single-seat air-superiority fighter. While the EAP, first flown in August 1986, had a pair of Rolls-Royce RB199 bypass turbofans, Eurofighter has two 20,250lb (9,185kg) thrust Eurojet EJ200s.

LEFT: First flown on 25 October 1991, the Airbus A340 long-range airliner entered service in March 1993. Carrying 250–350 passengers at a cruising speed of Mach 0.82, it is powered by four 31,200lb (14,152kg) thrust CFM International CFM56-5C turbofans.

RIGHT: Boeing's 777-200 long-range widebody airliner, powered by two turbofan engines in the 80,000lb (36,288kg) thrust class, can carry 300–400 passengers at a cruising speed at Mach 0.84 over a range of 4,520–5,500 miles (7,273–8,850km).

Chapter Ten

The Final Frontier

People began imagining the ultimate flight experience – travelling in space – centuries ago, with the Moon as the favourite destination. Dreamers and scientific writers suggested various means of propulsion into space, including waterspouts, evaporating dew, flying swans and even waxed feathers. French writer Jules Verne, in his 1865 story *From the Earth to the Moon,* chose the space cannon as the means to launch a craft to the Moon, uncannily siting it in Florida, close to where US astronauts would set out for the Moon a century later.

The truth is that only one method of space propulsion can work: only rocket motors can develop sufficient power to accelerate objects to the speed they require to overcome the Earth's gravity and get into space – at least 17,000mph (27,358kph). Only rocket motors can work in space, because they do not, like jet engines, rely on the oxygen in the atmosphere to burn their fuel. Rockets carry their own oxygen supply and so can work in airless space.

Although the rocket was invented by the Chinese in around AD1200, it was not until the latter part of the 19th century that anyone began to wonder if rocket power could be used for space travel. Russian scientist Konstantin Eduardovich Tsiolkovsky, born in 1857, became convinced of it while he was still in his twenties, and spent the next quarter of a century

working out the principles of space rocket flight. In 1903, months before the Wright Brothers achieved their epic flights, Tsiolkovsky set out, in an article for a scientific journal, the basic requirements. Much more powerful rocket propellants than gunpowder, used in the military rockets of the day, would be needed for spaceflight. Also, no single rocket would be able to achieve the speed necessary to travel into space; it could never have a high enough power-to-weight ratio. A space rocket would need to consist of a number of rocket units, or stages, joined together, and these would have to fire and separate in turn. By losing weight at each stage, the final unit could achieve the necessary speed. This is the concept of the multi-stage, or step rocket, which is used in all space launches.

A scientist most influential in developing propulsion capable of launching an object into space was the American Robert Hutchings Goddard (1882–1945), who built and fired the first rocket using liquid propellants. Although his rocket, burning gasoline and liquid oxygen, fired for only a few seconds, and rose just 185ft (56m), it paved the way for the future, being the type of rocket that has since carried men to the Moon and instruments to the planets. By 1937 Goddard's rockets were reaching speeds of 700mph (1,126kph) and heights of 1.7 miles (2.7km).

Unbeknown to him, and to most of the rest of the world, Goddard's work was being eclipsed in Germany. On the Baltic

island of Peenemunde, a team under the direction of the brilliant Wernher von Braun was developing a series of advanced liquid-propellant rockets. By the time the Second World War broke out in 1939, von Braun's team were working toward a practical ballistic missile capable of delivering a high-explosive warhead over a distance of several hundred miles. The first successful firing of this weapon, designated A-4, (V-2) took place in October 1942.

At the end of the Second World War, as part of their booty, the USA and the USSR shipped unused V-2s to their respective countries, taking with them members of the German rocket development team.

ABOVE: **This head-on view emphasises the small wingspan of the Space Shuttle Orbiter compared with its bulky fuselage, which incorporates a large payload bay.**

ABOVE: **The first Orbiter to fly in the atmosphere was *Enterprise*, which was used for the Approach and Landing Test programme in 1977. These began with unmanned captive flights, with the Orbiter, fitted with a streamline tail fairing, carried pick-a-back on the Boeing 747 Shuttle Carrier Aircraft.**

Milestones

1961

Russian Yuri Gagarin becomes the first man in space, orbiting the Earth in *Vostok 1*.

1969

US astronaut Neil Armstrong sets foot on the Moon from *Apollo 11's* lunar module.

1981

Space shuttle *Columbia* is launched from Kennedy Space Center on the first shuttle mission.

Wernher von Braun went to the USA and directed further rocket research at the US Army's White Sands Proving Ground in New Mexico. In 1949 his team fired the world's first multi-stage rocket, Bumper. Later flights took place from a new launch site at Cape Canaveral in Florida, a site that would develop into the famous Kennedy Space Center.

THE SPACE RACE

During the following decades of Cold War between the West and the East, many more rocket launches took place from within the USA and the USSR (at Kapustin Yar near Volvograd), leading to a race into space between the world's two greatest powers. With the *Sputnik* launches the Russians won the first heat, and also the second when, on 12 April 1961, Russian pilot Yuri Gagarin sped into orbit to become the first astronaut, or cosmonaut as the Russians call their space travellers. He circled the Earth once in the capsule *Vostok 1* on a flight lasting 108 minutes.

During the next fifteen years both countries rocketed men into space with great frequency, the highlight being the Moon landing by the lunar module of the American *Apollo 11* spacecraft on 20 July 1969. The words of the first man to walk on the Moon, Neil Armstrong, are engraved in history: "That's one small step for a man," he said, "one giant leap for mankind."

The three-man crew were accommodated in a cone-shaped, pressurised command module. This was connected with a cylindrical service module housing equipment, propellants and a powerful engine. The two sections together formed the Apollo mother ship, the Command and Service Modules (CSM). The third section was the lunar module. With the crew on board, the CSM weighed close to 45 tons. To lift such a weight and accelerate it to the 25,000mph (40,230kph) necessary to escape from the Earth's gravity required a massive launch vehicle, the *Saturn V*. This leviathan of a rocket, which stood 36 storeys high on the launch pad and weighed nearly 3,000 tons, was the last in the Saturn series of heavy launch vehicles developed by von Braun's team at the Marshall Flight Center in Alabama.

Over the next two and a half years US astronauts embarked on five more successful landing missions, and there were three further missions planned, but budget cutbacks and dwindling public interest (by then a Moon shot was no longer big news) forced their cancellation. There was a lot of surplus hardware, and two further missions were dreamed up that would use this up. The first was an experimental space station called *Skylab*. The second was an international space mission – the Apollo-Soyuz Test Project (ASTP) – with the Russians, who had also continued their experiments in space exploration. Any "space race" was forgotten on this 1975 mission, as a three-man American crew in an Apollo CSM met up with a two-man Russian crew in a Soyuz spacecraft. Astronauts and cosmonauts worked

ABOVE: **A dramatic shot of** *Endeavour* **(OV-105) in the vast Vehicle Assembly Building at Kennedy Space Center in March 1992 as it is mated with the external tank and twin Thiokol solid rocket boosters.**

together in a spirit of camaraderie. This was the way to explore space: co-operation, not competition.

THE SPACE SHUTTLE

The ASTP mission was for the USA not only the end of the Apollo era but also the end of the expendable era in manned spacecraft. In the USA experiments began with lifting body craft, such as the Northrop X-24, in which the fuselage is designed to provide aerodynamic lift. It is hoped that this type will eventually be capable of entering space orbit under the power of its own engines and re-enter Earth's atmosphere to return to base as an aircraft. While test flights with the X-24 were progressing, NASA contracted Rockwell to design and construct the world's first reusable space craft. This new craft, the Space Shuttle, would revolutionise space travel.

The final design chosen for the Shuttle system comprised three main pieces of hardware. Crew and cargo would be housed in a delta-winged Orbiter about the size of a medium-range airliner. It would take off like a rocket, but return to Earth as a glider. The Orbiter's rocket engines would be fed with liquid oxygen propellants from an external tank. Extra thrust for lift-off would be provided by twin solid-rocket boosters (SRBs) strapped

to the sides of the tank. Shortly after lift-off the SRBs would separate and be parachuted back to Earth for re-use. When the external tank emptied it would be jettisoned.

Work on the Shuttle started as the last Apollo Moon landings were taking place, but it was not until 1977 that the first Shuttle took to the air. This craft was the prototype Orbiter, named *Enterprise* to the delight of "Star Trek" fans. Flights in the atmosphere proved its aerodynamics, and work forged ahead on the first operational Orbiter, named *Columbia*. Technical problems, particularly with the main engines and the insulating tiles that formed the heat shield of the Orbiter, wreaked havoc with the schedules, and it was not until 12 April 1981 that *Columbia* blasted off from the Kennedy Space Center on the first Shuttle mission, designated STS-1 (STS for Space Transportation System). Close to a million people watched as veteran astronaut John Young and Robert Crippen rode the new "bird" into the heavens. After a flawless mission, *Columbia* touched down at Edwards Air Force Base in California two days later.

Columbia was ferried back to Kennedy atop a modified Boeing 747 carrier aircraft and by November was back on the launch pad. On 12 November it was again punching its way skywards. It was the first time any craft had flown into space more than once. The following year the Orbiter repeated the feat three more times. On the last flight (STS-5) it became officially operational, carrying two commercial satellites into orbit.

A second Orbiter, *Challenger*, went into service in April 1983, making three trips into space in the year. The following November *Columbia* was back in harness, this time carrying a science laboratory called Spacelab, built by the European Space Agency, in its payload bay. Its record crew of six included the first European to travel on a US spacecraft, Ulf Merbold.

It was in 1984 that the remarkable versatility of the Shuttle became apparent. In April spacewalking astronauts working from the *Challenger* captured an ailing satellite named *Solar Max* and repaired it in the payload bay before relaunching it. They did so using a jet-propelled backpack called the Manned Manoeuvring Unit (MMU) and with the help of the Orbiter's manipulator arm. In November, on the second flight of a new Orbiter, *Discovery*, Shuttle astronauts captured two

RIGHT: **The first lifting body test aircraft was built as a glider, whilst the Northrop/NASA X-24 was fitted with an engine. The X-24 was carried to 50,000 ft (15,240m) under the wing of a Boeing B-52 and air-launched. By using its engine the X-24 could reach over 100,000ft) (30,480m) and then glide back to its base.**

satellites that had become marooned in uselessly low orbits, and this time brought them back to Earth.

The Shuttle fleet expanded to four in 1985 when *Atlantis* became operational in October. With a fleet of four, Orbiters would soon be shuttling into orbit every few weeks, or so it seemed.

But it was not to be. On 28 January 1986 *Challenger* rose from the launch pad on its 10th and the Shuttle's 25th mission, designated 51-L. Only 73 seconds into the flight, the Shuttle assembly exploded in a fireball in the Florida skies. *Challenger* was blasted apart and her crew of seven died instantly, becoming the first in-flight casualties in the US space programme.

The remaining Shuttle fleet was grounded as then President Reagan set up the Rogers Commission to investigate the disaster. The immediate fault appeared to be a defective joint in one of the SRBs, which allowed hot gases to escape and torch the supporting structure. The SRB swung round and ruptured the external tank, which immediately exploded. The Rogers Commission recommended extensive modifications to the Shuttle to prevent such a thing happening again, as well as operational changes prior to launch.

The fleet remained grounded until September 1988, when *Discovery* blasted off from the launch pad on mission STS-26, spearheading the USA's "return to flight". Its four-day mission was flawless, drawing collective sighs of relief throughout the world. Nine years on, the Shuttle would be celebrating its 80th flight and preparing for its next major role in space, which was to aid the construction of the International Space Station.

On *Discovery's* launch day in 1988 the Soviets tried to steal some of the thunder, announcing that they were about to launch a shuttle craft of their own, called *Buran* (Snowstorm). It would be an unmanned, automated flight. A planned October launch slipped into November,

and *Buran* finally made it into orbit on 15 November, circling the Earth twice before landing near its launch site at the Baikonur Cosmodrome. Though outwardly a Shuttle lookalike, *Buran* did not use its own engines for lift-off. It rode into space pick-a-back on what had become the world's most powerful launch vehicle, *Energia*. Its own engines fired on the fringes of space to thrust it into orbit. *Buran's* maiden flight, however, was also its last. (The only *Buran* now resides in a children's playground at Baikonur.) Plans for manned missions in this and other *Buran* craft were eventually abandoned because of lack of funds following the break-up of the Soviet Union.

SPACE STATIONS

However, while the USA had been concentrating on developing the Space Shuttle, the Russians had been accumulating vast experience of long-duration flights in a series of space stations, building up to a continuous presence in orbit. Using automatic supply craft, they delivered fresh supplies to the crews of these stations, setting the stage for long-duration

flights. In November 1978 two Soviet astronauts completed a record 139-day mission, followed in 1979 by a 175-day mission, 184 days in 1980, 211 days in 1982, and 237 days in 1984. These were all achieved in Salyut space stations.

In February 1986 a new-generation space station called *Mir* (Peace) was launched into orbit. This had a multiple-docking module at one end, with six docking ports, as well as a single port at the other. This construction hinted at the spacecraft's purpose, as the base unit for a more extensive space complex. It would house the living quarters of the crew, while the main experimental work would be carried out in the add-on units that were to follow. The first unit, Kvant 1, docked with the base unit in 1987, followed by Kvant 2 (1989), Kristall (1990), Spektr (1995) and Priroda (996). With Priroda added, the *Mir* space station was at last complete, although, at ten years old, starting to show its age.

Mir has been continuously inhabited since its launch, with its cosmonauts continuing to smash space duration records. In December 1988 Musa Manarov and Vladimir Titov became the first space

travellers to spend a year in orbit. This feat was bettered by Valeri Polyakov, returning to Earth in March 1995 after 437 days.

JOINT OPERATIONS

Another feature of missions to *Mir* have been visits by "guest" cosmonauts from many different countries. They have included European Space Agency astronauts such as Ulf Merbold (1994) and Thomas Reiter (1995) on the so-called EuroMir missions. In March 1995 US astronaut Norman Thagard flew on *Mir*, the prelude to the first international space link-up since the ASTP mission two decades before. This happened in June 1995 when space shuttle *Atlantis* docked with the Russian space station, a suitable spectacular to celebrate the 100th United States manned flight. It was the most extensive assembly of space hardware ever in orbit, with ten astronauts and cosmonauts coming together for the first time. There was also an exchange of crews, with two cosmonauts transferring from *Atlantis* to *Mir* and two others, along with Thagard, transferring from *Mir* to *Atlantis*.

Further shuttle missions to *Mir* took

place, to accumulate experience in joint operations as a prelude to working together in the launch, assembly and operation of the upcoming International Space Station (ISS), also known as Alpha. On later Shuttle/*Mir* missions the shuttle ferried up astronauts for a long-term stay in *Mir*, beginning with Shannon Lucid in February 1996. She remained in orbit for 188 days, the longest any female astronaut or cosmonaut had remained in orbit.

In the immediate future the efforts of the major spacefaring nations in the sphere of manned space travel will be concentrated on the construction of the ISS, which is scheduled to become fully operational in the year 2003. When complete, the ISS, orbiting between about 220 and 280 miles (350 and 450km), will have a mass of more than 400 tons and measure some 330ft by 250 ft (100m by 75m). It will be operated by an international crew of six, with crews rotating every few months. The Shuttle will be the prime vehicle for assembly tasks.

But, if the history of spaceflight – or even of manned flight itself – has taught us anything, it is that dreams become a reality, and sooner than expected.

Space Shuttle

It leaves Earth like a rocket, operates in orbit as a spacecraft and then returns to land as an aircraft.

SPECIFICATION
Wingspan
78ft 1in (23.80m)

Length
122ft 1in (37.21m)

Height
56ft 7in (17.25m)

Weight
171,419lb
(77,756kg) empty
254,449lb
(115,418kg) with cargo
fuel tank and booster
rockets

Engines
Three Rocketdyne SSME
Two Aerojet Liquid Rocket
Engines (Orbit
manoeuvring Engines)
38 Marquardt reaction
control engines

A retractable manipulator arm fitted to the left-hand side of the payload bay (a second arm can be fitted on the right if needed) is used for deploying or retracting satellites and other payloads. The bay is also equipped with closed-circuit television.

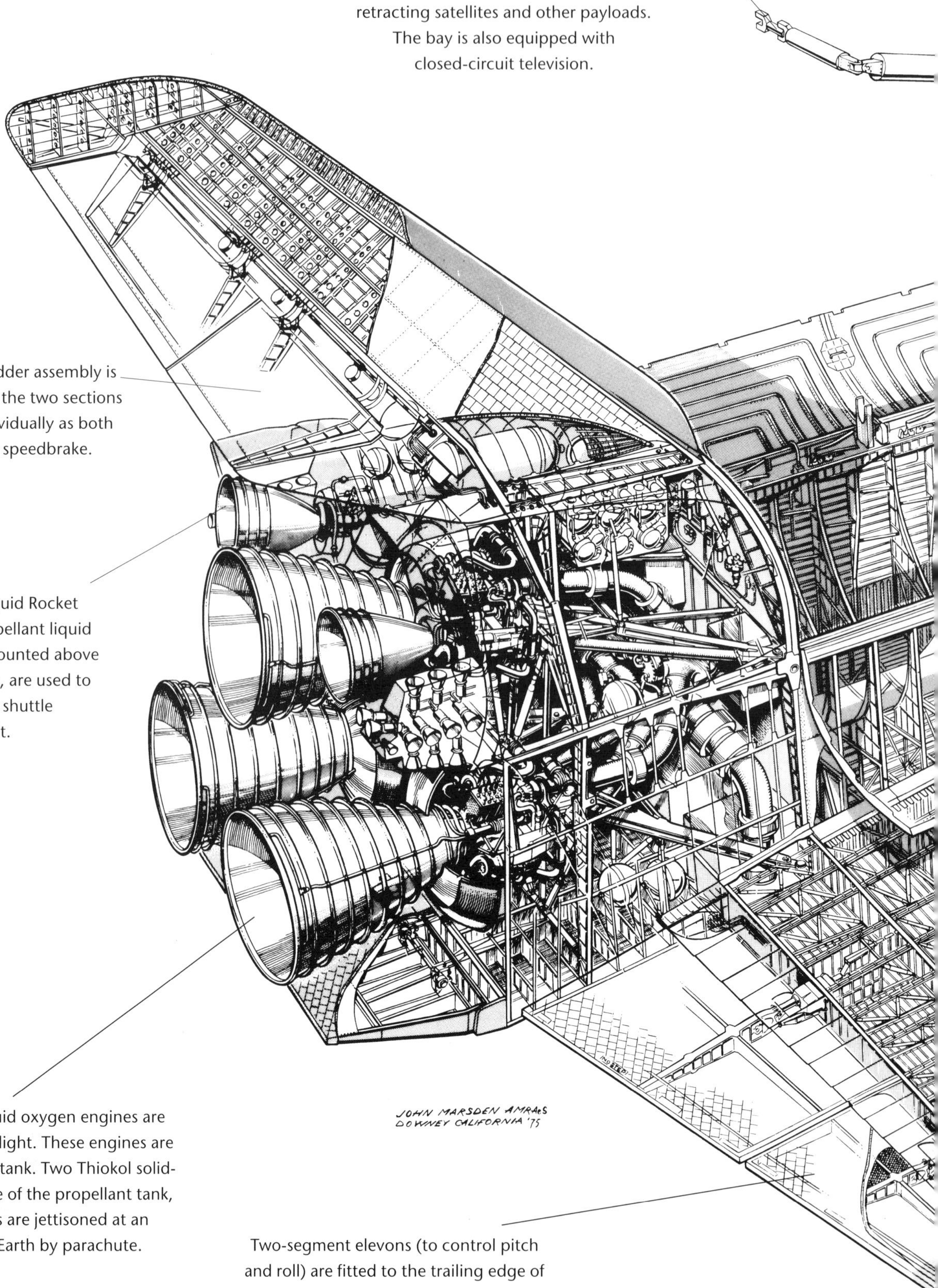

The two-piece rudder assembly is split vertically and the two sections are actuated individually as both rudder and/or speedbrake.

Two Aerojet Liquid Rocket Company bi-propellant liquid rocket engines, mounted above the main engines, are used to position the shuttle in orbit.

JOHN MARSDEN AMRAeS
DOWNEY CALIFORNIA '75

Three Rocketdyne SSME liquid hydrogen/liquid oxygen engines are used during the lift-off into orbit stage of the flight. These engines are supplied with fuel from an external propellant tank. Two Thiokol solid-propellant booster rockets, mounted each side of the propellant tank, provide extra thrust. The tank and boosters are jettisoned at an altitude of 27 miles (43km) and return to Earth by parachute.

Two-segment elevons (to control pitch and roll) are fitted to the trailing edge of the wing. These are only operated after re-entry when the craft is manoeuvring to land.

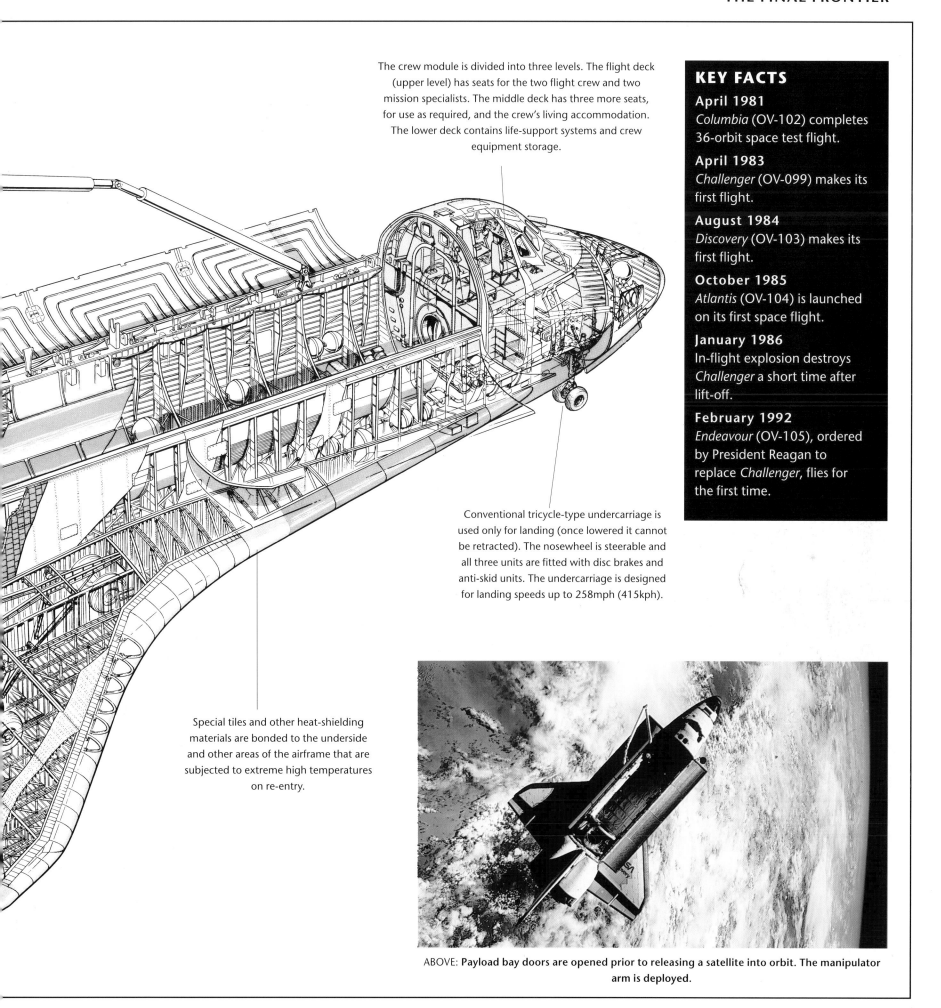

The crew module is divided into three levels. The flight deck (upper level) has seats for the two flight crew and two mission specialists. The middle deck has three more seats, for use as required, and the crew's living accommodation. The lower deck contains life-support systems and crew equipment storage.

KEY FACTS

April 1981
Columbia (OV-102) completes 36-orbit space test flight.

April 1983
Challenger (OV-099) makes its first flight.

August 1984
Discovery (OV-103) makes its first flight.

October 1985
Atlantis (OV-104) is launched on its first space flight.

January 1986
In-flight explosion destroys *Challenger* a short time after lift-off.

February 1992
Endeavour (OV-105), ordered by President Reagan to replace *Challenger*, flies for the first time.

Conventional tricycle-type undercarriage is used only for landing (once lowered it cannot be retracted). The nosewheel is steerable and all three units are fitted with disc brakes and anti-skid units. The undercarriage is designed for landing speeds up to 258mph (415kph).

Special tiles and other heat-shielding materials are bonded to the underside and other areas of the airframe that are subjected to extreme high temperatures on re-entry.

ABOVE: **Payload bay doors are opened prior to releasing a satellite into orbit. The manipulator arm is deployed.**

LEFT: The Space Shuttle's principal role is that of transporting satellites into space and releasing them into Earth orbit. Should a satellite develop a fault, it can be repaired in space by Shuttle mission specialists and put back to work, saving millions of dollars.

RIGHT: *Discovery* (OV-103) in space orbit. The manipulator arm is extended ready for satellite launch.
INSET: Scientists at work aboard *Skylab*. Although launched by rocket, *Skylab* was supplied from Earth by Space Shuttle flights.

BELOW: The USSR's *Buran* space shuttle was transported pick-a-back on the massive, purpose-built Antonov An-225 Mriya. Flights with *Buran* began on 13 May 1988. It completed its first orbital mission (unmanned) on 15 November 1988. The Soviet craft's dimensions are almost identical to those of the US Shuttle.

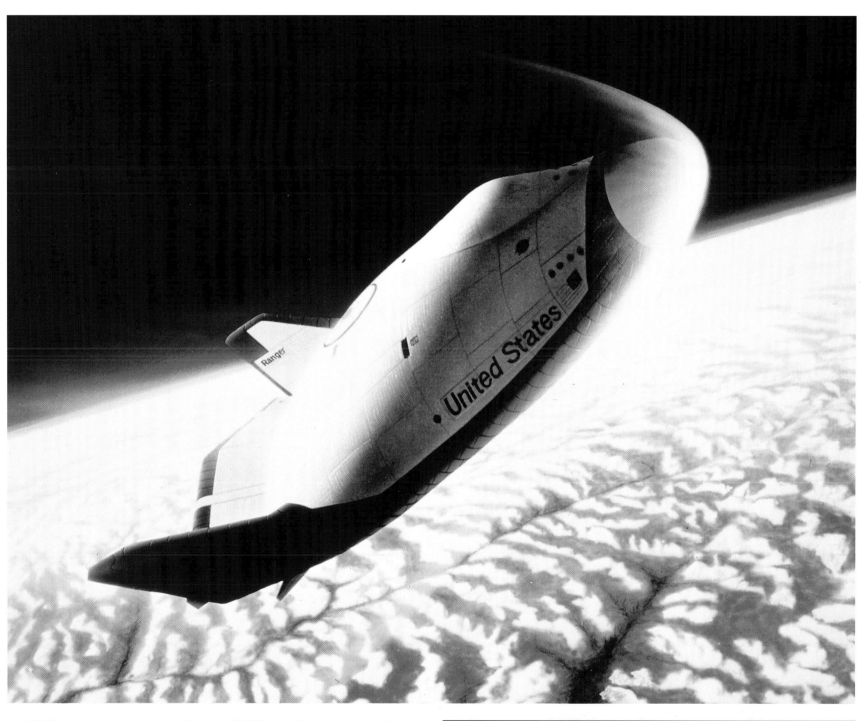

LEFT: The European Space Agency's concept for the re-useable space vehicle was the Hérmes. Designed to be launched on top of an Ariane 5 rocket to an altitude of 31 miles (50km) it could carry a crew of three and a payload of 3,527lb (1,600kg). The cone structure at the rear of the craft contained manoeuvring engines, cooling system and docking mechanism. This Module de Resources Hérmes (MRH) was jettisoned before re-entry.

ABOVE: An artist's impression of NASA's X-36 space station project. Designed to take-off and leave the earth's atmosphere to orbit under its own power, it would return to base as a glider for use again. The X-33 is probably the only lifting body space vehicle to be considered for production.

RIGHT: Venture is a wingless lifting body concept designed by Lockheed's famous 'Skunk Works'. It is capable of lifting a payload of 40,000lb (18,144kg) into low orbit. Like the Space Shuttle it lands conventionally after gliding to base.

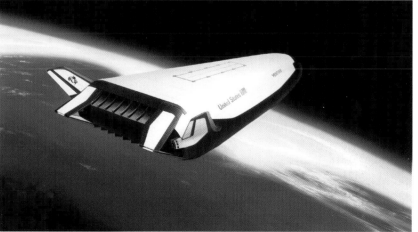

Index

Photo credits

The publishers would like to thank all those who have kindly supplied photographs and illustrations for use in this book.

Prelims

Endpapers Quadrant; Half-title page Philip Jarrett; Title page Quadrant; Foreword Tim Furniss/ Genesis; Contents pages (top left) Philip Jarrett, (centre left and bottom left) Quadrant, (top right) Hugh Cowin, (centre right) Quadrant, (bottom right) Tim Furniss/Genesis.

Introduction

Page 12 (top) Philip Jarrett, (bottom) Bruce Robertson; page 13 Bruce Robertson; pages 14 and 15 Philip Jarrett.

Chapter One First Flights

Pages 16 and 17 Philip Jarrett; pages 18 and 19 Philip Jarrett; pages 20 and 21 Philip Jarrett; page 22 (top) Bruce Robertson, (centre) Philip Jarrett, (bottom) Philip Jarrett; page 23 Philip Jarrett; page 24 Philip Jarrett; page 25 Bruce Robertson, (inset) Philip Jarrett.; page 27 Quadrant; pages 28 and 29 Philip Jarrett; pages 30 and 31 Philip Jarrett; page 32 Philip Jarrett; page 33 (top) Philip Jarrett, (bottom) Bruce Robertson; page 34 (top) Bruce Robertson, (bottom) Philip Jarrett; page 35 Philip Jarrett; page 36 Philip Jarrett; page 37 (top) Hugh Cowin, (bottom) Philip Jarrett; page 38 (top left) Philip Jarrett, (top right) Bruce Robertson, (bottom) Bruce Robertson; page 39 (top) Bruce Robertson, (centre) Philip Jarrett, (bottom) Bruce Robertson.

Chapter Two The Pace Quickens

Page 40 Philip Jarrett; page 41 Mike Vines/Photolink; pages 42 and 43 Philip Jarrett; page 44 (top) Philip Jarrett, (centre) Philip Jarrett, (bottom) Bruce Robertson; page 45 (top) Mike Vines/Photolink, (bottom) Bruce Robertson; pages 46 and 47 Philip Jarrett; page 48 (top) Hugh Cowin, (bottom and inset) Mike Vines/Photolink; page 49 Mike Vines/Photolink; page 51 Philip Jarrett; page 52 Philip Jarrett; page 53 (top) Mike Vines/Photolink, (bottom) Philip Jarrett; pages 54 and 55 Philip Jarrett; page 56 (top) Mike Vines/Photolink, (bottom) Philip Jarrett; page 57 (top) Philip Jarrett, (bottom) Mike Vines/Photolink; pages 58 and 59 Philip

Jarrett; page 60 Philip Jarrett; page 61 (top) Philip Jarrett, (centre) Mike Vines/Photolink, (bottom) Philip Jarrett; page 62 (top) Bruce Robertson, (bottom) Philip Jarrett; page 63 Philip Jarrett.

Chapter Three Peace Returns

Page 64 Philip Jarrett; page 65 Philip Jarrett; page 66 and 67 Philip Jarrett; page 68 Bruce Robertson; page 69 Philip Jarrett; page 70 (top) Bruce Robertson, (bottom) Philip Jarrett; page 71 Philip Jarrett; pages 72 and 73 Philip Jarrett; page 74 (top) Scandinavian Airlines System, (bottom) Philip Jarrett; page 75 (top) KLM, (bottom) Philip Jarrett; pages 76 and 77 Philip Jarrett; page 79 Philip Jarrett; page 80 (top) Philip Jarrett, (bottom) Hugh Cowin; page 81 (top) Philip Jarrett, (bottom) Hugh Cowin; page 82 Philip Jarrett; page 83 (top) Colin Cruddas, (insets) Philip Jarrett, (bottom) Philip Jarrett.

Chapter Four Spanning the World

Page 84 Philip Jarrett; page 85 Hugh Cowin; page 86 Philip Jarrett; page 87 Hugh Cowin; page 88 Philip Jarrett; page 89 (top) Bruce Robertson, (bottom) Philip Jarrett; Page 90 (top) Philip Jarrett, (bottom) Hugh Cowin; page 91 (top) Philip Jarrett, (bottom) Hugh Cowin; page 92 (top) Philip Jarrett, (bottom) Lufthansa; page 93 Philip Jarrett; page 94 and 95 Philip Jarrett; page 96 (top) Philip Jarrett, (bottom) Colin Cruddas; page 97 (top) Philip Jarrett, (bottom) Lufthansa; pages 98 and 99 Colin Cruddas; page 101 Philip Jarrett; page 102 (top) Philip Jarrett, (bottom) Hugh Cowin; page 103 (top) Philip Jarrett, (bottom left) Mike Vines/Photolink, (bottom right) Philip Jarrett; page 104 (top) Bruce Robertson, (bottom) Boeing; page 105 (bottom) Philip Jarrett; page 106 (left) Mike Vines/Photolink, (right) Philip Jarrett; page 107 Philip Jarrett; page 108 (top) Jay Miller, (bottom) Philip Jarrett; page 109 Philip Jarrett; page 110 Hugh Cowin; page 111 Boeing; pages 112 and 113 Philip Jarrett; pages 114 and 115 Philip Jarrett; page 116 Philip Jarrett; page 117 (top) Hugh Cowin, (bottom) Bruce Robertson; page 118 (top) Bruce Robertson, (bottom) Philip Jarrett; page 119 Philip Jarrett; pages 120 and 121 Philip Jarrett; page 122 Philip Jarrett; page 123 (top) John M. Dibbs, (bottom) Philip Jarrett; pages 124 and 125 Philip Jarrett; page 126

(top) Philip Jarrett, (centre) Hugh Cowin, (bottom) Philip Jarrett; page 127 (top) Philip Jarrett, (bottom) John M. Dibbs; pages 128 and 129 Philip Jarrett; pages 130 and131 Philip Jarrett; page 133 Andrew Dickson.

Chapter Six Defence and Attack

Page 134 John M. Dibbs; page 135 Philip Jarrett; pages 136 and 137 Philip Jarrett; page 138 (top) Philip Jarrett, (bottom) John M. Dibbs; page 139 (top) John M. Dibbs, (bottom) Philip Jarrett; pages 140 and 141 Philip Jarrett; page 142 John M. Dibbs; page 143 (top) Philip Jarrett, (bottom) John M. Dibbs; pages 144 and 145 Philip Jarrett; page 146 John M. Dibbs; page 147 (top) John M. Dibbs, (bottom) Philip Jarrett; page 149 Philip Jarrett; page 150 Philip Jarrett; page 151 (top) John M. Dibbs, (bottom) Philip Jarrett; pages 152 and 153 Philip Jarrett; page 154 John M. Dibbs; page 155 (top) John M. Dibbs, (bottom) Philip Jarrett; pages 156 and 157 Philip Jarrett; page 158 (top) John M. Dibbs, (bottom) Philip Jarrett; page 159 (top) Philip Jarrett, (bottom) John M. Dibbs; pages 160 and 161 Philip Jarrett.

Chapter Seven The Jet Era Begins

Page 162 Philip Jarrett; page 163 Philip Jarrett; pages 164 and 165 Philip Jarrett; pages 166 and 167 Philip Jarrett; pages 168 and 169 Philip Jarrett; page 170 Quadrant; page 171 (top) Quadrant, (centre) Jay Miller, (bottom) Jay Miller; pages 172 and 173 Philip Jarrett; page 174 Philip Jarrett; page 175 (top) John M. Dibbs, (centre left and right) Philip Jarrett, (bottom) John M. Dibbs; pages 176 and 177 Philip Jarrett; page 178 Philip Jarrett; page 179 (top) Philip Jarrett, (bottom) BEA; page 180 (top) Philip Jarrett, (bottom left) Hugh Cowin, (bottom right) Philip Jarrett; page 181 Philip Jarrett; page 182 (top) John M. Dibbs, (bottom) Philip Jarrett; page 183 (top) Philip Jarrett, (bottom) Jay Miller; page 185 Philip Jarrett; page 186 Hugh Cowin; page 187 Philip Jarrett; pages 188 and 189 Philip Jarrett.

Chapter Eight Defending the Peace

Page 190 Philip Jarrett; page 191 Hugh Cowin; pages 192 and 193 Philip Jarrett; pages 194 and 195 Philip Jarrett; page 196 (top) Philip Jarrett, (bottom) Jay Miller; page 197 Philip Jarrett; pages 198 and 199 Philip Jarrett; page

200 (top) Philip Jarrett, (bottom) Hugh Cowin; page 201 (top) Hugh Cowin, (bottom) Philip Jarrett; page 203 Philip Jarrett; page 204 (top) Philip Jarrett, (bottom) Hugh Cowin; page 205 Hugh Cowin; pages 206 and 207 Philip Jarrett; page 209 Quadrant; page 210 Hugh Cowin; page 211 (top) Hugh Cowin, (bottom) Philip Jarrett.

Chapter Nine Advanced Technology

Pages 212 and 213 Philip Jarrett; page 214 Mike Vines/Photolink; page 215 Philip Jarrett; pages 216 (top) Philip Jarrett, (bottom) Hugh Cowin; page 217 (top) Hugh Cowin, (bottom) John Cassidy/RAF; page 218 (top) John M. Dibbs, (bottom) Hugh Cowin; page 219 (top) Mike Vines/Photolink, (bottom) Philip Jarrett; page 220 Bournemouth Evening Echo; page 221 (top) John M. Dibbs, (centre right) Philip Jarrett, (bottom) Philip Jarrett; page 222 (top) Philip Jarrett, (bottom) Hugh Cowin; page 223 (top) Philip Jarrett, (centre) Quadrant, (bottom) Hugh Cowin; page 224 Hugh Cowin; page 225 Philip Jarrett; page 226 (top) Philip Jarrett, (bottom) Mike Vines/Photolink; page 227 (top) Philip Jarrett, (bottom) Mike Vines/Photolink; page 228 (top) Quadrant, (bottom) Philip Jarrett; page 229 (top) Philip Jarrett, (bottom) Hugh Cowin; pages 230 and 231 Quadrant; page 232 (top) SAAB, (bottom) Mike Vines/Photolink; page 233 Mike Vines/Photolink; page 235 Philip Jarrett; page 236 (top left) Philip Jarrett, (top right) Mike Vines/Photolink, (bottom) Philip Jarrett; page 237 (top) Philip Jarrett, (bottom) Mike Vines/Photolink.

Chapter Ten The Final Frontier

Pages 238 and 239 Jay Miller; page 240 Jay Miller; page 241 Tim Furniss/Genesis; page 243 Tim Furniss/Genesis; page 244 Mike Vines/Photolink; page 245 Tim Furniss/Genesis; pages 246 and 247 Tim Furniss/Genesis.

Jacket

Front panel (main picture) John M. Dibbs/The Plane Picture Company, (left to right) Mike Vines/Photo Link, Hugh Cowin, Frank Munger, Philip Jarrett; Back panel (main picture) Philip Jarrett, (left to right) Philip Jarrett, John M. Dibbs, Philip Jarrett.